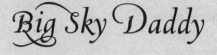

Big Sky Daddy

LINDA FORD

HARLEQUIN® LOVE INSPIRED® HISTORICAL

Recycling programs
for this product may
not exist in your area.

 LOVE INSPIRED BOOKS

ISBN-13: 978-0-373-28290-6

Big Sky Daddy

Copyright © 2014 by Linda Ford

Printed in U.S.A.

"I'll take good care of Teddy. We all will," Lilly said.

"He has a special fondness for you."

The words melted her heart. "And I for him."

Caleb touched her hand and rode away. He lifted his hat at the crest of the hill and waved to her. She waved back and stood watching until he was out of sight.

He would return tonight, just as he said.

Because of Teddy, she reminded herself. Not because of her.

She would not expect any man to return to her. That led only to disappointment and pain. As Rose had pointed out, she'd learned that lesson at a very young age and she'd had it reinforced throughout her life.

She was more than content living on the farm with her family, tending the garden and the animals. But she'd accept the company and care of Teddy and his father for a short time, even knowing it couldn't last.

The pain would be worth the joy of the moment.

Books by Linda Ford

Love Inspired Historical

The Road to Love
The Journey Home
The Path to Her Heart
Dakota Child
The Cowboy's Baby
Dakota Cowboy
Christmas Under
  Western Skies
    "A Cowboy's Christmas"
Dakota Father
Prairie Cowboy
Klondike Medicine Woman
*The Cowboy Tutor
*The Cowboy Father
*The Cowboy Comes Home
The Gift of Family
  "Merry Christmas, Cowboy"

†*The Cowboy's Surprise Bride*
†*The Cowboy's Unexpected*
  Family
†*The Cowboy's Convenient*
  Proposal
 The Baby Compromise
†*Claiming the Cowboy's Heart*
†*Winning Over the Wrangler*
†*Falling for the Rancher Father*
**Big Sky Cowboy
**Big Sky Daddy

*Three Brides for Three Cowboys
†Cowboys of Eden Valley
**Montana Marriages

LINDA FORD

lives on a ranch in Alberta, Canada. Growing up on the prairie and learning to notice the small details it hides gave her an appreciation for watching God at work in His creation. Her upbringing also included being taught to trust God in everything and through everything—a theme that resonates in her stories. Threads of another part of her life are found in her stories—her concern for children and their future. She and her husband raised fourteen children—four homemade, ten adopted. She currently shares her home and life with her husband, a grown son, a live-in paraplegic client and a continual (and welcome) stream of kids, kids-in-law, grandkids and assorted friends and relatives.

He brought me up also out of an horrible pit,
out of the miry clay, and set my feet upon a rock,
and established my goings.
—*Psalms* 40:2

My father taught me many things: how to shoot a gun, how to drive a car, how to find fossils in a gravel bed, how to recognize the constellations in the sky, but most of all, through his example, he taught me how a noble, kind man should act. This book is dedicated to his memory.

Chapter One

Bar Crossing, Montana
Fall 1889

Did he hear gunshots? Caleb Craig jerked toward the window. "Listen." He held up his hand, trying to cut short the storekeeper's detailed description about the young woman who had stepped out of the store as Caleb and his son, Teddy, went in.

"Lilly Bell," the storekeeper had said. Twin sister to Rose, the two were the least alike, though to be sure, both were sweet and generous and loyal. Their parents were elderly, but that didn't mean they were feeble. Oh, far from it.

A series of pops convinced Caleb someone had set off firecrackers. They were not as deadly as gunshots, but they were enough to start a dangerous chain reaction.

Before he reached the window, Caleb knew it had already started. Several women screamed. A deeper voice called out. The rattle and creak of wood and harnesses signaled frantic horses.

"You stay here," he ordered five-year-old Teddy, and then raced through the door.

The young woman, whose virtues the storekeeper expounded on even as Caleb hustled out of the shop, wrestled with a rearing horse hitched to a swaying wagon. Packages and sacks tumbled out the back. A redheaded woman raced toward the struggling gal. *That must be the twin sister, Rose.* An older man hobbled across the street toward them while other people huddled on the sidewalks, watching but doing nothing.

Caleb saw it all in one glance as he jumped to Lilly's side and grabbed the harness, his hand right next to hers.

"Steady there," he ordered, his voice stern yet kind— something animals understood.

Breathing raggedly, the horse allowed Caleb to pull his head down. Still holding tight to the animal, as was she, Caleb turned to the young woman. The name Lilly suited her. Blond hair, unblemished skin, blue eyes flashing like lightning.

She was understandably upset.

"What idiot set off firecrackers?" he demanded.

She snorted. "That Caldwell cowboy."

Ebner? His boss? Caleb glanced about but saw no sign of the Caldwell foreman. "Is anyone hurt?"

The redhead rushed to their side. "Lilly, are you okay?" She rubbed her hands over the young woman's arms. "I saw the whole thing." She jammed her fists to her hips. "I can't believe anyone would do such a stupid thing. Not even a Caldwell."

Caleb's neck tensed. He'd been working at the Caldwell ranch a couple of weeks now. Ebner was tough, allowing no slacking and objecting to Caleb keeping Teddy with him as he worked. Caleb had reminded Ebner several times it had been part of the agreement before Caleb had taken the job.

Mr. Caldwell was away on some errand, leaving Ebner

in charge. The foreman ran the place with efficiency. Caleb had certainly seen no sign of such wanton disregard for the safety of man and beast.

"I'm fine," Lilly said. She sucked in air as if to calm her nerves and faced Caleb. "Thank you for your help. I saw you at the store, didn't I?"

"Yes, ma'am." He gave his name.

"Pleased to make your acquaintance." The smile she gave him could have changed rain to sunshine.

"Papa." Teddy's trembling voice made them all turn toward his son. Both ladies murmured, "Ah," as they saw Teddy.

Caleb understood how the boy would pull at one's heart. Big blue eyes, tousled hair that refused to be tamed, a look of innocence, though it was impossible there could be any innocence left after what the boy had been through. Teddy leaned on his crutches, his right leg not touching the floor.

"Son, I asked you to stay inside."

"I know, Papa. But what if something happened to you?"

Lilly's attention flickered between Caleb and Teddy. Rose's lingered on the boy.

"I don't intend for anything to happen to me."

Teddy nodded, his expression more worried than relieved.

"You stay there while I help these ladies collect their packages."

"Yes, Papa."

"That's my boy."

An older man approached them. "Are you girls okay?"

"We're fine, Pa," the pair chorused.

So this was Mr. Bell. Caleb introduced himself. In turn, Mr. Bell introduced his daughters.

The horse had settled down. Caleb left Mr. Bell holding him and strode to the back of the wagon to gather up parcels and return them to the box.

Lilly scurried around to pick up things as well. "I hope nothing was damaged."

Teddy hobbled along the sidewalk to see better what Caleb was doing.

Lilly lifted a sack and paused to watch the boy. There was no mistaking the question in her eyes. She was wondering why the boy wasn't walking.

If only someone could provide that answer.

"Caleb." Ebner rode toward the wagon. "Leave them people to gather up their own stuff. You get our wagon on home now. Hear?"

"Yes, boss."

Lilly glowered at Ebner as he rode away laughing. Then she turned toward Caleb. "You work for them?" She grabbed the package from his hands and shook it as if his mere touch had somehow soiled it.

"Yes, ma'am. 'Fraid I do." And if he wanted to keep his job, he needed to do as the boss said. "Glad no one was hurt."

She snorted. "I'm sure your boss won't agree."

If only he could explain. But what could he say? His job with the Caldwells was too important to risk losing over a few packages in the dirt. He needed the money to take Teddy to a new doctor down east. Perhaps this special doctor would be able to say why Teddy still wasn't using his leg though it had healed up. At least on the outside. The several doctors he'd already seen suggested there was nerve damage. Or something. They had all been vague and none had helped in any way.

"Goodbye." He included the sister and father in his nod and joined Teddy on the sidewalk. "Let's get going."

The walk toward the wagon couldn't be hurried even though Teddy had gotten good at walking with his crutches over the past few months. At the wagon, he scooped Teddy up and set him on the seat. "Now don't you be driving off without me."

Teddy laughed. "You know I can't drive a wagon." He leaned forward as if to take the reins. "Unless you let me."

Caleb climbed up and sat beside his son. "Seems to me it's about time you learned." He pulled the boy to his lap and let him hold the reins, his big hands firmly on Teddy's small ones.

Teddy turned his face up to Caleb and gave him a smile as wide as the sky.

Caleb's heart caught the smile and clung to it, determined not to let the past steal the joy of this precious moment or any others yet to come with his son.

If only he could go back and undo the past. But he couldn't. He couldn't bring back his wife, nor could he stop the thugs from breaking in and taking her life. He'd discovered them and shot them, but in the gunfight Teddy had been injured. Caleb's throat constricted with the same mire of emotions he'd experienced when he found his son, his leg bloody, his little face filled with terror.

Caleb swallowed hard and forced air into his lungs. He'd never know if he had been the one who fired the shot that hit Teddy. He lived for only one thing—to see Teddy's fears end and the boy walk normally again.

If that required him to work for the Caldwells knowing Ebner could stoop to such dastardly deeds, well, that wasn't his concern now, was it?

As if suspecting Caleb might be having second thoughts, Ebner rode up beside him.

"You've got to understand something. The Caldwells don't get along with the Bells. We've been feuding ever since the Bells had the gall to file claim to a piece of land right plumb in the middle of Caldwell land. Seems some ignorant file clerk made a mistake. But will the Bells do the right thing and go farm somewhere else? Nope. They've got to keep on causing trouble. No one who works for the Caldwells can figure on being friends with the Bells. Understand?"

Caleb nodded. "Don't see I've got any cause to have truck with them."

"See that you don't." Ebner rode away, leaving Caleb to muse about his words.

"Papa, that man at the store, Mr. Frank, he said the Bells were nice people."

"Uh-huh. I expect they are." The way Rose and Mr. Bell had clustered around Lilly to make sure she wasn't hurt sure made him think so. It'd been a long time since he'd seen such care and devotion. Or rather since he'd experienced it. Amanda had been an efficient housekeeper and a good mother to Teddy, but she'd been distant and critical when it came to Caleb. He stilled his thoughts. One didn't speak evil of the dead even in his mind.

They rumbled down the road toward the Caldwell ranch, Teddy so focused on handling the horse that he never lifted his eyes from the animal.

Something in the bushes to the side of the road caught Caleb's attention. At first he thought someone had discarded a cow hide and wondered if there were rustlers about, but then he made out a nose and ears. A pup. Dead by the look of it.

He didn't want Teddy to notice, so he leaned over the boy. "Remember, you must always hold the reins as if something could startle your horse. Never get so relaxed he could get away from you."

Teddy pulled his hands from Caleb's and straightened,

leaning hard into Caleb's shoulder as he turned to look to the side. "Papa, it's a dog."

"Don't you want to drive the wagon still?"

Teddy patted Caleb's shoulder. "He's hurt."

"Son, we have to get back." *Please, Teddy. Let it go. You don't want to see any more suffering and death.*

"Papa, he needs our help."

When Caleb continued onward, Teddy pounded his shoulder. "Papa, you can't leave him. You can't. He's hurt. You have to help. Stop. Please stop." Tears mingled with Teddy's demands.

Caleb pulled the wagon to a stop and held Teddy by the shoulders. "Son, he's dead and I don't want you to see it."

Teddy flung his father's hands off his shoulders. "You don't know that. What if he's only hurt?" He pursed his lips and gave Caleb a narrow-eyed look. "You ain't gonna just leave him there to die, are you?"

"He's already dead." How could such a small body hold so much stubbornness?

"Then we need to bury him."

Caleb would have protected his son from ever again seeing blood and death and burial, but the boy seemed to have other thoughts on the matter. "Very well." He jumped down, lifted Teddy to the ground, handed him his crutches and grabbed a shovel out of the wagon. He followed his son to the dog.

A pair of eyes opened and followed their approach.

"Papa, he's alive."

Caleb knelt by the dog. It had been slashed, and whimpered as if in pain. He saw it was a female. "Teddy, she's barely alive and she's hurting." He pushed to his feet. "I want you to come back to the wagon." He waited for the boy to obey, but Teddy only looked at him in puzzlement.

"Why, Papa?"

"Just do as I say." Caleb's feet felt heavy as rocks as he went back to the wagon and reached under the seat. He had to do what he had to do. *It will be a kindness. The poor animal shouldn't be allowed to suffer.*

Teddy hobbled after him, saw Caleb reach for the rifle and screamed. "No. You can't shoot my dog." He scrambled to the animal so fast Caleb held his breath for fear he'd fall and further injure himself.

"She's my dog." Teddy huddled forward. "Ain't nobody ever gonna hurt her."

"Son, she isn't going to live."

"You're wrong."

He tried every argument to convince Teddy of the futility of trying to save the dog, but his son would not relent. Though Caleb saw nothing ahead but sorrow and regret, he couldn't stay at the side of the road any longer. He wrapped the injured dog in a gunny sack and carried her gingerly to the wagon. "We'll take her home and stay with her so she doesn't die alone." He made the animal as comfortable as possible.

"I'll stay with her."

Knowing when to concede defeat, Caleb lifted Teddy in beside the dog and continued on his way. At the ranch he pulled up to the storage shed and unloaded the supplies. Thankfully Ebner wasn't around to demand he explain why it had taken so long to get back. It also saved Caleb from confronting the man about how he'd treated the Bells.

His task done, he carried the dog over to the covered wagon he shared with Teddy. He could have joined the others in the bunkhouse, but it wasn't the sort of atmosphere he wanted Teddy exposed to. It would soon get too cold to sleep in the wagon—he counted on having enough money to head east before then.

"You know what Mr. Frank said?" Teddy sat beside the dog, rubbing a spot behind the animal's ear.

"He said a lot of things." The man had seemed bent on informing Caleb about the "beautiful Bell girls." He'd overlooked one tiny detail—the Bells and the Caldwells didn't get along.

"He said that pretty lady you helped knew how to fix things."

"Things?" Was she a blacksmith? He couldn't imagine it, but he'd encountered stranger things in the West.

"Hurt things." Teddy must have thought he needed to explain her abilities more. "Mr. Frank said she helps people, too, and all kinds of animals."

Caleb smiled at his son's enthusiasm. "Hurt people, too, huh?" He wondered if she could help him. He silently laughed in derision. It was those around him who would need her help. People who got close to him tended to get hurt.

"But especially hurt dogs." Teddy gave Caleb a wide-eyed, pleading look that brought a smile to Caleb's lips. How long had it been since Teddy had cared enough about something to use that special look of his?

"What are you saying, son?" As if he didn't know. But he dared not give the boy any encouragement. The dog looked beyond saving.

"We could ask her to help my dog."

"It might not do any good." But what harm would it do? Perhaps Lilly *could* help. Perhaps Caleb could protect his son from more pain.

"Couldn't we try, please?"

Lilly put the last of the packages into the wagon and then stared after Caleb and his son. Poor little fellow was limited by having to use crutches. Had he broken

his leg? Perhaps he had a severe cut. She hoped, whatever the cause, the injury was temporary. *God, please
help the little fellow get better.*

Caleb was so tender with the lad. He had lifted him to
the wagon seat and laughed at him, and then had taken
him on his lap as they drove away, little Teddy almost
bursting with pride as he gripped the reins.

There was a time she'd hoped she'd have a little boy
or girl of her own. But thanks to one Karl Mueller, she'd
given up such dreams.

Tightness weaved around her spine. How could she
have let herself care so deeply? And in hindsight, so foolishly? She could put it down to age. She had been a mere
sixteen years old when she'd been thrilled and somewhat
surprised at the attention he'd paid her. After all, he had
been handsome and so grown-up at eighteen. So atten-
tive. He'd made her feel important when he tipped his
head to listen to her talk. She'd told him her dreams and
her fears. He'd assured her he understood. They'd agreed
that when Lilly turned eighteen they would marry. And
she'd trusted him. Sometimes she wondered if Karl really believed the things he'd promised, or if they'd fallen
off his tongue simply because he thought they would
please her. One thing Karl liked was to know people
were happy with him.

Karl had saved his announcement for her eighteenth
birthday, as if it might have been a reason for celebration.
He'd revealed he had other plans. He'd been employed by
Mr. Fry at the hardware store for a year. Mr. Fry said how
much he appreciated Karl's work and asked him to go to
Oregon to take over the operation of another Fry store.
Karl's chest had expanded three sizes as he told Lilly this.

Karl had never once suggested she accompany him.
His words made it very clear that it wasn't part of his

plan. "My time and attention must be on this business. I intend to make this the most successful store Mr. Fry has. He'll be so pleased he'll make me a partner." Karl fairly glowed with self-satisfaction. He'd never expressed a word of sorrow over ending their plans so abruptly. Never suggested they keep in contact. Never even—she sucked in air heated by her anger—asked if she'd like to join him once he'd settled into his new job.

She'd finally learned her lesson, one she should have learned at a very young age. She and her sisters had been abandoned by their birth father after their mother's death, and had been left alone on the prairie to find their own way in life when the twins were three and Cora was five. It had set the tone for Lilly's relationships. Easy come, easier go.

Ever since Karl had left her, she had guarded her heart. That meant no man of her own. No child of her own. But never mind. She had Ma and Pa and her sisters and the many animals she took care of. That was enough for any woman.

Rose nudged her. "Stop staring at him. Have you forgotten he's a Caldwell cowboy?"

"I haven't forgotten. At least he had the decency to help us." She and Rose climbed to the seat of the wagon and Pa got wearily into the back. He had mentioned several times how the cold hurt his bones and it was only October. When they got home, she'd ask Ma to give him a tonic.

She guided the wagon out of town. "I wonder what's wrong with his boy."

Rose turned to face her squarely. "Don't you go getting all interested in them."

Lilly snorted. "I don't intend to." She glanced back. Pa

had stretched out, his head resting on one of the sacks, and fallen asleep. "I haven't forgotten Karl, you know."

"He wasn't the right man for you. He only cared about himself."

Lilly tried to remember what it was that had attracted her, but after a moment's thought she realized a couple of things. Although Karl had let her talk about her dreams, he had done far more talking than listening, and more importantly, her insides no longer wrenched at the sound of his name. She'd finally been able to push the sharp pain of his leaving from her mind.

She didn't intend to ever again give someone the right to hurt her like Karl had. "He certainly didn't think I was right for him. Good thing I found it out when I did."

"Karl is completely forgettable."

"Guess it goes both ways." Lilly's thoughts turned back to the events in front of the store. "I don't think he knew Ebner threw the firecrackers." Caleb had seemed somewhat surprised.

Rose chuckled. "I don't think we're talking about Karl anymore."

Lilly laughed. "He's forgettable, remember?" Though she wouldn't so readily forget how it had felt to watch him walk away with barely a wave.

Rose giggled. "He certainly jumped to obey when Ebner ordered him to stop helping you."

Lilly knew Rose was back to talking about Caleb.

"I almost expected him to pull his hat off and bow a little," Rose added.

Lilly chuckled, though she didn't find it all that amusing. She'd been surprised and not a little disappointed to realize he worked for the Caldwells and was eager to obey Ebner, the man who had been responsible for so much of the damage inflicted on the Bell farm. Though he was smart enough and cautious enough to always make it look like an accident.

"How can a man with any integrity work for that crew?" Lilly asked. "Wouldn't he have to take part in some of their activities?" Her voice hardened. "Like driving the sheep into the river. I'm not apt to quickly forget that one of the lambs died as a result of it." Not once but twice, the Caldwell cowboys had shepherded the sheep into the river while the Bells were away.

Rose squeezed her hand. "We both know the Caldwells are a bad bunch."

There was no need for Lilly to reply. They all knew the truth about the Caldwells. They insisted it was a mistake made by some inexperienced clerk that a quarter section of land right next to the river had been left off the Caldwells' land title. The Bells should have realized that was the case, Mr. Caldwell insisted, and not taken advantage of the mistake. The Caldwell cowboys had done their best to drive them off before Pa could prove up on the homestead. They'd failed. Even then they hadn't given up.

She realized she was clenching her teeth—something she did every time the Caldwell name came up. Why couldn't they leave the Bells alone? They had thousands of acres. The quarter section Pa owned shouldn't matter.

Over the years, she'd decided the Caldwell quest had nothing to do with reason. Some people weren't happy unless they had everything.

They approached the farm and Lilly allowed herself to study the place with pride. She and her sisters had a hand in developing the few acres into a Garden of Eden along the river despite the Caldwells' objections to their presence. She studied the place hard. The sheep were grazing placidly in their pasture. The milk cows looked up at their approach but didn't move, contentedly chewing their cuds. The hay was safely in the barn, and the oats were harvested and the grain stored for winter use. The garden was almost done as well—only the root vegetables were left to be brought in.

She let out a sigh of relief. "Everything looks the way it should."

"For now." Rose sounded dubious. But then they all knew it was only a matter of time before the Caldwells struck again.

"I hope Ma's all right." Lilly passed the new barn. "It's not like her not to go to town with us."

"She said she was tired."

Lilly glanced back at Pa, who was still asleep. "So is he."

"I think they're missing Cora." Their older sister had married a few weeks ago and moved with her husband, Wyatt, to a nearby ranch.

"Pa thinks he has to take over Cora's chores." Lilly tried to persuade him that she and Rose could manage without his help, but he still offered it constantly. "The cold bothers him. I'm going to ask Ma to give him a tonic. Maybe I'll suggest she take it, too." They drew up before the house. Ma watched from the window.

Pa woke and eased from the wagon. Rose and Lilly hopped down and scurried around to get the packages before Pa could do it.

"Did you sell all the produce?" Ma asked as they entered the kitchen. They took garden produce and medicinals to town each Saturday.

"Every bit of it," Rose assured her.

"Did you see Mrs. Andrews? How is she feeling?"

Lilly answered Ma's question. "She's much improved. I gave her some more cough syrup and I looked at little Andy. He's got a bad case of thrush."

Pa sat at the end of the table and sorted through the mail—mostly newspapers and a farm magazine.

Ma scurried about to make tea and they all sat down to enjoy it. "What's new in town? Did you see Mrs. Rawley?" Ma was speaking about her dear friend the pastor's wife.

"She asked after you," Lilly said.

Rose plunked her teacup on the table. "Ebner threw firecrackers under the horse."

"Goodness." Ma glanced around the table. "Is everyone okay?"

Rose chuckled. "A very handsome cowboy came and helped us."

Lilly squinted at her sister, knowing Rose meant to tease her. "I could have managed on my own."

Rose gave a dismissive shrug. "I didn't see you telling him to leave you alone." She turned to Ma. "Lilly could hardly tear her eyes off the man."

Ma studied each of the girls. "Is this a nice man? Should we invite him to join us for Sunday dinner?"

The skin on Lilly's face grew tight. "Ma, no."

Between them, the two sisters related the events. "The boy doesn't use his right leg," Lilly told her. "He walks with crutches. But Caleb—Mr. Craig—is very patient and tender with him."

"He's a Caldwell cowboy." For Rose that was all that mattered. She, of all the Bells, bore the most resentment toward their neighbors. Probably because Duke Caldwell, the son and heir, had teased Rose throughout school.

Ma held up her hand. "You can't judge a man solely because he works for the Caldwells. A man should be judged by his actions and his choices."

Rose grunted. "He chooses to work for the Caldwells. Guess that says a lot about him."

"Nevertheless," Pa said, with final authority. "We will

be fair and give the man the benefit of the doubt until we have reason to think otherwise."

Rose pursed her lips.

Lilly knew her twin didn't think anything good could come from the Caldwell ranch. But finally Rose lowered her challenging gaze from Pa's patient one. "Yes, Pa."

Pa turned to Lilly. "We'll give him the benefit of the doubt, won't we?"

Lilly nodded. "Yes, Pa." She agreed readily enough. For one thing, she'd like to know why Teddy didn't walk. Maybe she or Ma could help. She'd also like to know how a man who obviously had tender feelings could work for the Caldwells. Or perhaps his feelings were for Teddy and no one and nothing else.

There was one thing she would be clear about. She would not let her interest in the pair go beyond surface curiosity and concern.

Not that she expected she'd see them again unless they happened to bump into each other in town. So guarding her feelings shouldn't be a problem.

A few minutes later she went to the barn to start feeding the animals. She smiled as she stepped into the interior. The barn was cozy and warm and solid. The animals were safe in there.

If she could turn her heart into a solid barn she could keep her feelings safe and warm, too. She chuckled at the silly thought.

When she was done with the feeding, she stepped back outside and blinked as a wagon approached with Caleb in the seat. Teddy peered out from behind his father.

She stared. "What are you doing here?" Her words sounded rude, though she didn't mean them to.

But what was a Caldwell cowboy doing on Bell land?

Chapter Two

Teddy nudged Caleb. "Papa, tell her about my dog."

Caleb's heart swelled as he took in the pretty little farm—the decent-sized, new-looking barn, the outbuildings, the house surrounded by yellow flowers, the garden with pale cornstalks and orange pumpkins still on the vine. Once, he'd had a little ranch similar to this with a herd of cows that had increased in number each year. It was all he'd ever wanted.

His dream of settling down and raising cows and children had vanished the day Amanda had died and Teddy had gotten injured. After that, he couldn't abide the place. He'd taken care of Teddy as his leg healed, and then he'd begun looking for a doctor who could fix his son so he could walk.

"Papa." Teddy's voice brought him back to his task.

He wondered if she would welcome him or ask him to get off their property simply because he worked for the Caldwells. But surely she'd be moved by the needs of an animal and a small boy. He didn't expect or welcome any sympathy regarding his own losses.

He cleared his thoughts and spoke to the woman who was waiting patiently in front of him, her expression rife with caution. "We got us an injured dog. Mr. Frank told us you help injured animals."

Lilly nodded. "I do my best. Where's the dog?"

He jumped down and went to the back of the wagon to gingerly lift the limp dog out of it. The poor animal whimpered. "Hang on, buddy. We'll help you."

Lilly hovered by his side, her attention on the pup in his arms.

"What happened to it?" Her nearness rattled his insides. He'd vowed to never again think of sharing his life with a woman, but sometimes it was hard to remember that. Like now, as she tenderly ran her fingers over the furry dog. When her arm brushed his, his mouth went dry. He drew in a strengthening breath and righted his thoughts.

"This animal has been neglected." She fired a hot look at him, as if to silently accuse him.

"We found her by the road." He wanted to make it clear he wasn't responsible for the condition of the animal.

"Can you make her better?" Teddy asked.

Thankfully she shifted her powerful gaze to Teddy, and Caleb pulled his thoughts back to where they belonged—finding help for the dog, finding help for his son and preventing any woman from entering his life.

She smiled at Teddy. "I'll certainly do my best."

Her gaze returned to Caleb, warm with a compassion that slowly cooled as she looked at him. He understood her kindness was aimed at Teddy and likely this unfortunate pup. Toward him, she seemed accusatory.

Well, it wasn't like he wasn't used to accusations, mostly from his own thoughts. At twenty-five years of age, he had a number of failures to his name. Likely more than a man twice his age ought to have. He'd failed to protect his wife. He'd failed to help his son with his problems. Letting this dog die in his arms was not another failure he meant to endure. "Can you help?" His question rang with more harshness than he felt. She had no way of knowing he only wanted to make this turn out right.

"Follow me." She hurried toward the barn, seeming to expect him to follow.

He didn't move. He couldn't carry the dog and help Teddy down, too.

"I'll wait," Teddy said.

"See that you do." Caleb gave him a look that ought to have pinned him to the wagon box, but Teddy's eyes lingered on the dog.

Caleb hustled after Lilly. The woman moved like a whirlwind. By the time he caught up she was already inside the barn, a scrap of old blanket on the floor in front of her.

"Put her here. Gently," she urged as if she thought he'd drop the dog.

It was on the tip of his tongue to point out he'd rescued the dog and brought her here for the animal's good and he wasn't about to do anything to make things worse. Instead he knelt and eased the dog to the mat.

She examined the poor critter with gentle fingers. The dog moaned and opened her eyes briefly.

"What do you think?" Sure looked to him like the pup was about to draw her last breath.

"She's very weak. There are a number of cuts on her. She's got some nasty bruises. And she's been badly neglected." Her voice grew harder with each word. "Who would do this to a dog?"

"Same sort who would hurt a woman or child." He heard the strangled sound of his voice but hoped it wasn't noticeable to Lilly. He kept his attention on the suffering

animal as a thousand pictures flashed through his mind.
Amanda's blood pooling on the floor. Teddy's pale face as
Caleb cradled Amanda and tended to his son's wounds.

Lilly nodded her head in decision. "Let's get to work."

"You're gonna save her, aren't you? She's my dog. I
want her to live."

They both jerked toward Teddy, who stood in the doorway. Without waiting for an answer, he hobbled toward
them.

Lilly's eyes filled with pity.

Caleb stiffened. Pity would not do Teddy any good.
The specialist down east had promised to fit the boy with
a brace that would teach the leg to work again. Or so the
man had claimed. Caleb had long since lost his faith in
doctors. "Let's get started."

Lilly bent over the dog, but her hands didn't move.
He wondered what she thought about it all—Teddy, the
dog, him. Well, he already knew what she thought of
him. He worked for the Caldwells. That made him part
of the wrong side in a land feud. Good thing she didn't
know his past or she'd have reason to think even more
poorly of him.

"You want me to get water?" he asked.

She let out a gust of air and nodded. "There's a bucket
by the door and the pump is toward the house."

Caleb scrambled to his feet and then hesitated.

She glanced up, a question in her eyes.

"Is it all right if I leave him here?" He gestured with
his head toward Teddy.

She looked at his son and her mouth curved into a
smile as warm as the morning sun on the horizon.

His breath caught partway up his throat at her gentle,
sweet regard for his boy, who had been hurt so badly. He
closed his eyes against the rushing memories. The boy

was without a mother because Caleb had been unable to save Amanda. He'd been away from home when the cowboys had entered, set on punishing him for interfering after he'd caught them tormenting the young man running his father's store. If Caleb hadn't come along, the pair would have helped themselves to whatever they liked from the shelves without paying. In hindsight, he should have known they were the sort who would want revenge, but he thought the incident was over with when he rode away. Later he'd arrived home and come face-to-face with their blazing guns. He'd shot the two men in self-defense after they'd murdered his wife, and he lived with the agony that he might have been the one who shot the bullet that injured Teddy. His hope, his prayer, was that he could make up for it by getting Teddy the best of care. *God, let this doctor be one who can really help.*

He strode out to get water. He pumped with such vigor the water splashed out of the bucket, and he realized he was angry. What was the use of anger anyway? His energies would be better spent getting help for Teddy. And if that meant working for the Caldwells while seeking Lilly Bell's care for the dog that Teddy had claimed as his own, well, so be it.

He wouldn't let a feud that meant nothing to him stand in the way.

Lilly smoothed the dog's fur across the top of her head, which was about the only place that wasn't soiled with dirt and blood. "Poor puppy. You'll be okay now." She'd do her best to make sure that was true.

Teddy scooted closer and leaned over to put his face close to the dog's. "You're my dog and you ain't gonna die. You hear?"

The dog stuck out her tongue. It touched the tip of Teddy's nose and the little boy laughed.

Lilly wanted to pull both of them close and shelter them in her arms. Seemed life had been unfair and cruel to the pair. "I'll do my best to make sure she gets better."

Teddy studied her so intently her lips twitched with a smile.

"The man in town said you had a special way with sick animals. Do you?"

She laughed. "If taking care of them means I do, then yes."

"But nothing special?"

She studied him carefully. He was such a sweet-looking child. What had happened to his leg? She'd ask his father the first chance she got. If she or Ma could do anything to help… "I just use the skills my Ma taught me."

Caleb returned and set the bucket down. He squatted next to his son.

She turned from the pair, dipped a rag in the cold water and began to sponge away the dirt and blood from the pup.

"Can I help wash her?" Teddy asked.

"If it's okay with your papa."

After a moment of consideration, Caleb gently said, "It's okay."

She handed Teddy a wet rag and showed him a place where it appeared only dirt had smudged the fur.

"After all," Teddy said as he dabbed at the spot, "she's my dog. I should take care of her." Teddy sounded so serious she ducked to hide her smile.

"Teddy." Caleb's voice held warning. "You just found her. And she's in pretty bad shape."

"But Miss Lilly can fix her. Can't you? That man in town said you could."

She caught his hands and held them until he met her eyes. "Teddy, we will do our very best. Sometimes the best thing we can do is love our friend."

"I love her."

She felt the depth of his yearning in the pit of her stomach. He needed this dog. She prayed the injuries weren't too bad and she'd survive. *God, give me hands to heal and words to strengthen.* She meant both the dog and his young owner.

Grub padded in at that moment. The silly dog never noticed people coming, and usually barked a warning upon their going. But the big, clumsy, lop-eared dog was dearly loved by the entire family. Grub saw Caleb and Teddy and gave a halfhearted *woof.* He noticed the injured dog and ambled over to smell it. He then sat two feet away and watched.

"This is Grub. He's our dog." She'd never tell a stranger how useless he was.

Caleb snorted. "Johnny-come-lately, I'd say."

Lilly let the comment pass. "What's your dog's name?" she asked Teddy.

"She's a girl, right?"

"Yes."

"A girl might not like being with two boys."

"Two boys?" Was there another one hiding in the wagon?

"Me and Papa."

Caleb made a noise like he was holding back a laugh.

Lilly dared not look at him for fear of revealing her own amusement and offending Teddy. "Oh, I see. I don't think a girl dog will mind."

"That's good. You know any good girls' names?"

"Well, let me think." She continued to wash the dog as she talked, thankful she'd discovered nothing but cuts so far, though some of them were deep enough to make infection a real possibility. "My sisters are named Cora and Rose, but those aren't very good names for a dog. The girls I know have names like Nancy and Katie. I know a little girl called Blossom."

Teddy nodded and smiled. "I like Blossom. It sounds like a pretty flower and my dog is as pretty as a flower. You like it, Papa?"

"I like it fine." He knelt beside Teddy and patted Blossom's head gently, earning him a grateful swipe of the dog's tongue.

Lilly studied the man. He had dark brown hair, curly and tangled like it hadn't seen a brush in several days. His dark brown eyes set off a face full of determination. She felt a flash of sympathy. No doubt he worried about his son. It was on the tip of her tongue to ask where Teddy's mother was, but it didn't matter to her except where it concerned the boy.

Caleb met her gaze. "Blossom is a fine name for a dog who looks to be half collie and half bulldog, or something equally—"

Afraid he'd say "ugly," she quickly inserted her own word. "Strong."

He nodded and grinned.

She blinked. My, how his eyes did darken and flood with warmth when he smiled. His whole face underwent such a transformation she was almost tempted to say he was handsome. Which had been her first thought when she'd seen him at the store. Good thing Rose hadn't been there to take note of the way her cheeks had warmed as he brushed past with an apology.

She thought about how strong and kind he had been when he'd helped her calm the horse. Her feelings had been struck again with awareness of tenderness and strength when he took his son on his knee and drove from town.

Despite all those wonderful virtues, he had so much working against him. He was obviously married, even if she'd seen no evidence of a wife. He worked for the Caldwells, which put a barrier as big as the Rocky Mountains between them. Not that any of that mattered, because she had no intention of ever again getting close to anyone outside her family.

If you get close to people, you will just suffer more losses down the road.

She'd help the dog. She'd even help Teddy if Caleb let her and if she could. But she would not let her heart be drawn to either one of them.

She'd keep on repeating her vow every day if necessary.

Chapter Three

Blossom! Caleb had almost laughed at the name. The animal looked more like trash than a flower, but he would respect Teddy's devotion and hope the boy wouldn't end up with a broken heart.

Lilly bent over a cut on the pup to examine it more closely, and then let out a sigh. "It's not deep."

"Blossom sure likes me washing her." Teddy wiped at the fur. Indeed, the dog opened her eyes and focused on Teddy, who leaned closer. "You're so pretty. Prettier than any other dog I ever seen."

Caleb chuckled. The dog would likely grow into a good-sized animal with long silky hair like a collie. Her face, on the other hand, would probably look like she'd run into a train. "Beauty is certainly in the eye of the beholder."

Lilly made a sound—half grunt, half sigh. "Seems to be true on many levels."

Caleb considered her at length. It sounded like she had personal experience with the old saying, but it couldn't be on her own behalf. She was quite the most beautiful woman he'd ever seen. "I met your twin this morning. What about your other sister? Is she older or younger?"

"Cora. She's two years older. She got married a short time ago and she and her husband, Wyatt, live on a small ranch not far from here."

"How old are you?" Teddy asked, the question so out of the blue and so inappropriate it shocked Caleb.

"Son, we don't ask personal questions." He needed to give the boy some lessons on how to carry on a conversation with a woman. Not that he would mind knowing the answer. There was something about Lilly that made it impossible to guess her age. She had a twinkle in her eyes and a freshness about her that spoke of young innocence, but several times he'd glimpsed wisdom lurking in the depths of her gaze.

Lilly chuckled. "It's a perfectly natural question. I'm eighteen."

Teddy considered it a moment. "Mr. Frank said you and that girl you were with are twins. So your sister is eighteen, too?"

"That's correct."

"I'm five."

Caleb ducked his head to hide his smile at how Teddy delivered his announcement. As if it carried a huge amount of importance.

"My pa is twenty-five. Isn't that right, Papa?"

Caleb didn't know whether to laugh at his son's audacity or to scold it. The boy had developed a sudden need to tell Lilly everything. Everything? He hoped not. He did not want Teddy informing Lilly that his mama had been murdered and his papa had shot two men. And worst of all, that his papa might have been the one to injure his leg. Perhaps he could distract the boy. "Blossom is watching you."

Teddy smiled at his dog and patted her back. "My

mama was twenty-four when she died." Teddy cocked his head as if thinking about Amanda's death.

Caleb held his breath. Teddy had refused to say a thing about the day of her murder ever since it happened. *Please don't start talking about it now. Not in front of a stranger.* How would Caleb deal with the press of regrets and the weight of sorrow if he had to confront his past before this beautiful woman? He swallowed hard and gritted his teeth. He would not let his emotions escape into the open.

"Papa, does that mean she's still twenty-four?"

His lungs relaxed and released the pent-up air. "I suppose it does." Forever twenty-four. For some odd reason the notion gave him a measure of comfort.

Lilly touched Teddy's head. "I'm sorry about your mama." She shifted her gaze to Caleb. It was soft, gentle, full of compassion. He tightened his jaw. Her expression would have shifted to horror if she'd known the details. Lilly rubbed Teddy's back. "I'm so sorry, Teddy. I lost my own mama and papa when I was three."

He looked at her. "You did? I thought that man was your pa." He was referring to Mr. Bell.

"He is. He and my ma found us and adopted us."

Teddy studied her unblinkingly.

Lilly met his look with a kind smile.

Finally Teddy spoke. "I've never known anyone who was adopted. I found Blossom." He turned to Caleb. "Can I adopt her?"

Caleb chuckled. "I don't think it's called that when it's an animal." Teddy already had his heart set on keeping the dog. The animal wasn't as sorry looking as she had been when they'd found her, but she still looked mighty poor. "How is she?" He directed his question at Lilly.

She continued examining the dog. "There are some

serious cuts, but nothing is broken that I can tell. She's awfully tender over her ribs, though, so it could be some of them are broken. They're certainly bruised. I'll get some ointment to apply to the cuts. She needs to rest and get some proper food in her."

"Lilly, you have guests. I didn't notice anyone drive up." The sound of a new voice drew Caleb's attention. Mr. Bell stood in the doorway.

"Hi, Pa. You remember Mr. Caleb Craig and his son, Teddy? They found this dog and brought her to me for some care."

"Of course, the Caldwell cowboy."

The man's voice revealed no emotion, but Caleb felt condemned by the statement.

Mr. Bell rumpled Teddy's hair. He knelt by the dog and ran his fingers through her fur. "Found her where?"

Caleb answered the man. "Down the road about three miles."

Mr. Bell grunted. "Close to where the Bixbys live. He's a man with no regard for God's creation. Lets his animals suffer. Uses his land unwisely. What's your verdict?" He asked the latter to Lilly and she repeated what she had told Caleb.

Mr. Bell nodded. "He might benefit from Ma's tonic. She gave me a shot of the stuff and I feel better already." He chuckled. "Might be the nap and a hot drink of tea helped, too."

"I was going to ask her for some."

Mr. Bell planted a hand on Lilly's shoulder. She smiled up at him. Their love was obvious. It seemed neither of them regretted finding the other.

A found family full of tenderness and love. It was almost enough to give a man hope—

He jerked his thoughts away from that trail.

Mr. Bell headed for the open barn door and then paused. "Lilly, you need any help with the dog?"

"I think I can manage on my own."

"Then I'll be in my shop." The man disappeared through the door.

Lilly went to the neat room in the corner and returned with a jar and a roll of bandage. She looked from Caleb to Teddy.

He felt her hesitation and wondered what she wanted. He didn't have to wait long to find out.

She knelt in front of Teddy and commanded his attention. "I am going to fix Blossom's cuts." She explained how the ointment would help the wounds heal. "Now Blossom might not like me touching them." She let the information settle in Teddy's brain.

"Sometimes you gotta do what's best, even if it's hard." The words seemed to come from a dark place inside Teddy.

Feelings of pride and pain warred inside Caleb.

Lilly squeezed Teddy's hand. "You are exactly right. And very wise."

Teddy beamed.

"Now here's where you have to make a choice. Do you want to stay even if you have to see Blossom crying, or do you want to have your papa take you outside and wait until I'm done?"

Caleb jerked forward. "May I speak to you?" He indicated that they should retreat to the tack room.

She rose slowly. Leaving her supplies behind, she joined him, though she hovered just inside the door as if ready to take flight.

"I don't think he should have any choice in this. I'll take him to the wagon or over to the pump for a cold drink of water."

She refused to meet his eyes. "I'm sorry I spoke out of turn. But I've already given him the choice." She shot him a look of defiance.

"Papa, Miss Lilly, I've made up my mind."

Caleb knew he wasn't mistaken in thinking Lilly was relieved about the interruption. Maybe he was, too. He had no desire to engage in an argument with her about what was and was not appropriate for his son. All he wanted was assurance the dog Teddy had adopted on sight would live.

Teddy sat up, his expression eager.

"Son," Caleb began, intending to warn the boy that they were leaving the barn, but Teddy had already started to talk.

"I decided. Blossom is my dog. She wants me to stay."

Caleb jerked back. How could he disagree with that kind of conviction? "Very well. But you must be brave."

Teddy looked so determined that Caleb stifled a chuckle.

"I can. I remember how. Mama told me."

Caleb stared. In the past nine months, Teddy had steadily refused to talk about Amanda's death. Many had suggested it might help the boy if he did. Seems finding this dog had done something for Teddy that Caleb, the doctors and even Amanda's parents had not been able to do.

Lilly squeezed Teddy's shoulder. "Blossom will be much happier with you here."

Teddy beamed.

Another thought surfaced. Maybe Lilly had played a role as well, with her gentle kindness and direct way of talking to Teddy. If she and Blossom combined forces, could they help his son? He didn't expect the pair could figure out what Teddy needed in order to walk again, but it seemed at least they might help him come to grips with Amanda's death. That would be worth something.

Would she agree to spend more time with his son? But even if she did, how could he ask her without risking his job at the Caldwells'? Ebner made no secret of his antagonism toward the Bells.

Lilly knelt beside the dog, her knuckles white as she held the jar and supplies she'd brought.

Caleb's heart went out to her. She had a difficult job to do, applying ointment and dressings to the wounds. It would be doubly difficult with Teddy watching. Maybe she regretted allowing Teddy to stay. "Teddy, it's not too late to change your mind," he said.

"No. I gotta do this. Big boys don't let hard things stop them from doing what they have to."

He narrowed his eyes at the boy. Where had Teddy heard those words? Had Caleb spoken them to his son? He didn't remember doing so, but then a person can say a lot of things carelessly that a listener might take seriously. He'd best watch his words in the future. He didn't want to make the boy feel he had to take on a load too big for his little shoulders.

Lilly gave the boy a gentle smile. "Then let's get it done."

"Is this when she cries?" Teddy's voice was clogged with sadness.

She sat back to study him. "You don't have to stay."

He blinked back tears. "I can be brave."

"Very well."

Caleb sat behind the boy and held him close. "You won't be alone."

Lilly studied him. He wished he could read her expression. Did she see his care for Teddy and approve of it? Or was she able to see past all that to his pain and guilt?

He was getting plumb foolish. Of course she couldn't see anything of the sort.

She ducked her head and set to work. She screwed the lid off the jar and dipped her finger into a thick yellowish ointment and applied it to the first wound.

As expected, Blossom yipped.

Grub ambled over to investigate. He shoved his nose into Lilly's neck as if to inform her she'd hurt the other dog. She elbowed him aside. "Grub, go lie down. Everything is just fine here."

Grub padded back to his spot in the patch of sunlight pouring through the open door.

As Blossom whined, Teddy smoothed the fur on her head and whispered, "It's okay, little one. We're going to make you better."

Lilly kept her attention on her task. She applied the ointment to many of the wounds, flinching when Blossom cried. Some of the cuts she left open to the air, and a few she wrapped with bandages. When she was done, she sat back. "That's the best I can do for now. I'll get her some of Ma's tonic. But first, I'll bring her water."

Teddy looked at her with eager eyes. "I'll take good care of her."

"I know you will." She shifted her gaze to Caleb. "I really think she needs to stay here a few days so I can watch for infection."

Teddy let out a small cry. "She has to come with us."

Lilly caught his hand. "Teddy, I promise I'll take really good care of her for you."

"No. No." Teddy shook his head. "I'm not leaving her." He turned to Caleb, his eyes wide. He plucked at Caleb's shirt front. "Don't make me leave her. Please, Papa."

Lilly closed the ointment jar and tidied up the bandages. She took them back to the tack room and then stood at the doorway. "Caleb, may I speak to you in private? Teddy, will you watch Blossom carefully while I get her some water?"

Caleb took Teddy's hands and waited for the boy to look him in the eye. "I'll be right back. You hear?"

Teddy nodded. His eyes remained too large. His pulse beat frantically in the veins of his neck.

Caleb followed Lilly outside to the pump, where she already had a pail full of water.

She faced him. "I know this might seem presumptuous, but why not leave Teddy here? I can make sure Blossom doesn't get infected and he can be with his dog."

Caleb stared. This was what he wanted, wasn't it? But he couldn't leave Teddy alone.

Nor could he afford to lose his job by risking Ebner's ire.

What was he to do?

Lilly almost choked the words of invitation out. Not because she didn't welcome Teddy's company or think it would do him good to be with his dog.

But because she knew it would inevitably mean seeing more of Caleb, and there was something about him that made her heart pull at its moorings. A dead wife. A son who, for whatever reason, needed crutches to walk. Yet rather than seeing a man wallowing in self-pity she'd seen numerous glimpses of a tenderhearted man. She'd seen it in the way he'd held Teddy as she ministered to the dog. She'd seen it in the way his eyes filled with concern that Teddy might be upset by watching her work. And she saw it now in the way his expression went from surprise to interest to doubt and finally to decision.

"I couldn't leave him. He's not been away from me since…"

She waited, but he didn't seem about to explain further. "I understand. But the dog…"

He looked past her to the horizon. "Yes, the dog. It'll upset him some to leave her."

She nodded. But there was little more she could offer. "If you leave Teddy here, perhaps Ma and I could help with his leg."

Interest flared in his eyes and then faded. "I've been to a dozen doctors and they've not helped." Doubt and hope seemed to cling to his words.

"Do you mind telling me what happened? Is his leg broken?"

Caleb turned so she saw only his profile—he swallowed hard and sucked his lips in. "His ma was murdered."

A gasp tore from her throat. "I'm sorry."

He nodded but continued to stare at something far off. "I found two intruders. They came at me with guns. I used mine." He sounded as if he were working hard to grate his voice from his throat. "When it was over they were dead. Amanda was already dead—murdered by the pair."

"And Teddy?" she whispered, hardly able to take it in.

"Amanda must have seen the intruders coming and made him hide in the closet. When I found him, he'd been shot in the leg."

"Oh, no." Pain and sorrow twisted through her with such vengeance she couldn't breathe. "How awful." Caleb's face contorted and she knew he was reliving the horror. The only comfort she could offer was the one thing Ma had taught her. Sometimes all a person could give another person in pain was presence and touch. She pressed her hand to his arm. "Caleb, I am so sorry. It's too dreadful for words."

A shudder shook him hard. He turned to face her, his eyes dark as a summer storm, his mouth a white line.

She too shuddered at the frank agony she saw.

"That's not the worst part." His voice was a hoarse whisper. "I'll never know if I was the one who fired the shot that hurt him."

She nodded, understanding this feeling of guilt must edge every thought, every glance at his son. What comfort could she offer him? Only the truth.

"You have no way of knowing it didn't come from some other gun, either."

He nodded, but she could tell the words had not gone farther than his ears.

"How long ago did all this happen?"

"Nine months. Almost ten."

That long and the boy's injury still remained? There had to be something wrong, likely an infection. One that long-standing was unusual and—she shuddered—usually life threatening.

"Has the wound not healed?"

"It's healed, but he can't use the leg. And I have no idea why. No doctor has been able to help me." He told her about the many trips he and Teddy had taken to find help. "I have to get him to a doctor down east." He stepped away as if he were already on his way. "I can't leave him here. I need the job at the Caldwells in order to pay the special doctor."

She nodded. She and Ma used only common sense and old-fashioned remedies, along with herbs and poultices. Surely a special doctor would have newer things to offer. But if the infection had gone to the bone…

She shivered. If she could do anything to help, she would. She opened her mouth to ask him to reconsider taking Teddy away for the night.

Caleb turned on his heel and strode toward the barn before she could utter the words.

She rumbled her breath out. She'd been about to suggest he stay, too.

How had she so quickly forgotten that he was a Caldwell cowboy? Rose would be shocked.

Worse, she'd shocked herself by how much she'd been drawn to this man and his pain.

She could see Teddy through the open barn door, leaning over his dog, crooning words of comfort when he himself needed those same words. Likely some of Ma's medicinals wouldn't do his leg any harm, especially if infection had gone deep inside, but that type of deep infection usually resulted in severe pain, and the boy didn't appear to be suffering.

She or Ma could at least provide comfort measures to Teddy until Caleb took him to the special doctor.

Never mind that his father worked for the Caldwells.

Halfway across the yard, Caleb's feet slowed and he slowly came about to face her. With measured steps he returned to her, his expression full of determination.

"Tomorrow is Sunday. I don't have to be at the Caldwells'. If your invitation is still open, I accept for the day."

One day! What could she hope to do for Teddy or Blossom in one day?

"Unless you've changed your mind. Perhaps your family wouldn't welcome a Caldwell cowboy." He had clearly mistaken her hesitation.

Rose would have concerns, but she'd voice them in private. Ma and Pa would take a wait-and-see approach. As for Lilly, she'd make the most of the limited time, grateful in a way he'd not be there longer. The locked doors around her heart shuddered every time she thought of what he'd been through. "The invitation is still open."

Caleb gave a quick nod. "I'll deal with the consequences when I get back."

"I'm not trying to discourage you, but are you sure about this? From what I've seen of Ebner and the others, they won't be happy to know you're consorting with the enemy, so to speak. Only the Caldwells view the disagreement in such terms. We only want to be left in peace to farm our little bit of land."

"I only want to do what's right for Teddy. I'm sure I can make Ebner understand that." His words rang and his dark eyes flashed.

Lilly had her doubts, but she'd never before let the Caldwells stop her from doing what she thought was right.

She certainly wasn't about to let them stop her now.

Chapter Four

Caleb hadn't decided how he'd deal with Ebner should the man object, but he felt he should be able to do as he chose on a Sunday and return to his work at the Caldwells' on Sunday night without questions being asked.

He was a free man, after all.

He tried to dismiss the doubts cluttering his mind. At the moment, staying seemed the right thing to do.

Lilly's invitation had sounded sincere, but her eyes were now shadowed by second thoughts. Was she concerned about how the Caldwells would react? Or her family? Then she smiled and drove away every bit of darkness. "Let's make Blossom comfortable. Then I'd like Ma to look at Teddy's leg, if you don't mind."

He wouldn't have minded if he'd thought there was any chance they could help, but—

"He's been prodded and poked. Some of the suggestions for helping him have been absurd. And too many of them cruel. Hang him in a harness until he uses his leg. Use some kind of noxious rub that would burn a hole in the hide of a cow. Poke his legs to stimulate the nerves. Seems everyone had a cure. Too bad none of them worked." He sucked in air. "No more torture."

Her hand brushed his arm and stilled his rush of words. Her touch when he'd been almost overwhelmed by his memories had soothed him. He had noted, too, how she'd touched Teddy to calm him. He didn't know if he should object to the touch or thank her for it. But he couldn't pull words from his brain, so he simply stood there as she spoke.

"Caleb, I promise you neither my ma nor I will do anything to hurt Teddy." She held his gaze unblinkingly until he nodded.

"Very well."

Satisfied, she said, "I'll let you tell Teddy." She carried the water to the barn.

Teddy turned to them as they entered, his expression tight as if he expected Caleb to insist they had to leave.

Caleb's insides warmed at his ability to give his son one small gift—a yes to his request to stay. He squatted in front of him. "Teddy, I've decided we can stay until tomorrow evening. Then I'll have to go back to work and you'll have to come with me."

"One day?"

"I'm afraid that's all we have."

Teddy sighed softly. "Then God will have to make Blossom better in one day."

Caleb blinked. How could his son have any faith left after all the praying that had been done over him to no avail? But he would not rob his son of it. *Please, God, honor the faith of this little one.*

"I brought water." Lilly had poured some into a little dish.

"Can I give it to her?" Teddy reached for the dish.

"Of course you can. In fact, I think she might prefer it."

She helped him place the dish close to Blossom's nose.

Grub came over and lapped at the water. Lilly pulled him close to her. "I'll fill your dish in a minute. Let me help this little girl first."

Grub plunked down at her side and watched. "Good dog."

Caleb had his doubts about Grub's qualifications as a guard dog, but he certainly passed with flying colors as a friendly, obedient pet.

Teddy leaned over Blossom, patting her head. "Come on, Blossom. You have to drink so you can get better. We don't want you fading away to a shadow, do we?"

Lilly choked back a chuckle.

Teddy was repeating something Caleb had said often when Teddy was mending and didn't want to eat. "At least he listened to some of what I said."

She laughed. "I expect he takes in everything you say and do."

Caleb nodded, smiling at his son, filling with pure pleasure. With a jolt he realized he'd been so focused on getting help for Teddy's injured leg he had almost forgotten the joy that came from simply spending time with him. He opened his mouth, about to thank Lilly, for he knew it was because of her calmness in dealing with Teddy and Blossom that some of his tension had disappeared.

He closed his mouth again. How could he possibly hope to explain this feeling?

He studied Lilly out of the corner of his eye. She bent over Blossom, murmuring encouragement to the dog. She touched Teddy's head to encourage him as well. Grub pressed to her side.

It hit him like a sledgehammer.

This was a woman made for giving and receiving love. Not that he should care. But for her sake he was glad he

would only be there one day, lest she begin to care for
him more than she should. He did not want to think he
would bring sorrow or heartache into her life, as he'd
done to others'.

He could list a whole lot of times people had been hurt
because of him. Most of the events he hadn't thought of
until after Amanda's murder, and then the memory of
them had returned with a vengeance, as if to reprimand
him for having forgotten them.

The time he lied about taking eggs to one of Ma's
customers, instead having broken them while chasing a
gopher. The customer had berated Ma publicly and Ma
had gone home crying.

Then there was the time at school when he'd pulled a
chair out when his friend Toby had gone to sit down and
Toby had banged his head. Caleb had laughed until he
realized Toby had taken a long time to bounce up again.

He would not continue to list his guilty deeds. Suf-
fice it to say Caleb knew he was bad news to those who
happened to have the misfortune of hanging around him.

He'd be extra careful while at the Bells so they
wouldn't pay a price for helping him. Though it was
Teddy they meant to help.

Blossom lapped the water a few times and then ignored it.

"That's a real good start." Lilly patted Teddy on the
head and pushed to her feet. "I'll go to the house and get
Ma's tonic." She had only made it to the barn door when
Rose came out of the house and trotted toward them, carrying a dish. "Pa told us about the injured dog. I made
that gruel you like."

She handed Lilly the dish and the bottle of tonic. Her
look blared a challenge.

Lilly knew exactly what she was wondering. *Why is a Caldwell cowboy here and why are you helping him?* She backed up so Rose could step into the barn.

"Rose, you remember Caleb Craig and his son, Teddy?"

Rose snorted so softly Lilly hoped she was the only one to hear it. "The Caldwell cowboy from town. I'm not likely to forget." Her piercing look said, *But it seems you are.*

Caleb set Teddy behind him and got to his feet to face Lilly and Rose. "Sorry to intrude on your fight about the Caldwells, but we found this dog and my son instantly claimed him. Your sister kindly offered to help."

Rose met his gaze. Neither of them blinked as Lilly held her breath, wondering who would relent first.

Caleb spoke again. "She's even offered to let us stay the night so Blossom here can rest."

Oh, no. Now Rose would blurt out how much she disliked the Caldwells.

Rose blinked. "Blossom?"

"The dog."

"Overnight?" She glared at Lilly.

Lilly smiled, not at all deterred by her sister's shock. Rose would soon realize that Teddy and Blossom needed their help.

Caleb shifted his gaze to Lilly and gave her a smile full of gratitude. "Your sister is very generous." Beyond the smile, Lilly glimpsed an ocean's depth of sorrow.

She couldn't look away. This man had every reason in the world to have a furrowed forehead. She shivered at the thought of everything that had happened to him.

If it had been possible, she would have applied one of Ma's healing balms to this man's heart.

"Oh, fine," Rose grumbled, and moved toward Blossom and Teddy. "So this is the dog you found."

"She's mine," Teddy said.

"Then I'd say she is very fortunate."

Lilly smiled. Rose might have been one to fight and sputter, but she didn't have an unkind bone in her body.

Caleb looked at the thin mixture Rose had made—oats cooked with meat broth—and shuddered. "I sure hope you mean that for Blossom."

The twins laughed, though Rose did so with more abandon than Lilly, as if enjoying his suspicion.

"Yes, it's for the dog," Lilly murmured and knelt beside Teddy. Together they managed to get Blossom to lick up some of the concoction. Then she uncapped the tonic. "Teddy, I need to give her these drops. Think you can help?"

He nodded eagerly.

"That's good. You hold her head while I put the drops in her mouth."

Teddy did as instructed and Blossom swallowed the drops and drank more water. Wearily, the dog closed her eyes.

Teddy glanced from the dog to Lilly to Caleb and then did it again.

"Papa?"

"What is it?"

"Wasn't that stuff supposed to make her better? She's still just lying here."

Lilly touched Teddy's head and smiled at him, her heart brimming with sorrow and tenderness at his question. How many times had this child been promised something would make him better and then been disappointed? She pushed her lips together as Caleb's words echoed in her head. The treatments the poor boy had endured. And his father along with him.

"Healing takes time. It can't be rushed."

Teddy gave Lilly a look of frank admiration. "You sure do know a lot about taking care of sick animals."

Rose laughed again. "She's had lots of experience. When we lived in town she rescued all sorts of dogs, cats, birds, chickens and even mice, and she nursed them. We were ten when we moved to this farm and she's collected all sorts of critters since."

"Like what?"

"Well, she raises sheep and pigs. People bring her animals that are doing poorly. Mostly she fixes them up and sends them back home, but sometimes we keep them. That's how we got our horse, and we have a motley collection of cats she's rescued. You should see this place at milking time. Say, I think you will. Lilly, when are you bringing in the cows?"

Ignoring the reminder of chores to be done, Lilly glowered at her sister. "Rose, please don't tell them everything you know about me."

Rose's smile widened. "Only the interesting stuff."

Lilly gave her a hard look. "That would be everything."

Rose opened her mouth as if to argue and instead burst out laughing. "You almost had me that time. One of these days you are going to convince me with that deadpan way of yours." Her expression grew thoughtful. "Maybe our first pa was a gambler. You might have learned that from him."

Lilly shook her head. "You've had him be everything from a wild horse wrangler to a traveling preacher. And now a gambler."

"I'm just curious, you know?"

"No, I don't. Seems to me what's in the past is best left in the past." They had loving parents in the way of Ma and Pa Bell. That was enough for Lilly.

But it had never been enough for Rose. She constantly tried to discover something about their birth parents.

Lilly dismissed the direction of the discussion.

"I'll bring in the cows," she said. Rose left the barn to do her own chores.

"Can I go with you?" Teddy asked. Then he sagged. "I guess I should stay with Blossom."

The dog was sleeping peacefully. "There's not much to do for her right now but let her rest. You're welcome to accompany me," Lilly said. "Both of you."

Teddy scrambled to get his crutches and hurried to her side. Caleb followed after.

Lilly didn't know whether to be grateful for his company or annoyed he probably didn't trust her alone with his son. Then again, she had invited him. And it really didn't matter either way—her only interest was in seeing Blossom get better and helping Teddy if that was possible.

Lilly led the way past the house. Out of habit, she scanned the pasture and fields. The cows waited patiently. Beyond them, the white sheep dotted the faded green pasture. The yellow and gold leaves on the fruit trees and bushes flapped in the wind. The garden lay peaceful.

Everything seemed in order. She allowed her breath to ease out even though it was only a matter of time until the Caldwells would do something.

"Is anything wrong?"

She startled at Caleb's question. "Just checking."

"For what? Are you expecting some sort of trouble?"

She snorted. "You might say that."

"Like what?" He squinted at her and edged closer to Teddy as if to protect him.

"Nothing to concern you. At least not directly." She shouldn't have said anything, but now that she had, perhaps it was best she told him the truth. Perhaps he had been unaware of how dangerous the Caldwells could be. "You should understand who you work for. The Caldwells are always up to mischief." Aware Teddy could hear every word, though he seemed more interested in watching the cows press toward the fence, she kept her words low and benign while frustration raged through her. Why couldn't they leave the Bells alone?

He nodded. "You're right. It's nothing to do with me. I need the job and who they choose to feud with is not my concern."

She wanted to argue. But what could she say? That a man of honor would not work for people like the Caldwells? But why did it matter one way or the other if he was honorable or otherwise? Yet somehow it did. For Teddy's sake, she reasoned, it mattered.

They reached the gate and she opened it. "Come on, girls. Milking time." Two dough-faced Jerseys cows lifted their heads. "Come, Bossy. Come, Maude," she called.

"Look, Papa, they come when she calls them."

She led the animals to the barn with Teddy and Caleb at her side. She scooped oats into the manger for each.

"Are you going to milk them now?" Teddy asked.

"I like to get it done before supper."

"Papa, Mama used to milk a cow, didn't she?"

"She sure did. She insisted you have milk so I got her a decent milk cow."

"She used to take me with her." Teddy's sad voice scraped Lilly's nerves raw. She'd lost her birth parents when she was three—one to death and one to abandonment—and had only a fleeting recollection of them. Or were they memories the girls had created over the years?

She didn't know. Perhaps it would have been better to not have any memories of her birth parents at all—they only made her sad.

Teddy brightened. "I used to give the cow oats just like Miss Lilly did."

Lilly pulled a three-legged stool close to the first cow. "This is Maude. She's gentle as a lamb."

"Can I pet her?"

"Best wait until I'm done milking." *Squirt, squirt.* The milk drummed into the bucket.

Meowing cats exploded from everywhere. A couple, seeing strangers, hissed.

"Mind your manners," Lilly scolded, shooting streams of milk at each cat in turn.

Teddy's eyes were round. His mouth gaped open.

Caleb laughed. "Guess you never saw so many cats at one time."

"I want to pet them." Teddy dropped his crutches and sat down amid the melee.

Seeing the concern in Caleb's face, Lilly reassured him. "It's okay. None of them will hurt him." She smiled at the pleasure in Teddy's face as the cats rubbed against him.

She might only have one day, but she'd do all she could to see he enjoyed every minute spent on the farm.

Caleb felt as if he had stepped back in time to a gentler, sweeter place where life followed familiar routines and his son enjoyed normal pursuits.

Two cats crawled into Teddy's lap, purring loudly. Teddy laughed. The purest laugh Caleb had heard from him in many months.

Caleb's eyes misted, no doubt irritated by the dust the cats were kicking up and nothing more.

Now satisfied with their drink, several cats hissed at Blossom. She opened one eye and closed it again but otherwise paid them no heed.

Grub cocked his head and watched the scene with a puzzled expression.

"Why do you have so many cats?" Teddy asked.

"Mostly because we had three batches of kittens this year."

"And you get to keep 'em all?"

"For a while. Usually once cold weather sets in and mice move indoors, people come and ask for a cat to keep the mice population down."

"Guess you don't have any mice around here."

"Not many."

"Would have to be an awfully brave mouse to come here." Teddy laughed so hard at his joke that tears trickled from his eyes.

Caleb watched in pure and natural pleasure.

Lilly chuckled as she finished with Maude. Then she stood at Caleb's side, a foamy pail of milk in one hand, and watched Teddy. "If that isn't the sweetest sound in the world, I don't what is."

He looked at her. She looked at him. And for a moment they shared something. Something he had not shared with anyone since Amanda died. A common delight in his son. It was temporary, he warned himself. But for now, he allowed himself to enjoy the moment. "His laughter is better than Sunday music."

She laughed. "Tons better than Sunday music if you happen to sit next to Harry Simmons, who sings like a hoarse bullfrog." She croaked out a few words of a song, then broke off and covered her mouth with her hand. "Oh, I'm so sorry. I should not be mocking anyone." Pink flared up her cheeks.

He'd laughed at her imitation of the poor Harry Simmons, whoever he was, but his laughter stalled in the back of his throat when he looked at her. The woman could go from straight-faced teasing, to lighthearted imitations, to apologies so fast it left him dizzy.

And more than a little intrigued.

Her eyes widened and then she ducked her head.

Oh glory, he'd been staring long enough to make her uncomfortable.

He bent over Teddy and stroked one of the cats. Lilly hurried over to the other cow and started milking.

"What's her name?" Teddy asked.

"This is Bossy."

Did Caleb detect a note of relief in her voice, as if she were happy to be talking about cows again?

Teddy seemed to consider the name for a moment. "Is that 'cause she's mean?"

"No, she just likes to do things the same way and if I try to change anything, she insists otherwise."

Teddy brightened. "That's like Papa."

Caleb stared at his son. "Me? Why would you say that?"

"You always put your boots in the exact spot every night. Once I moved them 'cause I wanted something and you made me put them back. You always make me sleep on the same side of you even when I want to sleep on the other side. And every morning, you stare at the fire until the coffee is ready. And you tell me not to talk until you have your coffee."

It was all true. "That doesn't mean I'm like Bossy. I can change if I want." He stole a glance at Lilly. She had her head pressed to the cow's flank, but—he narrowed his eyes—her shoulders were shaking. "You find this funny?"

She nodded without lifting her head.

He crossed his arms and considered the two of them. Teddy innocently petting a lap full of cats. Lilly trying to hide her amusement.

So his son considered him inflexible. Stuck in a routine. As for the coffee, he simply had to get his first cup before his brain started to perk. It didn't mean he was bossy or stuck in a rut.

Lilly gasped, tipped her head back and laughed aloud. She held up a hand to indicate she wanted to say something as soon as she could speak.

He waited, none too patiently. Did the woman intend to spend the rest of the day laughing?

She swiped her hand across her eyes. "I'm sorry. I shouldn't laugh, but if you could see your expression..." She chuckled some more and then tried to press back her amusement, but it showed clearly in her eyes.

From a deep well within, one that felt rusty with disuse, a trickle of laughter escaped. It grew in volume and intensity. He laughed. And laughed. And continued to laugh until his insides felt washed with freshwater. Until his stomach hurt. Until he realized Lilly and Teddy were watching him with wide smiles.

He sobered and drew in a deep breath. "I guess it is funny to realize a five-year-old has been taking note of my habits."

She grinned. "It's kind of sweet if you think about it."

He couldn't seem to break from her warm gaze. It was as if she approved of him. No. That wasn't it at all. Really, it was as if she approved of the way he and Teddy were together.

Bossy tossed her head.

"Okay. Okay." Lilly turned her attention to the cow. "I'm done. I'll let you go."

If Caleb had a lick of good sense left, he'd be done, too. He'd be on his way before his brain got any more affected by this woman.

Only he couldn't break the promise he'd made to Teddy. He'd stay the night, enjoy one day of being part of a normal family. Then he'd return to the Caldwells and his job with his resolve renewed and his face set to reach his goal.

He'd dare not linger overlong at the Bell place and risk losing his job with the Caldwells.

Not that he was tempted. Not at all.

Chapter Five

Lilly turned the cows out. "I'll take the milk to the house and let Ma know you're staying overnight. She'll expect you to join us for supper."

"That's not necessary," Caleb said. "We have supplies in our wagon. But could I turn the horse in to the pasture?"

"By all means." She wanted to kick herself for not suggesting it the moment Caleb had said he'd stay.

She would have accepted his refusal to join them for supper, but Ma would have had a fit if she didn't bring them.

"Ma's a very good cook."

Teddy got a look on his face that could only be described as hungry. "Papa, she's a good cook."

Caleb chuckled. "Are you saying I'm not?"

"I like your food." He sounded so uncertain that Lilly smiled.

Teddy brightened. "But it might be nice to try someone else's for a change."

Caleb gave his son such a loving, amused look that tears stung Lilly's eyes. She almost envied the boy such devotion, which was plumb foolish. Ma and Pa loved her every bit as much as Caleb loved his son. But oh, to see such a look meant especially for her. She shook her head hard, trying to clear her brain of such confusing thoughts.

Caleb and Teddy had followed Lilly as she put the cows in the pen for the night. He turned his horse in to the pasture, and then they returned to the barn.

"Look, Papa," Teddy chirped. "Blossom wagged her tail. Isn't that good? Means she's getting stronger." Teddy eased himself down beside the dog and petted her, murmuring encouragement. "You're safe here. Don't be afraid. No one will hurt you now."

Caleb pressed a fist to his chest as if, inside, his heart were hurting.

Lilly touched his arm. "He's safe, too."

Caleb nodded, but his eyes did not show relief. "I wish—" He shook his head.

She patted him twice. "I'll ask Ma to look at his leg after supper."

"Thanks."

"I'll leave you two with Blossom." She hurried to the house to strain the milk. As she passed through the kitchen, she stopped to speak to Ma.

"How's the pup?" Ma asked.

"She's a fighter. I think she'll be okay. Ma, I asked them to stay overnight so they could be with the dog."

Ma nodded. "Sounds sensible. Did you ask them to come for supper?"

"Yes. Ma, the little boy has something wrong with his leg." She repeated what Caleb had said. "I said we'd do what we could to help. Can you look at the leg after supper?"

"Certainly." She stirred a pot on the stove.

"Caleb was afraid we might torture his son." She told Ma the things Caleb had said.

Ma dried her hands on a towel and looked out the window toward the barn. "That poor little boy and that poor father. I hope you assured him we'd be very gentle with the lad."

"I did, but I warn you, he's very protective of his son."

"As well he should be." Ma returned to the stove and her meal preparation, her lips tight.

Lilly stared. Was she thinking of her three daughters? She had never said much about the circumstances of their adoption. She had only assured the girls over and over that they were loved, that they were a blessing from God to a childless couple. But no doubt she wondered what had happened to the girls' birth parents. Or more accurately, their father. Cora could remember their mother had died. Lilly figured it must have been something horrible that caused their father to abandon three little girls in the middle of the prairie. She went to Ma's side and brushed her hair off her forehead. "You're the best ma," she said. When had Ma's hair gotten so gray? Both her parents were in their seventies, but she didn't like the thought that they were getting old.

"I'm glad you think so. Now you get on with your chores so you'll be done in time for supper," Ma said. "It will be ready soon."

"Yes, Ma." Lilly went to the workroom, strained the milk and set it to cool. Pa would take the cans to the river after supper and hang them in the water, where the cold would keep the milk fresh and sweet for days. Soon that wouldn't be necessary. The workroom would be cold enough once winter set in. Many days it was so cold the milk froze. Lilly smiled. She loved spooning the crystalline milk from her cup. It was almost as good as ice cream, a rare treat they only enjoyed at community gatherings.

Although done, Lilly lingered. She didn't want to rush back to the barn and give anyone reason to think she was being overly curious or concerned about Caleb and his son. Though, of course, she had Blossom to check on, and she had said she and Ma would do what they could to help Teddy. It would be nice to have more than one day on which to help. But she'd tell them Ma would look at Teddy's leg after supper.

She turned, her reasons for returning firmly established. But still she hesitated. There was something about Caleb that upset her equilibrium. She might have said it was concern and sympathy over Teddy's plight, but it was more than that.

She might have said it was compassion because Caleb's wife had been murdered. Or she might have said it was because they had shared a good old-fashioned belly laugh at Teddy's description of his father's routine.

It was all of those things. But still more. Something about the man touched a tender, expectant spot deep inside that she hadn't been aware of before this day.

And that frightened her. She didn't like surprises, and this unexpected feeling left her off balance.

But why let it bother her? He'd soon be gone. He'd made that very clear.

Rose stepped into the room. "I can't believe you asked him to stay."

There was no mistaking the challenge in her sister's voice. "Only for one night, so Blossom has time to rest."

Rose made a dismissive sound. "Never thought I'd see the day you'd hang about a Caldwell cowboy." She didn't give Lilly a chance to answer before she grinned and spoke again. "Though he is rather handsome, and seems a decent sort of man." She grew glum again. "For a Caldwell cowboy."

Lilly shrugged. "Hard to judge a man after only a few hours, but I'm glad he's staying long enough for Ma and me to look at Teddy's leg and see why he doesn't use it." She explained yet again what had happened to the boy.

"Oh, that's terrible. I wouldn't wish that kind of disaster even on a man who works for the Caldwells."

Lilly chuckled. "Nice to know."

Rose studied Lilly long enough to make her squirm inside, but outwardly she returned the look, hoping she was managing to keep hidden every hint of her confusion about her feelings for Caleb and Teddy.

Rose's expression softened as if satisfied with what she saw.

Lilly might demand to know what exactly Rose thought that was, but she didn't care to encourage Rose's curiosity about the Caldwell cowboy and Lilly's choice to open their home to him.

"I came to tell you supper is ready," Rose said. "Will you let the others know?"

"Certainly." Lilly left the house and stopped at Pa's shop to tell him, and then made her way to the barn. She paused outside the door. Why hadn't Rose informed everyone of supper herself? Lilly narrowed her eyes. Was she purposely avoiding contact with Caleb and Teddy simply because Caleb worked for the Caldwells? His reasons were noble—to earn enough money to take Teddy to a special doctor. She'd have to tell Rose that and set the record straight.

Caleb was sitting near Teddy and Blossom, his back against a post, his legs stretched out halfway across the alley. He'd perched his hat on a nearby nail. He was watching his son, an affectionate smile curling his mouth. She drew in a breath at the depth of his devotion. Many men would simply accept the fact their son would only walk with crutches and get on with their lives. But not Caleb. It seemed he meant to move Heaven and earth to help his son. It was truly admirable and brought a sting of emotion to the back of her eyes.

Teddy fussed with the dog, petting her head and talking to her, urging her to eat more.

Neither of them had noticed Lilly in the doorway until Grub padded toward her.

She stepped inside. "Supper is ready."

Caleb tugged on the lobe of his ear. "We don't want to be a bother."

"It's no bother."

Slowly he rose. "If you're quite certain?"

"I most certainly am." More than anything, she wanted them to join the family for a meal. She wanted more time to observe them.... She meant, observe Teddy.

"Then we will come." He signaled for Teddy to join him and the pair fell in step with Lilly as she crossed the yard.

Teddy grinned up at his father. "I was afraid you would say no."

"Why would you think that?"

"'Cause sometimes you are so stubborn."

Lilly choked back laughter. Young Teddy must have really kept Caleb on his toes.

"Son, must you point out all my flaws and perceived failings in front of Miss Bell?" His voice deepened.

She couldn't say if it was from amusement or annoyance or perhaps a combination of both. "Please, call me Lilly." He'd used her Christian name several times already—perhaps not aware he was doing so. She certainly didn't want to revert to a more formal way of address.

"Lilly and Caleb it is, then."

She realized she, too, had easily used his Christian

name even without permission. Maybe working together over an injured pup erased some of the normal polite restraints.

"Papa, I only say what I see."

Lilly could not contain her amusement at Teddy's directness and burst out laughing.

Caleb rocked his head back and forth in dismay, but she understood it was only pretend because his eyes brimmed with mirth, and in a moment he chuckled.

Teddy grinned, pleased with himself for making them both laugh.

Ma and Pa would enjoy a young boy's presence at supper. Even Rose would see Caleb was a nice man.

She realized her smile might have appeared too bright as she entered the house, so she forced a bit of seriousness into her expression.

Still chuckling, Caleb followed Lilly to the house. Teddy had not once complained about the simple food they ate, but perhaps the meals, although adequate, were lacking in imagination.

He was willing to give his son a good meal tonight. Then it was back to their regular fare after tomorrow.

Lilly led him into the house.

The scent of roast pork, turnips and apples brought a flood of saliva to his mouth. The meals he'd had over the past few months certainly didn't carry such tantalizing aromas.

"Papa, it smells awfully good," Teddy whispered.

"It does indeed." Caleb glanced about. It was a usual-looking kitchen—cupboards to one side, a big stove belting out heat, a wooden table. But there were touches that revealed the family, too. A rocking chair with a basket of mending. A spinning wheel and a basket of carded wool.

A stack of papers teetering on a side table. And on the cupboard, four golden brown loaves of bread were cooling beside jars of applesauce and jars of dark blue-purple jam. He could almost taste the jam on the bread.

He and Teddy seldom had bread. A man on his own didn't have time to make bread, even if he knew how. They ate biscuits unless they found bread to purchase in one of the many towns he'd visited in his search for a doctor who could help Teddy.

The woman by the stove turned at their entrance.

Lilly pulled them forward. "Ma, this is Caleb Craig and his son, Teddy." Lilly and her mother's love for each other was evident in the way they each smiled. "Caleb, my mother."

Both Teddy and Caleb offered their hands and Ma shook them. "Pleased to meet you."

Mrs. Bell indicated two chairs at the table and he and Teddy sat down.

The others took their places. Rose and Lilly sat across from him and Mr. Bell sat at the end, facing his wife.

Caleb glanced around the table, but his gaze stalled when it landed on Lilly. She smiled as if to assure him they were welcome.

"Papa." Teddy tugged at his sleeve to get his attention. "This is like we used to have."

Caleb nodded. "Yes, son." They'd once known family. Though Amanda admitted she didn't love him and had married him only to get away from her overly strict upbringing. He'd tried to love her as a man should love his wife, but she had rebuffed every attempt, so they had lived together in peaceful coexistence, both committed to providing their son with a pleasant home.

But that home had never felt as warm and welcoming as this one did already.

Mr. Bell cleared his throat. "Welcome to our guests. I'll give thanks." He reached for Rose's hand on one side and Caleb's on the other. Seeing what Mr. Bell meant for them to do, Teddy reached for Ma's and Caleb's hands.

Caleb hesitated. Regret, refusal, confusion and pain all flashed through his brain. Being invited so intimately into this family circle had set his nerves to jangling. He had vowed to distance himself from people after Amanda's murder. Or maybe it had begun long before that, during the years when Amanda had remained cold to his love. Slowly, over time, he had closed his heart in order to protect it. Now he was grateful he had done that. It kept him from overreacting to this current family situation. He'd only be here one day. He sucked in air and allowed Mr. Bell to take his hand.

He sought Lilly with his eyes. She smiled and gave him a tiny nod. Confused by the way his heart tipped sideways at her gesture, he bowed his head as Mr. Bell asked the blessing. A question blared through his mind. Why had he looked to Lilly for reassurance? He didn't need or want assurance from anyone. And yet his insides felt soft and mellow knowing she was sitting across from him, and she cared enough to take note of his hesitation.

He jerked his thoughts to a halt. If he kept going in that direction he would lose sight of his every goal. He was only there to get a dog tended to, his son looked at and a savory meal or two eaten. Then he would return to the Caldwell ranch.

All that mattered was getting Teddy to that doctor down east.

"Amen," Mr. Bell said, and the word echoed around the table.

Throughout the meal Teddy raved about the food. He turned often to Mrs. Bell to ask questions.

Mrs. Bell helped him cut his meat and butter his bread. She filled his cup with milk three times. "You can have as much milk as you like," she said. "We have lots of it. Milk is good for strong bones."

"Would it make my leg work again?" Teddy latched his trusting, begging gaze on Lilly's ma.

She didn't answer at first. "It might depend on what's wrong with it, but it can't hurt."

"Then can I have some more?" He downed the contents of his cup and pushed it forward for a refill.

"Son, remember your manners." Caleb spoke softly, not wanting to spoil Teddy's enjoyment of this family meal, but needing him to be polite.

"Please," Teddy said. As Mrs. Bell filled his cup again, he added, "Thank you so much." He drawled the words to make sure Mrs. Bell understood he was terribly, terribly grateful.

Lilly and her sister glanced at each other and ducked their heads to hide their amusement.

Mr. Bell smiled at Teddy. "A young boy with a healthy appetite is a good thing to see."

Caleb murmured his thanks. He had no objection to the kindness and attention this family seemed prepared to heap on his son.

Mrs. Bell patted Teddy's hand. "You'll go far."

Lilly watched Teddy. She swiped at her eyes and glanced at Caleb. Then she ducked, as if uncomfortable that Caleb had seen her tears. Rose also swiped tears from her eyes.

The tenderness of this family's behavior toward his son stirred Caleb's heart. Perhaps the boy would find something here he hadn't had since his mother's death— the loving care of a mother figure. Only in this case, two mother figures, a grandma figure and a grandpa-type man.

Too bad he could only spend a day with them. No. He didn't want more time. He clanged shut the doors guarding his heart, doors he'd built with steel and sealed with rock. His future did not include a loving family and a warm home. He had Teddy. That was enough.

When the meal ended, Mr. Bell spoke. "We'll have our Bible reading now." He lifted the Bible from a nearby shelf and opened it.

"Papa," Teddy said, "you used to read the Bible every night. How come you quit?"

Caleb shrugged. "Things change." It hadn't been intentional. At first he'd been in shock. Then his energies had been bound up in caring for Teddy. Then the two of them had been on the move, going from one doctor to another.

Mr. Bell turned pages. "God changes not."

Caleb nodded. "For which I am grateful."

"Tonight's reading is from Job, chapter thirteen." He glanced about the table, giving each person a moment's attention. "May we each be blessed by the hearing of God's word." He read the chapter until he reached a verse that he emphasized. "'Though He slay me, yet will I trust in Him.' We'll stop there. Job, a man like us, faced troubles and trials most of us will never know, thank God, yet he chose to trust God through them all. Shall we pray?" He again reached out for the hands on either side of him and prayed that each be blessed, and each have a good night's sleep. "May we honor You in all we say and do. Amen."

Teddy clung to Caleb's hand even when the others started to push back from the table. He pulled at Caleb to draw his attention. Caleb leaned toward the child. "What is it?"

Tears flooded Teddy's eyes.

Caleb groaned inwardly. What had upset the boy so much? "Do you miss Mama?"

He nodded. "But that's not why I'm sad."

"Then what's wrong?"

The room had grown quiet. Caleb glanced up and met Lilly's gaze. Her lips lifted at the corner—it was not quite a smile, but there was no mistaking that she meant to encourage him. He nodded and turned back to Teddy.

"What is it?"

"He asked God to bless me."

"Yes. Mr. Bell asked God to bless each of us." He didn't understand why that had made Teddy cry.

"Can God make my leg better?"

Lilly hurried around the table and knelt beside Teddy. She touched his head and looked at Caleb. He felt her concern clear through to the bottom of his heart.

"Can He, Papa?"

Caleb pushed his chair back and pulled the boy to his lap. "God made you. I expect He can fix you."

Lilly hovered close. "God can do anything. Do you want my pa to pray for you?"

Teddy sniffed. "Would he?"

Mr. Bell had already moved to Lilly's side and placed his hand on Teddy's head. Rose scurried around to stand behind Teddy's chair and Mrs. Bell stood behind Caleb, her hand warm on his shoulder.

Mr. Bell prayed. "God of all mercies and love, look upon this little child of Yours and make his leg strong and well again that he might run and play like other little boys, and most of all, that he might love and adore You all his life. Amen."

For a moment no one moved, and then Mrs. Bell squeezed Caleb's shoulder and stepped back.

Teddy beamed up at Mr. Bell. "You know God real well, don't you?"

Mr. Bell chuckled. "I've known Him a long time."

Lilly leaned over and kissed the top of Teddy's head.

Caleb rubbed the bridge of his nose and kept his gaze on Teddy until the rush of emotions passed. He'd beseeched God to heal his boy, but he'd never felt as blessed and supported by the prayers of others as he did here in the Bell house.

Would God choose to heal Teddy?

For good measure he added a silent prayer. *Help me earn enough money this fall to take Teddy down east.*

As soon as he thought the words, he regretted them. A doubting man would not receive anything from God.

Would his prayer, expressing doubt as it did, be the reason Teddy's didn't heal?

A familiar sense of failure caught at his thoughts.

Chapter Six

Ma signaled to Lilly to join her. "God will do His part. Now let us do ours."

Lilly nodded. "Caleb, would you let my ma examine Teddy's leg and see what she thinks?"

Caleb pushed to his feet and handed the crutches to his son. "Where do you want him?"

"The cot." She indicated the narrow bed at the far side of the room.

Teddy remained beside the table. "You're not gonna hurt me, are you?"

Lilly sat on Caleb's chair and faced Teddy. "Did I hurt Blossom?"

"A little, maybe."

"But she had open cuts. Do you?"

He shook his head and leaned close to whisper to Lilly. "Will you look at my leg instead of your mama?"

"My ma knows more about such things."

"Nonsense," Ma said. "You are every bit as good as I any day of the week." She smiled at Teddy. "Certainly she will look at your leg. Do you mind if I watch her?"

"That's okay." Teddy hobbled toward the cot. "Do you want me to lie down?"

Lilly knelt before him. "First, can you pull your pant leg up and show me where you were hurt?"

He did so.

Caleb stood at Lilly's shoulder, his presence making her nervous. And yet she didn't want him to move away.

She saw the boy's scar, the skin pink and uneven. She checked the underside. The bullet had gone in and out, leaving two roundish scars in the fleshy part of the leg just above the knee.

She probed the area, watching Teddy for signs of pain or tenderness or evidence of the bone being injured. He never once flinched. There was no heat in the area, which was a good thing.

She cupped her hand under the knee. "Can you swing the leg in and out?"

He did so.

"Does it hurt anywhere?"

"No."

"You can lie down now, Teddy."

Once he was comfortable, she lifted his leg, put it through a range of motions, felt the muscles for any lack of mobility and again, watched for signs of pain. "Thank you, Teddy. I'm finished." She turned to consult with Ma. "I detected no infection. Every muscle is working, as far as I can tell."

Ma nodded. "I agree."

There might be nerve damage, but from the placement of the wound, it seemed unlikely. "Teddy, what do you think is wrong with your leg?" Sometimes people had an intuition about their own bodies.

"It's forgotten how to walk."

She smiled. "I think you're right." She turned to Caleb. "I think it needs a little help remembering."

"What kind of help?"

"Well, if he was to remain here a few days I would try some warm poultices to stimulate the muscles and I'd do some exercises to help the muscles remember how to work."

He shook his head, but she didn't give him a chance to voice his explanation again.

"I can teach you what to do and you can do it yourself."

"I appreciate that."

Teddy pushed his pant leg down and sat up. "Are you going to make my leg work again?"

"I'm going to help if I can. But it will be you and God that make it work again."

Teddy stole a glance at Pa, who was sitting at the end of the table while Rose cleaned up the kitchen. Teddy signaled for Lilly to lean close. "Can you ask your papa to talk to God about my leg again tomorrow?"

Lilly tousled Teddy's hair, which wasn't hard to do. The little guy had three cowlicks that gave his hair a permanently rumpled look. "Would you like me to ask my pa to pray for your leg every day until it's better?"

Teddy nodded eagerly.

Lilly turned to Pa and repeated the request.

Pa smiled. "Young man, it would be my privilege. You can ask Him, too, though. God likes to hear young boys pray."

"I'll ask Him when I say my bedtime prayers."

Lilly allowed herself to look at Caleb. She saw hope and despair in his gaze, as if he wanted to believe but was afraid to. She'd like to ask him why he couldn't let himself believe. But he wasn't going to be around long enough for her to ask those sorts of questions.

"I'd like to try a cowslip poultice."

Ma nodded. "I'll get it from the shed." Ma's medicinals were kept in the gardening shed, where she sorted, prepared and stored everything. She brought the tinctures that would freeze into the house for the winter.

Ma returned with a little jar. "The root is most effective, especially in cases like this."

Lilly knew she meant in cases of mild paralysis. Lilly had learned most of the remedies and herbs by heart, though Rose had begun a project to record all of Ma's medicinals. "For after she's gone," Rose had said. The words had brought a protest from Lilly. She did not want to think of that happening, but Rose was right. The remedies should be written down so others could use them.

"Thanks, Ma." Lilly went to the cupboard. "Caleb, I'll teach you what to do."

Caleb stood at her elbow as she spread a small amount of the ground root on a piece of brown paper and folded it to seal the edges. "We put that on Teddy's leg, cover it with a warm, wet cloth and leave it for about half an hour."

They went to the cot and she did as she had described, and then she looked about. Now what? How was she to amuse them for half an hour?

Pa put down the paper he'd been drawing on. He was always working on some kind of invention. Some had been successful. Others, less so. "Caleb," Pa asked, "where do you hail from?"

Caleb pulled a chair to the side of the cot and sat down. "I was raised in Nebraska. After I married I had a little farm there. I was increasing my cow herd…." His voice trailed off.

Lilly wanted to pat his arm to comfort him, but pressed her hands to her knees and sat stiffly in a chair by the table. Teddy lay on the cot, Caleb sitting at his side. They were so alone, while the Bell family was clustered together near the table. It didn't feel right.

Pa cleared his throat. "I heard of your misfortune. I'm sorry. Tell me about your family—parents, brothers, sister…"

Teddy perched up. "I have a grandmother and grandfather in 'Delphia."

Caleb smiled. "Philadelphia. Teddy's maternal grandparents. My own parents and brother are still in Nebraska."

"Philadelphia!" Rose snorted. "I suppose you heard that Douglas Caldwell has been there and is on his way home. I expect Philadelphia has had enough of him."

"Rose," Ma scolded without saying anything more. Rose hung her head, but Lilly knew she wasn't sorry for what she had said. Rose and Duke, as everyone else called Douglas Caldwell, the son of the Caldwell Ranch owner, had never gotten along.

"I've not heard a thing about Douglas Caldwell," Caleb said.

Lilly didn't want Rose to continue that topic of conversation. She went to Teddy's side and lifted the poultice. "How does it feel?"

"Nice and warm," Teddy said, straining upward to check on what she was doing.

"Good. A little longer and then you're done."

"I'll be all better?"

She chuckled. "It might take a little time."

Pa began to talk about the plans for Montana to achieve statehood and the time passed quickly.

She removed the poultice. "The skin is pink and warm." She showed Caleb. "Now I'll do some exercises." She did them while Caleb observed. "Sometimes it's hard to remember everything, so you do them now and I'll watch."

Caleb gently lifted Teddy's leg and bent it.

"You need to keep the leg properly aligned." Lilly placed her hands on Caleb's, her arms crossing his as she guided the movement. It was almost like a hug. Rather than think like that, she concentrated on the exercise. Caleb's arm muscles flexed. Strong arms that held a little boy, that lifted heavy sacks of feed as she'd seen him do in town and that felt warm and steady underneath her own.

Her cheeks grew hot enough to make her wish she could hide her face. Could she hope no one else would notice? Even Rose, who watched her every move?

"I think I've got it," Caleb said, and she jerked her hands away and stepped back.

"Good. I'll go through the instructions about the poultice again in the morning."

"How often you think this should be done?" He waved at Teddy's leg to indicate he meant the poultices and exercises.

"Best if it's done three times a day, wouldn't you say, Ma?"

"That's what I would recommend."

"I see." He helped Teddy sit up and then turned to Pa. "Lilly invited us to stay overnight so Blossom could rest. I trust that meets with your approval?"

"By all means. Stay as long as you like. Do you need a bed? The cot is narrow, but you're welcome to it."

"No, no. We're fine. We've got the wagon all set up." He gestured to Teddy and they went toward the door.

Teddy stopped. "Aren't you coming to see Blossom?" he asked Lilly.

"I haven't forgotten." Her first thought was to rush out the door with them, but she forced herself to wait, practicing her intention of guarding her heart against intimacy. "Shall I go with you now?"

"Yes, please."

She could hardly refuse a request like that.

"Rose, go with your sister," Pa said.

Lilly smiled at Rose, though she wished to go without Rose observing everything she did and said. How foolish. There'd be nothing for her to notice. All Lilly meant to do was give Blossom some more tonic, make sure the dog was comfortable, and then bid Caleb and Teddy good-night.

Caleb watched Lilly and Rose until they entered the house and closed the door behind them. They'd helped Teddy tend the dog and then left. He lifted Teddy into the wagon. The poor boy was exhausted. It had been a long day. They had gotten up early so Caleb could feed Teddy before doing chores, then they had made the trip to town. Teddy had been so excited by it that he'd bounced up and down on the wagon seat and talked nonstop. Then they'd found Blossom.

Caleb smiled. He'd had a dog growing up, both he and his brother, Ezra, claiming it as their own. They used to have contests to see which one of them the dog would go to, both boys using every imaginable treat to tempt the dog. Bacon had certainly worked well.

Teddy touched Caleb's cheeks. "You're smiling."

"I guess I am."

"You liked having supper with the Bells, didn't you? I sure did."

"It was awfully nice. Sorry I haven't been making better meals for you."

Teddy patted Caleb's cheeks. "You do the best you can. No one can ask more than that."

Caleb chuckled. Teddy sure had a way of picking up

wisdom from others. "How does your leg feel? Any different?"

"Not yet. Miss Lilly said it might take a while. Maybe in the morning it will be better."

"Maybe, but it might take longer than that." He didn't want Teddy to get his hopes up, but without hope what did the boy have? The possibility of finding something that would help kept Caleb going day after day. That and his determination to see his son walking on both legs again.

He helped Teddy remove his boots and trousers and put them on the trunk that held Teddy's things. Exactly where he always put them. He chuckled.

"What's so funny?" Teddy asked.

"I always put your things in the same place, don't I?"

"Uh-huh." Teddy pulled on his flannel nightshirt and sat cross-legged on the bedroll spread in the wagon box. "I want to pray like Mr. Bell does."

Caleb closed his eyes and sucked in a deep breath. Bedtime prayers were one more thing that he had neglected. No wonder God wasn't listening to his desperate pleas. Caleb had neglected his duty as a father. His sense of failure made his shoulders sag.

But there was no time like the present to change things. "Then let's pray."

Teddy knelt on the bedroll, his hands clasped before him, and squeezed his eyes tightly shut. "Dear God, I don't know You like Mr. Bell does, but I know You are strong and You can make me better. So will You, please?" He paused as if listening for a reply. "It's nice to be with the Bells. They're a good family. Bless them." He named each one. "And bless my papa. Help him to get better, too. Amen." He crawled between the covers and pulled them to his chin.

Caleb shook his head. "Son, I'm not sick or injured."

"But you're sad. I almost never hear you laugh anymore." Teddy sat up, surprise widening his eyes. "Until today. You laughed a lot today."

"I suppose I did." Lilly had a way of making him see and enjoy the humor in things.

Teddy twisted the covers in his hands. "Papa, are you mad at me?"

"Mad at you? How could you think such a thing?" He pulled Teddy to his lap and wrapped his arms about him. "I could never be mad at you."

"Even if I broke something like your knife that Uncle Ezra gave you?"

Caleb chuckled. "Well, I might be mad for a few minutes, but I couldn't stay mad for very long because I love you so much." He held the boy close. This child was all he had left of his family and his dreams.

"That's good." Teddy yawned.

"It's time you went to sleep." He tucked the boy in and kissed his forehead. "I'll just be outside." It was too early for him to go to bed, and he needed time to think. He slipped from the wagon, sat with his back to the wheel and stared at the star-studded sky.

His gaze went to the little house, where he could see golden light glowing from the window. Mrs. Bell crossed the room. Mr. Bell sat at the table. He couldn't see the twins, but he knew they were near their parents.

Hadn't he longed for such a home since the day he and Amanda married? A home filled with love and faith. He still did, but now he knew it wasn't possible. He carried too much pain and failure in his knapsack to ever again hope for such a home.

Mr. Bell had spoken about how Job had lost everything, yet still had vowed to continue trusting God. Caleb could do that as well.

"Papa. Papa." Teddy's screams rent the air and brought Caleb to his feet in one swift movement. He rushed into the wagon and scooped Teddy into his arms.

"It's okay. I'm here. You're safe. Shh. Shh."

Teddy sobbed and clung to Caleb. Finally he calmed enough to shudder out a few words. "I saw him again. He had a big knife." His crying intensified.

Caleb knew he meant one of the men who had invaded their home and murdered Amanda. He rocked Teddy and murmured comfort. Caleb's insides filled with bile. These nightmares occurred every night. If only he could erase the terror from Teddy's mind.

Teddy leaned back and looked at Caleb. "I wouldn't be scared if you brought Blossom in to sleep with me."

Caleb closed his eyes a moment and wished for patience. They were crowded enough in the wagon without sharing the space with a dog. Despite that, he knew he wouldn't be able to say no. But tonight was not a good idea. "Blossom is hurting too much to be moved right now."

He felt Teddy slouch. "I guess so. Maybe tomorrow?"

"Maybe." They'd be back at the Caldwells then. Blossom would have to sleep somewhere, and he kind of guessed Ebner wouldn't be all that welcoming of an injured dog.

"You won't go away, will you?"

"I'll never be where I can't hear you if you need me."

"Okay." Teddy allowed Caleb to tuck him back under the covers. "We'll take good care of Blossom, won't we?" Already he sounded half-asleep.

Caleb waited until Teddy's breathing deepened. "I'll

take good care of her, but I'll take even better care of you. I promise."

This was one aspect of his life where he couldn't allow himself to fail.

Chapter Seven

Ma and Pa retired to their bedroom and Lilly and Rose went to the room they shared. In companionable silence they prepared for bed. Both read a portion from their Bibles. They prayed silently and turned out the lamp.

Then, as they always did, they talked.

Lilly propped herself up on one elbow and turned to her sister. She could see her in the dim light of the moon. "I can't help feel the Bell family can help Teddy, but he's only going to be here one day. What can we hope to accomplish in that time?"

Rose studied Lilly for a moment. "You sure it's just Teddy you're interested in?"

Lilly bristled. "Of course. And Blossom, too."

"And perhaps the Caldwell cowboy? I noticed he couldn't keep his eyes off you during supper. And you pretended not to notice, but I know you did."

"He's had a lot to deal with. I certainly feel sorry for him. But that's all." She only partly believed it. But yet, something deep inside called out to him at every turn, every word, every sign of distress he hid admirably well.

"Well, don't feel so sorry for him that you forget he works for the Caldwells."

"Honestly, Rose. I fail to see what that has to do with it. He's a fellow human being. Shouldn't that count for something?"

"Don't you think it's rather convenient for Ebner to have someone visit us? Perhaps inform him as to where he could do the most damage?"

"It's not like that at all. Caleb is worried Ebner will find out he's here and fire him."

"So he says. Just be careful."

Lilly lay down and stared at the ceiling. The same ceiling she'd stared at for almost eight years. Ever since they had left Bar Crossing and Pa had built the house on this bit of land.

Rose spoke, slowly at first. "I think you feel a connection to Teddy because he's lost his mother. Just like we lost our parents. But don't let it cloud your judgment."

"Oh, Rose, can't you let it go? Cora says she remembers a wagon riding away with our father in it."

"She remembers that our mother was dead." Rose jerked up and stared at Lilly. "What if she'd been murdered? Maybe in an Indian attack."

Lilly shuddered. "You're always imagining something, and every time it gets worse. I wish you'd stop. Like I've said a hundred times, it might be better not to know what happened."

"More like a thousand times you've said that." Rose chuckled, as if to make sure Lilly knew she was teasing. Suddenly she sat up and stared at Lilly. "But that's what Teddy is dealing with. Poor little boy. I don't blame you for wanting to help him."

Lilly's insides twisted into a knot. "I can't imagine the horror. We must pray that Teddy's leg gets better."

Lilly sat up and reached for Rose's hands. They each prayed for Teddy's leg.

But Rose didn't immediately crawl under her covers again. "I wonder what Caleb does with Teddy while he's working."

Lilly had wondered the same thing, but knew whatever he did, Caleb would not let Teddy out of his sight.

"He'll return to his job tomorrow and that will be the end of it." Lilly knew it was for the best and said so.

"He might be okay if he didn't work for the Caldwells."

Lilly smiled. Coming from Rose, that was a big sign of approval. Her sister had grown quiet and Lilly turned to a more comfortable position. Tomorrow was all she had, and she meant to use it wisely.

The next morning, Lilly braided her hair more carefully than usual and considered winding the braids about her head like the girls in town often did. Then out of need to prove to herself she wasn't doing it because they had company, she tossed the braids down her back, and as she left to do the morning chores, she pulled on the oldest, rattiest straw hat she could find.

Rose, helping Ma prepare breakfast, stared at the hat and covered a giggle.

"What?" Lilly demanded.

"Did you have to fight the mice for that hat?"

She tipped her nose and sniffed. "My cats keep the mice down." Recalling Teddy's amusement at how brave a mouse would have to be to live around here, she chuckled as she crossed the yard toward the barn.

She drew abreast of the wagon and stopped. The wagon's rocking indicated someone was inside, but she heard no voices.

Then Teddy peeked out through the front opening.

"Good morning," she said.

He glanced over his shoulder. "Don't talk to Papa until he can make some coffee."

Lilly grinned. "Is he truly so cross before coffee?"

Teddy nodded, eyes round. "Like an old bear."

"I can hear you, son." Caleb's growly voice came from the wagon.

"Sorry, Papa." Teddy mouthed the words, "I told ya."

Lilly's grin widened and she raised her voice slightly. "Pa has coffee ready in the house if you care to join him."

"Well, why didn't you say so?" Caleb picked up Teddy and jumped out the back. His expression was grim as he looked toward the house. He strode past her, carrying his son and the crutches as if waiting for Teddy to cross the yard under his own steam would take too much time.

"Ma's expecting you for breakfast, too."

Caleb didn't slow a bit until he disappeared into the house.

Lilly turned back to her chores, a smile upon her lips.

And if she cared to notice and admit it, a song in her heart at seeing this amusing side of Caleb.

She went first to Blossom to get her to drink. The dog was weak and limp. "Girl, don't you dare die." She examined the dog again. The cuts showed no sign of infection.

She sat back on her heels. "You are in no shape to travel." But that afternoon, Caleb would take the dog and leave. *God, please don't let Blossom die. Poor Teddy has had enough death and pain to deal with already.*

She fed the pigs and chickens, milked the cows and returned to the house.

Caleb sat at the table with a cup of coffee between his palms, his back to her.

Teddy turned to look at her as she stepped into the kitchen. "He's okay now. You can talk to him."

She chuckled. "What happens if you run out of coffee?"

Caleb shuddered. "Perish the thought."

"We did once. Remember that, Papa?"

"Better'n I care to."

"What happened?" Lilly expected Teddy would be full of details.

"Son, some things are just between you and me."

Teddy paid no heed. "Pa hitched the wagon up real quick and ran the horse all the way to the first farm we came to. He bought a few beans off the lady for a whole lot of money."

"She drove a hard bargain," Caleb grumbled.

Every one of the Bells laughed.

Teddy grinned, pleased at the response he had gotten.

Caleb grunted. "There is no such thing as a secret with a five-year-old watching everything I do."

"And that's a good thing," Pa said, filling Caleb's cup again. "We learn to speak and act more wisely because of them."

Caleb nodded. "One thing I've learned…"

Lilly stopped pouring milk into a jug to listen.

He continued. "Always keep a good supply of coffee on hand."

His unexpected words brought another round of chuckles from the family.

Lilly saw Pa give Caleb a look of approval and her insides felt warm and sweet.

"Breakfast is ready," Ma announced, and they gathered round the table.

Teddy enjoyed breakfast with as much enthusiasm as he had his supper.

"I never tasted such good food," he managed to say between mouthfuls.

Caleb planted his hands on either side of his plate, a fork and knife clutched tight. He looked at Teddy with raised eyebrows. "The way you talk makes it sound like we eat poorly."

"You do the best you can," Teddy said. "But we don't eat anything like this."

Lilly pressed her lips together to stifle a laugh.

Caleb favored her with a scowl, though she saw amusement in his eyes and realized he enjoyed his son's comments as much as anyone. "What about Mama's cooking? Didn't you enjoy that?"

Teddy's fork paused halfway to his mouth. He looked thoughtful. "I guess it was okay, but only 'cause I hadn't eaten food as good as Mrs. Bell's." He gave Ma an adoring look.

Why, the little scamp was deliberately flattering her.

Ma smiled. "Thank you, Teddy. That's very generous of you. It's easy to prepare nice meals if there is lots of good food, and we have that here on our farm." She leaned closer as if speaking for Teddy's ears only. "But no need to pour on the praise. I'll feed you all you want as long as you and your papa care to stay."

"Well, young man," Caleb said. "Does that teach you anything?"

Teddy gave his papa a dismissive look. "Yes. Good cooks are generous and kind."

Caleb sent Lilly a look full of surprise and pleasure. "What am I supposed to do with him?"

Did he mean the question for her? Or maybe Ma or Pa? But his gaze rested on her as if he wanted her opinion.

"Seems to me you should keep doing whatever you've been doing. The results are rather pleasant," Lilly said. She meant Teddy. Didn't she? Though he and Caleb made a very nice package together.

He smiled, relief, gratitude and something more in his eyes. "Thank you."

Rose made a soft sound as if to inform Lilly she'd seen something as well.

Lilly ducked her head and wiped her plate clean with the last bite of her bread.

"Thank you for another wonderful meal," Caleb said, when they had all finished.

Teddy rubbed his tummy. "Thank you very, very, very much. I shall enjoy the memory of this meal when we eat something cooked over an open fire." He sounded so sad and regretful.

"You'll do just fine," Caleb said. He brought his attention to Lilly. "Would you show me again how to make the poultice and do the exercises?"

"Gladly." She pushed away from the table.

Caleb had rehearsed every step during the night. Spread the stuff Mrs. Bell supplied, fold the paper, cover it with a warm, wet cloth. It was fairly simple. He cut a piece of paper.

"It's a little small," Lilly said, peering over his shoulder. "But it will do."

He spread the mixture.

Lilly stepped forward. "That much would burn his skin. Use a very thin layer." She showed him. "There you go." She moved aside and let him fold the paper. She'd made it look so easy, but his effort resulted in a lumpy mess.

"Like this." She flipped and rolled until the poultice was smooth and flat. She handed it to him.

He realized she was waiting for him to take over and went toward the cot.

"You'll need a warm, wet cloth." She nodded toward the cloth sitting not more than four inches from where he'd been working.

"I went over every step during the night," he grumbled. "Now I can't remember anything."

"It will come with practice."

He didn't point out that there was little time for practice. He had to learn in a hurry.

He dampened the cloth and let her test it.

She nodded her approval. "You don't want it too hot."

Caleb was beginning to think there was far more to this whole procedure than he had thought. It had seemed so simple when he'd watched her the night before.

Teddy waited on the cot, his pant leg pulled up, and Caleb applied the poultice. Now to wait the half hour.

"Today is Sunday," Mr. Bell said. "We go to church in Bar Crossing."

Caleb hadn't attended church since his arrival at the Caldwells', and he thought longingly of sitting in a service with the likes of the Bell family. But perhaps they wouldn't want to be seen in public with a man who worked for the people on the other side of the feud.

"It would be nice if you came with us," Mr. Bell said, eliminating that possibility and leaving Caleb with another. Would the Caldwells object to him attending with the Bells? He would not let their opinion sway him except for one reason—he needed the job.

On the other hand, Ebner had not attended church since Caleb had started work and somehow Caleb didn't think it was something the man practiced. And Mr. Caldwell and his wife were away. Didn't seem as if there'd be anyone to object.

"I'd like that."

Teddy grabbed his hand. "We're going to church? Like we used to?"

"Yes, son." How many times had he deprived the boy of things he enjoyed or accepted as part of normal family life simply because he was on the move, or tired, or discouraged?

"Last time we went to church was for Mama's—what do you call it?"

"Her funeral." Caleb forced the words past the restriction in his throat.

Teddy nodded. "Mama would be glad we are going."

"Yes, she would be." Amanda had been rigid in her church attendance.

"Do you think God will talk to me?" Teddy asked, delivering a shock to Caleb's midsection. He didn't know how to answer the boy.

"What do you want to hear?" he asked.

Teddy glanced around the table and whispered, "I can't say."

Mrs. Bell took Teddy's hands and looked deep into his eyes. "Teddy, I believe God will tell you what you need to know."

Teddy held her gaze for a moment and then nodded.

Caleb's heart was so tight he didn't dare look at Lilly for fear it would burst open, but he heard her sigh and guessed she'd been as moved by the exchange as he.

Mr. Bell cleared his throat. "We leave in forty-five minutes."

"That's plenty of time to do Teddy's exercises," Lilly said. "We'll give the poultice a few more minutes." They waited a bit then she let him remove it. "Let's see how well you remember them."

"Not very well, I'm afraid."

"We'll do them together." She guided his hands. His arm cradled hers in many of the movements as he followed her lead. Would he ever remember how to do all these without her guidance? He must, of course. But her sure, steady hands and her calm words reached into his heart and strengthened him in a way he hadn't known since…he wasn't sure he'd ever felt so confident.

He tightened his jaw muscles. Had he forgotten his many failures? His hand faltered. She steadied it and smiled, thinking perhaps he had forgotten what he was doing.

But he'd remembered. *Don't let people get close to you. They'll get hurt.*

"That's enough for this morning," she said, and stepped back.

Little did she know how true her words were.

"Papa, can we go see Blossom now?"

"I tended her this morning," Lilly said.

Teddy grabbed his crutches. "Is she all better?"

"Not yet, I'm afraid."

"Oh." The word dripped with disappointment. Then Teddy brightened. "Good thing we're going to church. I can ask God to make her better."

"You can, indeed," Mr. Bell said. "But you don't need to wait for church. You can talk to God anytime."

Teddy nodded. "But it's better in church."

No one argued with his five-year-old wisdom as he headed out the door, Caleb and Lilly on his heels.

Lilly hung back and indicated she wanted to talk to Caleb.

He fell in at her side.

"I didn't see any improvement in her this morning. I'm sorry."

"Are you saying—" He couldn't imagine how Teddy would respond if the dog died. "I thought…I hoped." He stopped talking. What was there to say? She could only do so much. Isn't that what a dozen doctors had said to him about Teddy? Such futile, hopeless words.

She touched his elbow. "Don't give up hope. I haven't."

He nodded. Easy for her to say. It wasn't her son, her life. He shook away the troubling thoughts. She was doing her best. A person couldn't ask for more.

They followed Teddy into the barn. The dog lay limp and motionless until Teddy called her.

Then her head came up and her tail wagged.

"Look at that," Lilly said, her voice round with surprise. "It's like she'd been waiting for him."

Caleb grinned at the pleasure in Teddy's face. He only hoped Blossom wasn't saving the last of her strength for Teddy as a goodbye gesture.

But Blossom drank some water, ate the gruel Lilly had prepared and took the drops. She licked Teddy's hand then closed her eyes and went to sleep.

Caleb watched, praying the dog wouldn't die. Blossom's chest rose and fell in regular rhythm and the tension eased from Caleb's body.

"She's doing fine," Lilly said, brushing his arm. "Now I must get ready for church."

He realized he could do with some cleaning up, too, as could Teddy, and they headed for the wagon.

They each had one good set of clothes and he pulled Teddy's from his trunk first. His shirt and trousers needed to have a flatiron applied, but Caleb didn't have the means to do so.

"You bought me these for Mama's funeral," Teddy said as he donned his nearly new clothes. "Look, my pants are almost too short." Teddy grinned, smoothing his trouser legs.

"Why, I believe you've grown three inches this summer. Guess the food I serve you can't be so bad after all."

Teddy's hands stilled. He looked up. "I didn't mean it was bad."

Caleb chucked him under the chin and laughed. "I

know you didn't. Now, if you want to wait outside and give me room to change, that would be nice."

Teddy lowered himself to the ground and leaned on his crutches. "You gonna wear the suit you bought for Mama's funeral?"

He looked at the items in his trunk. "It's the only good clothing I have."

"You looked very handsome in it."

"Did I, now?" He'd have thought Teddy would be so consumed by shock and pain that he wouldn't notice or remember any details from that day. "I'm surprised you noticed."

"Well, I didn't," he mumbled, studying the ground at his toes. "But I heard some ladies talking and they said you were handsome."

"Hmm."

"One of them said something really strange."

"Really?" He couldn't imagine what.

"She said you were a good catch. Papa, what does that mean? I thought you caught fish. You're not a fish." He giggled.

Caleb pulled out his newish shirt and slipped into it. He removed his well-worn denim pants and pulled on the black trousers. For the last occasion he'd donned this outfit, he'd worn a Western bow tie with tails that hung down several inches. Now he chose it again and pulled on his black suit jacket. He brushed his hair back and took a clean black cowboy hat from the hatbox where he had stored it. He brushed the dust from it and planted it on his head. He grabbed a damp rag to clean his boots with and then jumped down to face Teddy.

"What do you think?"

Teddy studied him with narrowed eyes. "I guess you look handsome."

Caleb chuckled. "So do you."

Mr. Bell came out to hitch the horse to their wagon.

"I better get our horse, too," he said, but Mr. Bell heard him.

"No need to take two wagons to town. You can ride with us."

Caleb hesitated. Not that he minded riding with the Bells, but he didn't want for him and Teddy to become a nuisance. Besides, there was this feud with the Caldwells. Apart from his job at the Caldwells', though, this disagreement between neighbors had nothing to do with him, so why should he let it influence him? He realized he wanted to ride with the Bells, be part of the family, observe Lilly with her sister.... He cut the rambling, traitorous thoughts short. "Thank you. I appreciate it."

"Jump aboard."

At Mr. Bell's command, Caleb lifted Teddy to the back of the wagon and climbed in beside him. The elder man drove to the door.

Mrs. Bell came out wearing a dark blue dress and matching bonnet with a black shawl pulled around her shoulders.

Rose came next, her red hair coiled back and covered with a pale gray bonnet. Then Lilly stepped out and Caleb was glad he'd worn his suit. Lilly looked like a lovely flower in a cornflower-blue dress, her hair a golden halo framing her face, her eyes bright as the Montana sky.

Rose looked at him and then nudged Lilly.

He hoped it meant he had passed inspection. He had only Teddy's word that he looked his finest.

He assisted the girls into the back of the wagon, where they sat on quilts their father had put on the box to protect their clothing.

They arrived at the church and Caleb jumped down

to help the ladies. But when he reached for Teddy, the boy held back. "Pa, will people laugh at me 'cause I use a crutch?"

His insides crackled like old paper. If they did—well, he didn't want to think how he'd react.

Lilly answered Teddy. "No one will think anything of it."

Teddy nodded, pressed close to Caleb's side and gave Lilly a beseeching glance. "Will you stay with me?"

Lilly looked startled and looked toward her parents.

Caleb's jaw clenched. Did she object to escorting them? Was it because he worked for the Caldwells? Or did she have a beau who might object? Why hadn't he considered that? Of course she would. The young men of the community were probably lined up six deep hoping for a chance to court her.

Mrs. Bell smiled at her. "A little reassurance goes a long way."

Lilly nodded and stayed next to Teddy as the three of them followed the others inside.

Lilly crowded close as they walked down the aisle. Just like a regular family, Caleb thought. But then he hardened his heart. He would never again have a family.

They sat down, Teddy between Caleb and Lilly, and glanced about. There was something familiar and comforting about the place. It might have been the grinding of the pump organ, the greetings between friends and neighbors. Or maybe it was the sense of coming home. He hadn't attended church much since Amanda's funeral, but before that he'd missed it only in emergency situations.

He scanned the congregation and didn't notice any young men looking in Lilly's direction. Odd. He must have missed it. Or seeing him at her side, they'd guarded their interest.

The preacher stood behind the pulpit.

Teddy leaned forward, as if intent on hearing from God.

Caleb hoped he'd find what he sought.

They sang familiar hymns. Lilly and Caleb held the hymnal in front of Teddy. Although he could not read, he looked from Caleb to Lilly and wriggled with excitement. Oh, to be so eager to hear from God. He and Lilly shared a smile over the boy's head. Seemed to him they'd often shared pleasure regarding him. Caleb liked the feeling.

Pastor Rawley opened his Bible and Teddy fixed his eyes on the man. "When God speaks, do you listen?"

Teddy nodded vigorously.

Caleb stared. Had someone told the pastor of Teddy's desire to hear from God? No, that wasn't possible.

The pastor continued. "I expect most of you are saying you do. But is it true? Do you listen and obey when He says, 'Forgive others as I have forgiven you'? When He says, 'Fear not, I am with you'? Or when He says, 'Seek Me with all your heart and I will be found of you'?"

Teddy's mouth hung open. He turned to Caleb and indicated he wanted to whisper in his ear. Caleb knew such behavior was inappropriate, but he made an exception. "I knew God would talk to me," he whispered, his voice filled with awe.

Caleb patted Teddy's back and smiled. What exactly had God said to him? He listened intently to the sermon, hoping to understand. The words burrowed into his heart. Having faith, seeking God, forgiving others. What about forgiving oneself? The thought burned a path through his brain. He'd never thought of having to forgive himself. But Pastor Rawley pointed out that if God had forgiven a person, shouldn't the person also forgive his own failings or mistakes or sins or whatever lay like a burden on his shoulders?

He ended with a prayer while Caleb's thoughts churned with hope and possibility.

Teddy's face glowed. "I heard God."

"I'm glad for you."

They joined the others exiting the church. Lilly introduced him to Pastor Rawley and his daughter and several other young ladies. Caleb shook hands and continued on his way to the wagon. Several young men passed by and nodded a greeting, but he felt slightly smug when Lilly kept her attention on Caleb and Teddy without showing any interest in the possible beaus.

As he helped Teddy and the ladies into the wagon and climbed up to join them, his thoughts returned to the service. He felt as if he might have heard from God, too, but he wasn't sure he was ready to forgive himself. His failures were a heavy chain about his neck.

Lilly found the service refreshing despite her awareness of Teddy and Caleb at her side. She watched Teddy as he listened to the sermon. The little boy longed so much to hear from God. *Please, God, honor Teddy's desire.*

After the service, the town girls had whispered as they clustered around her, demanding to know who the good-looking cowboy was. She'd introduced them so they could find out for themselves, but they'd wilted at his lack of encouragement.

Cora and her husband, Wyatt, as well as Wyatt's sixteen-year-old brother, Lonnie, joined them. They had slipped in too late for any of the Bells to speak to them before church started.

Now Lilly introduced them to Caleb and Teddy.

Cora's eyes went from Caleb to Lilly and back again several times.

Lilly pretended not to notice, but she inwardly groaned. Cora would demand to know every detail. Not that Lilly had any reason to object. He was just a cowboy looking for help for his son and a pup. A Caldwell cowboy.

"Do you girls want to ride with us?" Cora asked.

Lilly hesitated. It seemed rude to leave Caleb on his own, but if Rose went and she didn't, who knew what kind of picture Rose would paint.

"I'll ride with Ma and Pa if you don't mind," Lonnie said. He'd claimed Lilly's parents as his own after Cora and Wyatt married.

Taking everyone's acceptance as a given, Lonnie trotted over to the Bell wagon and climbed up beside Caleb and Teddy. He spoke to Pa, who nodded and waved goodbye.

Lilly waved back, her gaze on Caleb and Teddy.

Rose climbed into Wyatt's wagon. "Now we can bring you up to date on all the news."

Oh, great. Lilly could hardly wait to hear Rose's interpretation of the previous day's events. She climbed up beside Rose and Cora, leaving Wyatt to drive the horses and listen to everything the girls had to say. Not that she minded. Wyatt had proven to be fair and noble. He might even be led to correct some of Rose's wild imaginations.

Rose had the good grace to wait until they left the churchyard behind before she started. "I tell you, he is every bit as good-looking as Wyatt."

Wyatt looked over his shoulder, a grin splitting his face. "I see your taste is as good as Cora's," he said.

Annoyed at being left out, Lilly said, "I think you're good-looking, too. But—"

Rose chortled and cut off Lilly's words. "Not as good-looking as Caleb? Is that what you were going to say?"

"No. I was going to say a little boyish."

Wyatt looked startled and then whooped with laughter, while the other girls grinned.

"Boyish?" Wyatt said. "So this Caleb is an old man?"

"A handsome old man?" Cora probed. "Does Pa approve?"

"He's not old." She'd asked him. "He's twenty-five. And why would I need Pa's permission to help his son? And care for his injured dog?"

"A dog?" Cora's eyebrows headed for her hairline. "You never said anything about a dog."

"He brought an injured pup for some doctoring." She explained about Blossom, causing Cora to chuckle several times at little Teddy's behavior.

"You know, that's very interesting." Cora's grin grew wider and wider.

Rose wore a look of triumph as she nodded and nodded.

"You're going to hurt your neck," Lilly warned. Then she squinted at Cora. "What's so interesting about an injured pup? More than anything, it's a pity that people would purposely or carelessly hurt an animal. There ought to be a law against it." She ran out of protests and glared at her sisters, who continued to smile as if they shared some superior knowledge.

"Let's see," Cora began. "Wyatt shows up with a horse that needs to rest and a brother who is afraid. Caleb shows up with an injured dog and an injured son. Seems to be a pattern here."

"Lots of people come for Ma's help," Lilly protested. "That's nothing new. Besides, what no one has mentioned is he's a Caldwell cowboy."

Cora's amusement died. She stared at Lilly for three heartbeats and then turned to Rose. "Is that true?"

Rose nodded. "It is." She spoke as if she'd lost her best friend.

"What's he doing at the farm? Are Ma and Pa in danger?" She pressed to Wyatt's back, peering down the trail to where the Bell wagon was rattling homeward.

Lilly let out a long-suffering sigh and explained yet again that Caleb worked for the Caldwells because he needed money to take Teddy to a special doctor. "In the meantime, Ma and I are teaching Caleb to spread a poultice, and to do exercises to stimulate Teddy's leg and maybe get it to work."

"You're teaching him?" Cora sounded incredulous.

"Yes. He'll have to do it himself when he gets back to the Caldwell ranch tonight."

Cora sank back. "My goodness. I barely get married and things go awry at the farm."

Lilly rumbled her lips. "Everything is fine. None of us is in danger. You can continue to be a happily married woman and we'll manage just fine."

Wyatt turned around and grinned at her. "I don't think Cora is about to change her mind about being married, are you, dear?"

Color flooded Cora's cheeks. "I'm quite happy where I am."

Wyatt gave Cora such a loving smile that Lilly turned away, feeling she had intruded on a private moment.

She stared at the passing scenery, seeing nothing.

She had closed her heart to the possibility of ever having a love like the one Cora and Wyatt shared. The knowledge brought her pain when she considered it, but she ignored the burning in the depths of her heart and reminded herself that being left behind hurt even more.

A door in some far corner of her heart cracked open slightly, but the fear of pain and rejection was too strong and she slammed it shut.

Love was too great a risk.

Chapter Eight

"I wanted to go with Lilly." Teddy watched the wagon following them, carrying the three sisters and Wyatt. He made it sound like he was riding by himself in the Bells' wagon, but Lonnie and Caleb were with him.

"She wanted to be with her sister." Caleb, too, watched the wagon. No doubt they would tell Cora about him and Teddy. What would they say? How he'd like to be a little mouse in the corner and overhear that conversation.

One thing he knew: Rose would make sure none of them forgot Caleb worked for the Caldwells.

What would Lilly say? Would she talk about the injured dog? Would she explain how Teddy's leg had gotten injured? Or would she mention how she and Caleb had laughed together at Teddy's antics?

"Cora misses her sisters," Lonnie said. "Except she mostly thinks about Wyatt. A body could get tired of it. Wyatt this and Wyatt that." His mouth drew down to a frown and then he laughed. "It's not much better when I'm with Wyatt, except it's Cora this and Cora that." The young man sobered, grew morose. "Sure hope I never fall in love like that."

Caleb nodded and smiled. He let Lonnie think he

shared the feeling, but to him falling in love seemed the best possible thing that could happen to a man.

His smile flattened. His teeth clenched. That sort of relationship was out of the realm of possibility for him.

Lonnie didn't seem to care if Caleb contributed to the conversation or not. He spoke of the older man who was Wyatt's partner—Jack Henry. "He says Cora and Wyatt put him in mind of the way he was when his missus was alive."

Lonnie spoke about coming to the Bell farm. "One of our mares was ready to foal so we couldn't keep going. Wyatt and I were looking to start our own place." He looked past Wyatt to a distant spot. "We were running from our past." He brightened. "But Cora helped us see we didn't have to keep running."

Teddy turned to Lonnie. "What were you running from?"

Caleb touched his son's shoulder. "It's not proper to ask personal questions."

"Oh, that's okay." Lonnie said. "We went through kind of a rough spot. I don't like to talk about it. I'll tell you this, though. My pa was nothing like Mr. Bell." His adoring glance rested on the older man driving the wagon. "Mr. Bell is a good, kind man."

"He is, indeed," Caleb agreed.

They arrived at the Bell farm and entered the house. A leaf was put in the table to extend it. The girls soon had it set and Mrs. Bell brought from the oven a roast surrounded by vegetables.

Wyatt, Cora and Lonnie sat beside Rose on one side of the table. Lilly sat between Teddy and Mrs. Bell to Caleb's left. Teddy grinned as if he'd been highly rewarded. Caleb had been busy guarding his heart. Maybe he should have been guarding Teddy's, as well. The boy looked ready to move in and settle down permanently.

Any hope of such would end this afternoon. They'd head back to the Caldwell ranch. End of story.

The conversation around the table was lively as the Bells told Caleb about the different people they'd spoken to at church. He didn't know if they were watching how they were talking about their friends and neighbors because Teddy was listening, or if they always spoke kindly, but he figured it to be the latter.

Lilly turned to help Teddy with his food. She poured him several cups of milk.

Caleb chuckled. "I think I'm going to have to find a milk cow." He meant it jokingly. A man headed down east didn't take a cow with him. The thought soured his insides. "If I ever put down stakes somewhere again, that is." He concentrated on his food, not wanting anyone to think he was feeling sorry for himself.

Cora laughed softly. "Wyatt had moving on his mind, too, until I made him see the folly of the notion."

Wyatt grinned. "Now I can't imagine why I thought it was a good idea."

Caleb noted the way Cora's eyes softened. He liked this couple. Cora had a mother-hen attitude toward her sisters and he guessed she'd felt responsible for them all her life. Wyatt had a brash, bold look that seemed to say he'd face whatever life placed in his path and deal with it. Even though Lonnie had hinted at a spot of trouble, Caleb thought it likely Wyatt's life hadn't tossed anything hard his way, or he might not have been quite so cheerful.

After dinner, Mrs. Bell served up generous portions of stewed fruit. She passed fresh cream so thick he spooned a dollop onto the delicious fruit mixture.

Everything about the meal and the company was

pleasant. But Caleb couldn't fully enjoy it. So many things were roiling inside him. Uppermost was worry about Teddy. Would he ever again walk on both legs?

Beyond that, deep inside, so deep it hid in blackness, lay his unacknowledged, impossible longing to share his life with a woman who loved him. A woman to whom he could freely express his love. Someone who would stand at his side in creating a family like the one the Bells had.

Thankfully the meal ended before his thoughts grew more hopelessly hopeful.

Lilly turned to Caleb. "I suggest we wait to take care of Teddy's leg until the kitchen is clean and the others have gone outside."

"I agree." He did not wish to have the others see his bumbling ways, nor did he want Teddy to have to endure curious stares, no matter how kind they were.

Besides, he wanted to be able to enjoy Lilly at his side without so many pairs of watchful eyes. He ignored the irony of wanting something he'd vowed to deny himself.

"Of course, you'll have to help with dishes." Lilly tossed him a tea towel and a challenging look and then plunged her hands into the hot, soapy dishwater.

He felt the others watching. "I've been known to dry a dish or two." He stood beside her.

"My papa makes me help with dishes when we're living in our wagon."

Caleb grunted. His son was turning into a real chatterbox. "You dirty half of them, so it seems you should wash and dry half of them."

"See?" Teddy crowed, as if Caleb had confessed to some terrible deed. Then he squinted at Caleb. "But he won't let me cook over the fire."

The girls giggled. Wyatt and Lonnie grinned widely.

Lonnie patted Teddy's shoulder. "I know exactly how

you feel, kid. Wyatt here always treated me like I couldn't take care of myself."

Wyatt gave his brother a long, measuring look. "I was only trying to protect you."

Finding someone on his side, Caleb met Wyatt's look. They considered each other a moment and each gave a little nod. Nothing had been said. No signal had been given. But Caleb knew they somehow shared a common bond of caring for a younger one—in Wyatt's case, a brother, in Caleb's, a son.

"I know." Lonnie grinned. "And I 'spect that's what your papa is doing, too."

Teddy nodded.

Lilly planted a wet dish in Caleb's hands and he brought his attention back to the task at hand.

Amid laughing and good-natured teasing, the dishes got washed and the kitchen got cleaned. Lilly shooed the others outdoors. Her parents said they were going to nap and disappeared into their bedroom.

"Now, let's see what you can do." She stood to one side and observed as Caleb prepared a poultice. "I couldn't do better myself," she said as he put it on Teddy's leg.

He concentrated on each step. He had to remember how to do it without supervision so he could continue the treatment back at the Caldwells'.

She pulled two chairs close to the cot and they sat side by side. "Sundays are my favorite day," she said.

He could see why that might be, but he wanted to hear her reasons, so he asked.

"So many reasons. For now, it means Cora and Wyatt and Lonnie can be with us for the day. I guess it won't be that way once the cold weather and snow set in." She brightened again. "Most of all I like the familiar routine of it." She ducked her head. "I don't like things to change."

He could understand that, too. "You have a nice family and a nice home."

"I know."

"Papa, how can you run away from the past?" Teddy's question halted their conversation.

Caleb explained to Lilly what Lonnie had said. "I don't know if you can, son. The past is always a part of us. Guess we can only learn how to accept it." Likely the boy was referring to the horrible events that had occurred in their once peaceful home—though it had lacked the warmth and joy the Bell home had. He wanted Teddy to learn to confine the horror of that day to a small corner of his mind and not let it rule his life.

Lilly leaned over Teddy and stroked his forehead. Her tenderness with his child made the back of Caleb's nose sting.

"Teddy," she said, "my ma once told me if I want to get rid of a bad picture in my mind, I have to replace it with a good one."

Teddy clung to her gaze. "How?"

"What's your favorite thing?"

"Blossom."

Caleb saw her flinch ever so slightly and knew she had the same awful thought he did—what if Blossom didn't make it?

She continued. "What you do when the bad picture comes is pretend to turn around so your back is to the picture and you think of the good thing instead."

"Did you do that?"

She nodded. "I used to wake up crying. I was so afraid I didn't want to go to bed. After Ma talked to me, I would think of one of my favorite things." She laughed.

"Strangely enough it was much like you and Blossom. I loved a furry little kitten I called Puff."

Teddy nodded. "Did your mama let you take Puff to bed with you?"

"Ma doesn't like cats in the house, but she did let me keep Puff in my bed a couple of times when I was especially afraid."

Caleb was again struck by the loving kindness in this family.

Teddy turned to Caleb. "See, I need Blossom with me."

Caleb laughed. Teddy certainly had a way of working things to get what he wanted.

"I suppose Blossom will have to sleep somewhere." It was time to remove the poultice and he did so.

Lilly checked Teddy's skin. "It's important to make sure we don't burn him."

We? Caleb would not acknowledge how good that sounded because there would be no 'we.' There would be only him. "I'll see if I can remember the exercises on my own."

He regretted his words immediately as Lilly stepped back and allowed him to manage on his own. Only twice did she correct him with verbal instructions. He could do this, he congratulated himself. On his own.

That particular victory fell flat.

Lilly watched Caleb's growing confidence with a mixture of pleasure and regret. If he meant to take care of Teddy on his own, he was proving capable. In the back of her mind she'd unwillingly harbored a hope he could struggle and decide Teddy needed to stay with the Bells. Wouldn't he then have to stay, too? Why would she think such a thing? Of course he wouldn't stay. He had a job and needed the money to take Teddy for treatment. Unless, of course, she and Ma could help Teddy, and then he wouldn't need to work for the Caldwells. Nor go east to see a doctor.

She jerked her gaze from Caleb, but she saw nothing except a twirl of confusion that came from inside her head. All that mattered was taking care of Teddy's leg using the best of the skills Ma had taught her. Where and when Caleb went afterward was of no concern to her. Hadn't she learned her lesson? *Don't get close to people. Don't care too much. It'll just be one more loss down the road.* The road she walked with Caleb and Teddy was to be just one day long.

She sucked in air and held it until her brain hammered for oxygen. She released her breath slowly, in firm control of her wayward thoughts.

The others returned to wait for Lilly to join them.

Their usual Sunday activity included wandering around the farm, letting Cora catch up with any changes and generally sharing the latest news each had. Soon the cold and snow would make them unable to get together on Sundays. Lilly did not welcome the thought. She enjoyed seeing Cora every week.

"Ask him to come along," Rose whispered, and Cora nodded.

"Yes, do."

She shook her head at her sisters' suggestion. Hadn't she only moments ago talked herself into keeping a distance from Caleb? Asking him to join them would put him squarely into her life, where she did not want him. "He'll want to stay with Teddy."

Ma stepped from the bedroom, patting her hair and then trying to hide a yawn. She headed for the stove to make herself some tea.

"Ask Ma to watch him," Cora said. "You know Ma would be glad to."

Ma noticed their conspiring. "What are you girls up to now?"

They turned as one.

Cora answered. "We wondered if Caleb would like to join us on our walk."

Lilly watched Caleb. His face lighted as if the thought pleased him, but guilt quickly replaced the pleasure. He lifted a hand toward Teddy. "I have to keep an eye on my boy."

Relief, along with a twinge of sadness, filled Lilly. For a moment she'd thought he would agree.

"Tsk. You don't have to spend the afternoon indoors," Ma said. "It'd be my pleasure to watch him."

He thanked Ma. "In that case, I'd love to go for a walk with all of you."

Lilly turned toward the outdoors, not wanting anyone to see her smile.

Rose hurried ahead, calling Grub to her side, Cora and Wyatt following arm in arm. Lilly glanced about for Lonnie, but he hung over the fence at the pig pen, watching his favorite animals.

That left Lilly no option but to fall in at Caleb's side and traipse after the others. She twisted her hands into a knot. Why did it matter if they walked together? It meant nothing to either of them. But something about caring for Teddy and seeing Caleb's tenderness toward his son had awakened a desire she had tried to bury a mile deep, where it would never surface.

However, if Caleb walked at her side, it would give her a chance to talk about Teddy, though she wasn't sure what she needed to say. Caleb could handle the poultice and exercises fine on his own. And she said so.

"It would be an answer to a prayer if this works," she said.

"I confess I move between hope and despair. I would dearly love to see him walk without having to endure any more pain and discomfort. I know God could heal him, if He so chooses. But is my faith enough?" He shrugged.

"I suppose it depends what you have faith in."

"Why, in God, of course."

"Oh." She purposely looked puzzled. "Didn't I hear you say you wondered if your faith was enough? Seems that means you're trusting in what you can do."

He stopped stock-still and turned to stare at her, surprise filling his eyes. "I never thought of it that way. Of course I don't think it depends on me." He considered it a moment and shook his head. "At least I don't mean to." He turned to follow after the others again. "You've given me food for thought."

She couldn't tell if he appreciated it or not. "I hope you didn't think me harsh or judgmental. I spoke without thinking."

"No, no." He strode on, his hands stuffed into his pockets.

In the lead, Rose guided the group toward the sheep pasture. They lined up along the fence and watched the animals grazing peacefully. Glad to be rescued from the uncomfortable conversation, Lilly counted her flock.

It grated at her nerves that one of the lambs had been drowned by the Caldwell cowboys.

Rose sidled up to her. "Those horrible Caldwells," she murmured, and cast an accusing look past Lilly to Caleb.

If Caleb heard the comment, he gave no indication.

"My little flock is expanding." She hoped to divert Rose from the attack she sensed was coming. "I'll spin this spring's wool as soon as the snow falls."

Cora explained to Caleb. "She makes sweaters and

mittens from her wool and sells them. She always has a ready sale for them. Settlers and ranchers stop at the store and admire her things and soon all her handiwork is gone."

"It sounds like a lot of work," Caleb said.

"I enjoy it." She especially enjoyed knowing people received a quality product in everything she made.

"Work isn't difficult if you enjoy it." Wyatt pulled Cora closer and planted a kiss on her forehead. "Or if you do it for the one you love."

Lilly rejoiced for the love her sister had found. But even so her heart ached. She couldn't pinpoint the exact cause. Was it regret over how things had changed? How Cora now had a life that didn't include her twin sisters? Or was it something more—longing to experience the same thing?

She shook her head. A love like the one Cora and Wyatt shared was nice to see, but was it worth the pain and risk it carried in its arms?

"Let's see how Pa's trees have fared." Cora turned toward the orchard.

As they walked by the various fruit and berry bushes, Lilly explained how Pa had tried to produce fruit trees hardy enough for the Montana climate. A few scrawny apples remained on the trees, pockmarked by hungry birds. "Pa always leaves some fruit for the birds and deer."

Caleb smiled. "I like that."

They continued on their way, going toward the garden shed.

Rose turned to Cora. "I've made good progress in getting Ma's medicinals and remedies on paper."

"Rose is the family diary keeper," Lilly said by way of explanation.

"Someday you will thank me for making sure they are written down."

"You're doing a good job," Lilly admitted. "Cora, you should see the beautiful leather notebook she is writing in." She'd only started the new notebook a few days ago. Before that she'd written her notes in a plain booklet.

Rose grinned. "Why, thank you, dear sister. For that compliment I promise not to tease you for the rest of the day."

Cora and Lilly grinned at each other.

"Do you believe her?" Cora asked.

Lilly chuckled. "Not for a minute. She can no more resist teasing me than she can stop breathing."

Rose flounced away. "Don't say I didn't offer."

Wyatt laughed and turned to Caleb. "They sound like they mean it, but be warned, don't ever try to come between any of them. They'd turn on you so fast you couldn't escape without bruises."

Cora gave him a playful shove. "You make us sound vicious and we never are."

Wyatt pulled her to him. "You're far more subtle, aren't you? But I'm not fooled." He planted a kiss on her nose.

Lilly's throat clenched and she turned her attention to the landscape. The sun was warm, the sky almost cloudless. Dry leaves crackled underfoot. The breeze off the river carried a chill, warning people not to grow complacent and forget about the approaching winter.

"There's snow on the mountains," Wyatt said.

Cora pressed her cheek to his shoulder. "You'll be warm and dry in our little home this winter."

He nodded and smiled down at her. "I shall enjoy every minute of it." He leaned over as if to kiss her nose again.

"Enough of that." Rose shepherded them along the riverbank amid laughing protests from Wyatt and Cora.

They wandered for a spell until they reached a grassy slope, a favorite spot for Lilly and her sisters, and they sat down. Autumn leaves rustled in the nearby trees. Birds chattered noisily.

"Look," Lilly said, pointing to the prairie across the river. "A herd of antelope moving south for the winter."

They watched the animals for a few minutes and then settled back to enjoy the rest of the afternoon. Apparently done with the pigs, Lonnie jogged over to join them. The conversation went round various topics, especially plans for the coming winter. For the girls, that included spinning, knitting and quilting. The men discussed Wyatt's livestock.

Throughout the conversation Lilly noticed that Caleb kept looking toward the house. She was about to suggest they return when the topic shifted, as it seemed to always do, to the Caldwells.

"We haven't seen any of their cowboys around in days," Rose said, glancing about, as did the others, to make certain today wasn't the day they showed up to do their mischief.

"Has anyone heard if Duke has returned yet?" Cora asked.

"Douglas." Rose refused to call the Caldwell son by the nickname everyone else used. "Maybe he got lost or changed his mind about returning. Philadelphia might suit him better than Montana."

"You know you're just dying for him to get back. You miss him so much." Lilly grinned at Caleb to invite him in on the family joke.

Rose spun toward Lilly. "I most certainly do not."

Her reaction drew a chuckle from the other sisters.

"But he so admires your red hair," Lilly teased.

"He mocks it." She turned to Caleb. "He used to chant 'redhead, redhead, fire in the woodshed.' I know what he meant." She tapped the side of her head and rolled her eyes. "As if having red hair means there's something wrong with my mind. *Phewt.* I could live quite happily never seeing him again."

Caleb's eyes sparkled, but he looked sincere as he leaned toward Rose. "I expect he's jealous of your beautiful hair."

His compliment brought a rush of pink to Rose's cheeks and more laughter from the others.

"Of course, Rose didn't take his teasing without retaliation," Lilly added.

"I would be surprised if she did." Caleb looked from one to the other. "What did she do?"

"She punched him in the stomach so hard he could hardly walk afterward." Lilly had been proud of her sister's actions, but at the same time she'd been a little afraid of what Ma and Pa would say.

"Ma and Pa made me write a letter of apology." Rose still grumbled at the idea. "I wrote it, but I never meant a word I said."

Caleb studied the three girls each in turn, his gaze resting finally on Lilly. "It sounds to me like things could get interesting when this Duke fella comes back."

"Douglas," Rose corrected. "And if he tries anything, he'll soon discover we aren't helpless little girls anymore."

"Tell me you won't do anything foolish," Cora begged.

"Depends what you call foolish." Rose looked away, silently informing them she would not reveal any plans she might have. She jumped to her feet. "Look, something's caught in the river."

They all hurried to the bank. Bright red and blue flashed in the water.

"They look like ribbons," Cora said. "Oh, I'd love some more ribbon."

Wyatt waded into the water and caught one strand as it fluttered by, a blue ribbon he gave to Cora. She rewarded him with a kiss full on his mouth.

The other ribbons drifted by but got caught on a rock. "Let's get them," Lilly called, running downstream.

"Let me." Caleb strode in and retrieved another length of ribbon, this one red. "It's for you." He handed it to Lilly.

"Thank you." She smiled, lowering her head and smoothing the wet ribbon. She might never wear it, but she'd cherish it as a keepsake.

She couldn't meet Caleb's eyes. But as she glanced past him, a bit of blue caught her attention. "The other ribbon is caught."

Caleb trotted to the river, waded in and rescued the yard of ribbon. He handed it to Rose. "One each. How fortunate."

Rose's eyes widened and then narrowed. Lilly wondered if she would accept a gift from a Caldwell cowboy.

Lilly released her breath when Rose took the ribbon and said, "Thank you very much."

Hopefully Caleb wouldn't be offended by her less-than-enthusiastic response.

He glanced down at his wet trousers. "I best go change. Then it's time I got back to Teddy." His gaze went toward the house. "He might be getting worried."

Lilly's attention was riveted on Caleb's face. The depth of devotion she saw there struck at her heart.

Was it possible a man could remain faithful in spite of challenges that would rock even the strongest person?

Chapter Nine

The afternoon had passed with lightning speed for Caleb. He'd enjoyed spending time with the Bell sisters, Wyatt and Lonnie, and he had found himself relaxing and feeling unburdened in their company.

Now his chest muscles tightened. Forgetting his responsibilities was not a good thing. He had a son who required his full time and attention.

Despite his mental warning, he smiled as he remembered the way Rose and Lilly had teased each other—all without rancor. His smile disappeared as quickly as it came when he flashed to Rose's struggle to accept the ribbon from him. He understood it was because he worked for the Caldwells.

And if he wanted to keep that job, he'd better pack up and get back there.

"It's time for me to leave," he said to the others.

They rose and followed him across the yard.

He hurried into the house, expecting to find an anxious Teddy. Instead, Teddy was sitting at the table with a glass of milk, an empty plate with some crumbs on it and Mr. and Mrs. Bell huddled close. They were listening intently as his son told them stories.

What stories had Teddy told?

Caleb's heart twisted. There were far too many sad, bitter tales in the boy's life.

Teddy didn't even glance up at Caleb as he continued regaling the elder Bells.

"Papa told me I catched the biggest fish any little boy ever caught." He saw Caleb. "Didn't I, Papa?"

"You did, indeed." The memory came with surprising joy. A lively little stream ran through his ranch. Caleb often caught a fish or two for the next meal. Teddy had started talking about fishing when he could barely walk. Despite Amanda's protests that the boy was too young for such adventures, Caleb had started taking him fishing as soon as he could toddle. He couldn't have been more than three when he caught his first fish. "I'm surprised you remember."

"I 'member real good," Teddy said. "Mama cooked the fish for breakfast."

Caleb remembered, too. It was a good memory. One where he had accomplished what he had hoped to, instead of failing his son.

"Son, we need to go. Say 'thank you' to the Bells."

Teddy did so and hobbled over to Caleb. "Blossom is coming, isn't she?"

"We'll load her in the wagon." He thanked them all for their hospitality.

Mrs. Bell handed him a jar of ingredients for making poultices. "Maybe you can come visit us again. We've really enjoyed your company." Her gaze rested on Teddy as she spoke.

Teddy turned his big blue eyes to Caleb. "Can we, Papa?"

"We work at the Caldwells." That said it all. Ebner would not look kindly at him consorting with the Bells.

The others hadn't followed him indoors. Although Rose was the only one who made her suspicions clear, the others likely shared her opinion.

He insisted on paying Mrs. Bell for the medicine she had given him, and made sure the amount indicated his appreciation for everything, including the hospitality they had offered to him and Teddy.

After another round of goodbyes and thank-yous, he managed to shepherd Teddy out the door and toward the barn. Cora, Wyatt and Lonnie were standing at the fence, watching the pigs and talking. Rose ducked into the garden shed. He saw no sign of Lilly.

Not that it mattered, except he wanted to thank her for her help.

He and Teddy stepped into the barn and he smiled. Lilly was kneeling beside Blossom, giving her some more tonic.

"I'm glad to see you before we leave."

Her eyes snapped toward him.

Had he sounded too eager? He hastened to explain. "I wanted to be sure to thank you for all you've done for Blossom and Teddy." More than that, she'd given him hope that there was something he could do to help his son, but he couldn't say that.

"It was my joy to help them both." Her gaze connected with his. A smile curved her lips and made him wish he could stay longer. Then she jerked her attention to the dog. "Blossom needs lots of rest and good food. You can take these drops with you. Give them to her three times a day. I'm sending along some ointment, too. Apply it every night to prevent infection." She handed him the items. Her fingers brushed his palm and he felt an incredible urge to curl his hand around hers.

Instead he thanked her and stuffed the things in his

pocket. "I'll hitch the horse to the wagon and get Blossom. Teddy, you stay here." He rushed out. He couldn't wait to get away while he still had his wits about him.

He hitched the horse and then drove close to the barn, hopped down and hurried in to get the dog and his son.

Lilly followed as he lifted the Blossom into the back of the wagon. "Don't hesitate to bring her back if you suspect infection. I can help you with that."

"I'm sure we'll be fine." They had to be. He had a job to protect and a boy to take care of.

And now an injured dog to tend.

Everything would have to fit in around his work. He didn't mean to give Ebner reason to fire him.

With that thought uppermost in his mind, he thanked Lilly again and bid her goodbye.

Teddy waved at her until he could no longer see her. "I like Lilly. Will we see her again?"

Not willing to give the boy reason to be sad, Caleb simply answered, "It's hard to say."

As he expected, Ebner was none too happy to discover Caleb had an injured dog with him. "A gimpy boy and now a half-dead dog. Have you forgotten you're here to work?"

Caleb silently objected to the way Ebner described his son, but he kept his thoughts to himself. He'd heard worse and so had Teddy. The world had more than its fair share of cruel people. "I haven't forgotten. I'll do my work as usual."

"Well, don't think you can waste time looking after that sorry mutt."

Caleb nodded, directing a steady look at his boss to inform him Caleb was his own man, even if he had to take orders from Ebner. "I'll give you no cause for complaint."

"Huh." Ebner stalked away.

Teddy glowered at Ebner's back. "Papa, I don't li—"

Caleb held up a hand to silence the boy. "He's my boss. No bad-mouthing him."

"Yes, Papa."

Caleb settled Blossom and Teddy, leaving them in the wagon, and then hurried to do the evening chores. It was late by the time he finished and turned his attention to making supper for them.

Teddy sighed softly when he saw it was to be beans, stale biscuits and peaches.

"I know I'm not the cook Mrs. Bell is, but I don't have time to make a proper meal."

"It's okay, Papa." Teddy's voice lacked even a hint of enthusiasm.

Caleb hurried through the meal knowing he still had both Teddy and the dog to take care of. He made the poultice and left it on Teddy's leg while he applied ointment to Blossom's wounds and got her to take the drops and some food. Then he did Teddy's exercises. It hit him how much time was involved in doing everything.

There was only one way to accomplish it without upsetting Ebner.

The next morning he rose before any men or animals had stirred and slipped from the wagon. He paused a moment and looked back at his sleeping son. *Don't wake up while I'm gone.* Teddy would panic if he found himself all alone.

Caleb glanced at the cold coffeepot. He took a step toward the place where he built a fire to make their meals then forced himself to turn away. He could wait for coffee. He'd ignore the pounding that entered his head at the thought.

He hurried to the barn and surprised the horses, who were still sleeping. They shuffled and stomped as he rationed out oats and hay for each of them. Then he grabbed the fork and cleaned the pens and alley. Satisfied that should give him enough time to take care of Teddy and Blossom, he trotted back toward the wagon.

Cowboys staggered from the bunkhouse, scratching and groaning. Caleb overheard grumbling about the horses waking early, but he didn't say anything about his part in it.

He jogged back to the wagon, anxious to drink coffee and take care of his son. Perhaps he could hope to have the first cup before Teddy stirred. At the wagon, he peeked inside to assure himself all was right.

At the sight greeting him, his heart fell like a stone.

Teddy was curled up beside Blossom, one hand pressed to the dog's head, the thumb of the other hand in his mouth. His eyes were wide as twin moons.

"Teddy, what's wrong? Did you have another nightmare?" Caleb jumped up and pulled the boy to his knee, holding and rocking him.

Teddy clutched at Caleb's jacket and burst into tears.

Caleb rocked back and forth and rubbed Teddy's back. He should have never left the child. But if he meant to do the things Lilly had suggested, he had no choice.

"I thought you'd gone," Teddy managed to say around his sobs.

Caleb tipped Teddy's face up toward him. "I will never leave you."

"Something bad might happen to you. Like it did to Mama."

Caleb pulled his son to his chest. He couldn't promise that nothing bad would ever happen to him. There simply weren't any guarantees in life. "I will do everything I can to make sure nothing happens to me, but if—God forbid—it does, you let Grandma and Grandpa know." Amanda's folks would come and get him.

"How?"

"Well." He shifted so he could reach the satchel containing letters and other important papers. "Everything you need to know is in here."

"Papa, I can't read." Teddy sounded like he couldn't believe Caleb had forgotten that little detail.

"You take this to some adult you trust and let them read it."

Teddy nodded vigorously. "Like Miss Lilly."

"Miss Lilly would be a very good choice."

Teddy sighed and curled against Caleb's chest. "I like Miss Lilly, but I don't want anything to happen to you."

Amen to that. No one must be allowed into Caleb's life who would turn one ounce of his attention from this precious little boy of his.

"Now I better make us some breakfast so I can get to work."

He hustled over to start the fire and set the coffeepot to boil.

Teddy watched his every move. "You ain't had coffee yet?"

"Haven't." He corrected Teddy automatically, his mind counting down the seconds until the coffee would have developed enough kick for his satisfaction.

Teddy sat back on the bed and bent over Blossom's head. "He hasn't had coffee yet. And he didn't even growl at me."

Caleb grinned to himself. *See,* he wanted to say to someone, *I can change. I'm not a creature of habit.* But there was only one person he cared to tell. And she was back with her parents and sister at the Bell farm.

The coffeepot hissed and spat. He poured a cupful

and sucked back the hot liquid, gasping when it burnt
his tongue.

From inside the wagon, he heard a little giggle and
smiled again. He let the liquid cool a bit and then drained
the cup. He quickly threw some sausage and potatoes
into a skillet and set it over the rocks he used as a stove.

"Now, young man, let's get this poultice done." He put
Blossom on the ground to do her business. Teddy had gotten into his clothes and sat with his pant leg rolled back.

That done, Caleb stirred the contents of the skillet and
then tended Blossom. Next he broke six eggs into the skillet and stirred the mixture. While he did Teddy's exercises, the eggs set. "Good enough," he declared. He had
no time to waste. He dished the food out and gulped his
down. He had barely finished when the cowboys started
to pour out of the cookhouse. The majority of them saddled up and rode away.

Ebner headed toward Caleb. Caleb grabbed his hat
and rose to his feet. No time to do dishes. "Teddy—"

"Papa, can I stay here with Blossom?" Teddy whispered.

Caleb gave it a moment's consideration. From where
he'd be in the yard, he would be able to see Teddy. Truth
was, he could accomplish his work a lot faster if he didn't
have a tagalong.

"Okay, but don't go anywhere." He hurried toward
Ebner, who immediately barked orders at him.

"Get the barn chores done, then—"

"They're already done, boss."

Ebner's only sign of acknowledgement was a narrowing of his eyes. "Good, because it's too late in the sea-
son to be mollycoddling a hired man just 'cause he's got
a gimpy kid. I want the big corral ready for use. When
yer done that we need about half a dozen gates built.

Then—" By the time Ebner finished, Caleb had enough work for most of the week. Did Ebner mean for him to do it all today? He didn't ask because he didn't want to know the answer.

With a quick glance over his shoulder to check on Teddy, Caleb hustled to begin his tasks.

He worked steadily all morning and then trotted back to the wagon to throw together some food, do the poultice and exercises and tend Blossom.

Ebner dogged Caleb's trail all afternoon. The minute one job was finished, he ordered him to do another.

Throughout the day, Caleb barely had time to glance at Teddy, let alone go over and see if the boy was doing all right. From what he could see, Teddy wandered about the wagon and sat next to Blossom most of the time.

This was no life for a child. But what choice did either of them have?

He finished his chores. Ebner had disappeared into the cookhouse, allowing Caleb to escape being assigned any more tasks. He rushed over and threw some food together for supper. Teddy needed to be fed better. No doubt he was thinking longingly of the meals at the Bells', even as Caleb was. But Caleb had plumb run out of time and was getting a little low on energy, too.

It was dark before he finished tending Teddy and Blossom and cleaned up the dishes from three meals.

He lay beside Teddy in the wagon, too weary to do anything but seek the bliss of forgetfulness in sleep.

This was the way things would be now. He'd manage somehow.

But after two more days of rising early, two mornings of ignoring the complaints of those who'd had their sleep disturbed by the horses thumping about before dawn and two days of work that could keep two men busy, Caleb came to a conclusion.

He couldn't do everything and be everywhere, and Teddy was the one suffering.

As suppertime and the end of the day approached on Wednesday, Caleb found Ebner. "Boss, we need to talk."

Ebner crossed his arms and faced Caleb. "So talk."

"I can't manage taking care of Teddy and doing the amount of work you expect."

Ebner had been saying so since Day One, and now he wore a gloating look. "You quitting?"

"No, sir." The man would have to fire him to get rid of him. Although he hoped Lilly's methods would help Teddy, he wasn't prepared to cancel his plans to go east to see that doctor Amanda's folks had found. He needed this job to accomplish that. "But if I get someone to look after Teddy during the day it would sure help me."

Ebner studied him intently a moment and nodded. "You do that." He strode away without asking who Caleb meant to ask, and Caleb wasn't about to tell him.

He jogged back to the wagon, hurriedly tossed his belongings aboard and lifted Blossom and Teddy into the back.

"Papa, are we leaving?"

"Son, I'm taking you where you can be properly looked after while I work."

Teddy's face drained of color. "You're leaving me behind?"

"I think you'll like what I have in mind. Now, wait here while I get the horse." When he returned, Teddy sat on the bench, grinning at Caleb.

"I know what you're planning," he said.

Caleb climbed up beside him and smiled at his son's joy. "Let's see if you're right."

* * *

"Company coming." Pa, about to come in for supper, paused at the doorway.

Lilly stirred the pot of stew that simmered on the stove and then joined Pa in the doorway. It was a covered wagon. She knew of only one person in the area who traveled about in such a fashion.

Caleb.

"It might be someone passing through," she said, as much in explanation to herself as to her pa.

"Could be," Pa agreed.

Rose and Ma emerged from the garden shed where they had been the past two hours, as Rose continued to catalogue Ma's herbs and remedies.

Rose shot an accusing glance at Lilly.

Lilly shrugged. If it was Caleb, she had nothing to do with his return. When he'd left Sunday night, she thought it would likely be the last she saw of the Craigs and their dog.

The wagon drew closer and she could see it was Teddy and Caleb. Teddy waved and grinned.

She lifted her hand to return the greeting. Then curled her fingers and lowered her arm, pressing it to her stomach. Her initial curiosity had bounced to gladness to see them again, but just as quickly she'd quelled the feeling. After all, he hadn't come to see her.

Why had he come?

The wagon passed the barn and drew up before the house.

"Evening," Pa said.

"Evening." Caleb nodded and continued to sit beside Teddy.

He'd come all this way to say that? Lilly almost laughed.

"What can we do for you?" Pa asked as Rose and Ma joined Lilly.

Lilly realized she was holding her breath, and she eased it out slowly and quietly so Rose wouldn't notice.

Caleb got off the wagon and came to face Pa. He clutched his hat in his hands. "Sir, Mrs. Bell, ladies." He nodded to each of them. "I have a very large request to make." He sucked in a breath. "I find I can't take care of Blossom, do Teddy's extra care and keep up with my chores." The hat twisted round and round. "Lilly said to come back if I needed anything." He swallowed hard.

Lilly suspected he wanted to ask for help, but the Bells waited, letting him do it in his time and his way.

"I'm here to ask if I can pay you to look after Teddy for me while I work." His gaze caught and held Lilly's, as if he meant the question solely for her.

Ma and Pa looked at each other and then Pa said, "Why, of course we'll help with your son and the little dog. Bring them in."

"Thank you." He planted his hat on his head but didn't move. "Shall I put Blossom in the barn?"

Ma turned to Lilly. "What do you think?"

"Do you plan to leave Teddy here overnight?" Lilly asked, thinking Blossom might provide Teddy with comfort if that were the case.

The hat came off again and twisted round and round. Caleb's mouth pulled up at one corner. "I don't want to, but what choice do I have?" Agony tightened each word. "How can I bring him here each morning and get back to work then come get him each evening after work? It wouldn't take much to convince Ebner to fire me and I simply can't have that."

Lilly reached out a hand to him and then she pulled it back. Her sympathy must be contained, for if she expressed it as deeply as she felt it, she would squeeze his arm and smile reassuringly. Rose would object on the sole basis he worked for the Caldwells. Ma and Pa would warn her to be more circumspect. Instead of following her instincts, she slipped to Ma's side. "We can make sure he's safe and happy, can't we, Ma?"

"To the best of our ability. Bring them both inside."

Caleb again put his slightly battered hat on his head and turned to Teddy. "You want to visit the Bells for a while?"

Teddy nodded and grinned and then almost leapt into his father's arms. As soon as Caleb set him on the ground, Teddy put the crutches in place and headed for the house. "I knowed he'd bring me here."

Lilly went to the back of the wagon, from which Caleb lifted Blossom. The dog raised her head and licked Caleb's hands.

"She's looking better," Lilly said.

Caleb grinned. "Must be all the loving she gets from Teddy."

"I expect you've done your part by tending her wounds." Even a quick glance revealed they were clean.

"There's been no change in Teddy's leg."

"I'm sorry. But it's only been a few days."

Caleb held the dog, his gaze on Lilly as if seeking something from her. Was he discouraged? Perhaps he felt he'd failed.

"It's a lot of work to take care of an injured dog and a boy needing special attention." She hoped he'd find her words reassuring.

He nodded. His eyes darkened, and then he shifted his gaze to Blossom. "Where do you want me to put her?"

"I suppose Teddy will sleep on the cot, so why don't you put her on the floor beside it?"

"Good. She'll keep him company."

They went indoors and settled the dog. Lilly brought water and food for her and grinned at how eagerly Blossom took both. "It's good to see her gaining strength."

Teddy hurried over and sat on the floor beside her. Blossom wriggled from nose to tail. Teddy patted her head. "She's going to be better soon, so then she can run and play with me."

Caleb slowly brought his gaze up to meet Lilly's. She read the despair there, knew he was wondering if Teddy would ever be able to run and play again.

Ma observed them. "Love and proper care work wonders. Have you had your supper?"

Teddy answered immediately. "Pa's been awfully busy. Says there's no time for cooking."

Caleb groaned.

"It's okay, Papa. I'm not 'plaining."

Caleb rolled his eyes.

"We were about to eat," Ma said. "Please join us."

Teddy was on his feet headed for the chair he'd formerly occupied before Ma finished her sentence.

Even Rose chuckled at his eagerness.

Soon they were gathered around the table. Pa held out his hands and Caleb took the one on his side.

As Lilly took the hands of Rose and Ma, she thought how Caleb and Teddy fit right in, how the family seemed livelier with them there. And how glad she was to see him across the table.

Thankfully, Pa said grace at that moment, preventing her from examining the thought.

After the meal, Caleb grabbed a towel and helped dry the dishes.

"Just like Wyatt used to do," Rose murmured.

What did she mean by that? But she couldn't ask and get an answer in front of everyone else.

After the kitchen was clean, Lilly helped Caleb prepare the poultice. They took care of Blossom and then she supervised Teddy's exercises.

"You're doing good."

He smiled, but it did not reach his eyes. "If I didn't need…"

She understood what he didn't say—if he didn't need the money, if he didn't need the job, he would make different choices. He'd take care of Teddy himself. But wishing didn't change anything. If it did, she could wish for a man to love her like she wanted. She could hope for a family of her own. But she knew the folly of wanting those things. She'd never forget the disappointment and pain of opening herself up to those dreams, only to have them snatched from her.

Caleb finished Teddy's exercises and stepped back. "I'll bring Teddy's things in."

Lilly glanced around. Pa was reading. Ma was knitting. Rose was writing in her book of cures. That left her to accompany Caleb. "I'll come with you." She sensed how difficult it was for him to consider leaving Teddy.

They went outside to the wagon. Caleb reached into the back for a small trunk, groaned and stepped back. "I don't want to leave him. I'm all he has."

She rubbed his arm. "He has Blossom. We'll take good care of them both."

"I have no doubt of that, or I wouldn't even have considered this. But he's just a small guy who has lost his mother. I don't want him to think I'm leaving him, too."

"You can make him understand."

"I'll put him to bed before I leave." He hoisted the trunk and returned indoors with Lilly following.

She couldn't imagine how hard this was for both of them. If only she could do something to make it easier.

Caleb put the trunk at the end of the cot. "I'll help you get ready for bed, Teddy."

Teddy stood at Pa's side, looking at something Pa had drawn. At his father's word, he went to Caleb.

"Am I going to sleep here?"

"Is that okay?" Caleb asked.

He nodded. "Blossom will want me to stay close." He slipped into his nightshirt and Caleb folded his clothes neatly and put them on top of the trunk.

Teddy sat on the bed with an expectant look on his face. He signaled for Caleb to move closer so he could whisper something.

Caleb nodded. "I'll ask." He turned to Lilly. "Teddy wants to know if you will listen to his prayers."

"Me?" The request slammed her in the middle of the chest and then the feeling eased, leaving her insides quivering with yearning and pleasure. She could love this boy. If she let herself.

"Please," Teddy begged.

She'd stood lost in contemplation long enough to make him think she'd refuse. "I'd be honored." She sat on the bed and Teddy crawled into her lap and closed his eyes.

She closed hers as well, more to contain the bittersweet joy of being near this child than to prepare for prayer.

Teddy prayed for his father, Blossom and each one in the Bell family, and then he asked God to make his leg remember how to work. "Amen."

A still quiet filled the room.

Lilly slowly turned her gaze to Caleb. His dark eyes were filled with hope and despair. She knew her own eyes must have shown her feelings of joy and pleasure, because she could not contain nor control them. He smiled as if he were correctly reading the tender feelings his son brought to her heart.

He turned away. His expression softened as he studied Teddy. "I'll tuck you in."

Lilly scurried out of his way.

Teddy crawled under the covers. "Cozy," he said, his voice soft with contentment.

Caleb tucked the blankets tight and bent over to kiss him on the forehead. His hand lingered, brushing Teddy's hair back, wiping an imaginary spot of dirt from his son's face. He sucked in air and straightened. "Good night, Teddy. I'll be back tomorrow evening. Be a good boy." He wheeled around and headed for the door.

Teddy sat bolt upright in bed, the cozy covers tossed aside. "Papa, you're going?"

"Yes, I thought you understood that. But I'll be back."

"No, Papa. You said you'd always be close enough to hear me. You can't go. You can't." Tears and sobs intermingled with Teddy's anguished words.

Caleb hesitated at the doorway.

Lilly held her breath. Would he leave? What choice did he have? Her heart echoed Teddy's cries. Her birth father had left her and Rose and Cora. Wasn't he supposed to stay close and take care of them? She pushed her fist into the pit of her stomach in an attempt to stop the pain. Was she so unimportant, so unlovable, so forgettable that even her own father could walk away?

She wanted to pull Teddy into her arms and shelter him from such fear, but she was riveted to the spot as firmly as if someone had driven nails through her shoes.

Chapter Ten

Caleb stood in the doorway, Teddy's cries tearing wide wounds through his heart. He had promised Teddy he would never leave him, he would always be close.

But he had to work.

Who would comfort his son when he cried in the night?

"Papa, Papa, don't go," Teddy sobbed.

Caleb closed his eyes as pain seared from the soles of his boots to the top of his head. He couldn't do it. He couldn't leave his son. Somehow he had to work things out. He turned slowly and faced the Bells. "I can't leave him."

Mr. and Mrs. Bell nodded. "We understand."

Teddy's sobs shuddered to a stop. He swiped at his tears.

Lilly jumped to her feet. "Ma, Pa, why can't Caleb stay?" She flung about to face Teddy. "If your papa stayed here overnight, would you be happy to stay with us during the day?"

Caleb shook his head. "My job—"

"You can ride back and forth. It's not far on horseback. Go back in the morning. Come here after work."

She turned to her parents. "Don't you think that would be good?"

The older couple looked at each other, stayed silent for a moment and then nodded at the same time. Mr. Bell answered. "You're welcome to stay and leave Teddy here during the day."

It sounded like a good idea, but Caleb shifted his attention to Teddy. His son would have to approve. "What do you think, Teddy?"

"Could Blossom stay with me?"

Lilly answered his question. "She certainly could."

"And you'd come here every night?" he asked Caleb.

"Every night."

"Then I guess it's all right."

"Good. I'll park the wagon and come back and get Teddy." He meant to sleep in the wagon as they had done previously.

Mr. Bell waved away Caleb's plan. "No need for that. Teddy is already settled. You can sleep with him if you don't mind being crowded, or better yet, bring your bedroll in and sleep on the floor beside him. Unless you object to sleeping on the floor."

Caleb laughed as much with relief as with amusement. "No objection at all. Teddy, I need to take care of the horse and wagon and then I'll be back. Okay?"

Teddy nodded. "I'll wait for you."

He almost told the boy to go to sleep, but he understood Teddy would not settle until he saw Caleb ready to sleep beside him. "I'll be back in a few minutes."

Lilly followed him to the door. "I'll get your horse some feed." Caleb left the wagon parked beside the barn and then led the horse inside, where Lilly put out a bit of grain and some hay.

She leaned on the pitchfork handle, her chin resting

on her clasped hands. "Caleb, I hope I haven't put you in an awkward position."

He brushed the horse down. "How's that?"

She made a sound, half snort, half laugh. "I can't see the Caldwells being happy about you riding over here every evening."

He turned the horse into the manger for its feed, using the time to consider his reply. Ebner most certainly would raise a ruckus if he knew where Teddy was staying. "What is good for Teddy is more important to me than what Ebner thinks."

"Very noble. But you might lose your job." She cleaned up a bit of scattered hay, making it impossible for Caleb to see her expression. Did she approve of his decision or consider him foolish?

He felt he needed to explain his behavior to her. "I promised Teddy I would always be close enough that he could call me."

She studied him with a look of confusion. "But you won't be here in the daytime."

"He's okay during the day. Night is when he gets scared and has frightening nightmares. I can't imagine what he'd do if I wasn't there to hold him and tell him he was safe." Memory of the horrors that plagued his son gripped Caleb so hard he struggled to breathe. "I can't leave him." He choked out the words.

She stood beside him and rubbed his arm.

He could not deny himself this bit of comfort. He covered her hand with his and pressed it tight to his forearm.

"No father should ever leave his children."

Her words sounded as if her throat were as tight as his. Her mouth twisted.

"I will never leave him. It's a promise I made to both myself and him."

"I didn't mean to suggest you would, but not every child is so fortunate. Thank God for people like Ma and Pa who took us in."

If he wasn't mistaken, her words conveyed regret as much as gratitude. He curled his fingers about her hand where it lay on his forearm. "Lilly, what happened to your parents?"

A jolt shook her and he held her hand tighter, narrowing the distance between them to only a couple of inches. Whatever had happened, it still had the power to shatter her world.

"My mama died. My papa left us in the middle of the prairie and rode away."

Did she realize when she spoke of them she still sounded like a little girl? He ached to pull her into his arms and comfort her as he would have Teddy.

"We never saw him again. Don't know what happened to him or why he left us." She shook herself a little, pulled her hand away and squared her shoulders. "So you see, I know that not all fathers promise to never leave their children, and even fewer keep that promise."

He stood silent and waiting, hoping she would open her past a bit more. Somehow he knew, though he couldn't explain how, that inside she had a room full of sorrow she needed to empty.

But she placed the pitchfork in the tack room, dusted her hands off and faced him, her expression serene, as if all her thoughts were joyful and peaceful.

He knew otherwise.

"Are you ready to go back to the house?" she asked.

He nodded. "Teddy will be anxious."

They stepped into the dusky evening and closed the barn door behind them. A cat slipped inside just before the door shut. Grub sat waiting for them and almost fell over his own feet in his rush to get to their side.

Caleb chuckled. "Don't suppose he'll teach Blossom his ways, do you?"

She laughed. "Are you suggesting that would be a bad thing?"

"Hmm. Let me think." He rubbed his chin. "I guess it depends on whether I want a big clumsy animal or a dog who will protect my son."

She stopped and rubbed her chin, imitating his contemplative action. "I'd think the answer would be obvious. Isn't it your job to protect Teddy?" She didn't wait for him to answer. Not that he needed to. The question had been purely rhetorical. "So it seems what Teddy needs from Blossom is a playmate. Besides, Grub isn't clumsy. He's just…" She pressed her lips together to search for a word she liked. "Overeager."

"If you say so."

Grub, sensing they were talking about him, turned around in an excited circle and ended up on his back with a silly grin on his face.

Caleb chuckled as Lilly patted the dog.

"You're a good old dog, no matter what he thinks."

Grub scrambled out from underfoot and they continued on their way to the house.

"How do you know what I think?" he asked.

"You've made it plain you think our dog is useless."

"Only as a guard dog," he said. "He's very good at… other things." He purposely made the words vague, matching his voice.

"Yes, he is."

When they reached the door, Grub flopped down beside the house and Caleb and Lilly stepped inside.

Teddy sat with Rose beside him looking through a

book. Mrs. and Mr. Bell had pulled chairs close to the cot and were looking at the pictures along with them.

Caleb ground to a halt. He'd once dreamed of such a homey scene.

He and Amanda had loved this child. Her murder had robbed Teddy of this sort of attention. Was he doing the boy a disfavor by letting him enjoy it here with the Bells, knowing it would be temporary? He answered his own question. He couldn't deny him the joy, nor could he take the boy back to the Caldwells' knowing he would have to neglect the poultices and exercises if he meant to keep his job.

Mr. and Mrs. Bell pushed their chairs back to the table. "Girls, it's time for bed," Mr. Bell said. "This little fellow needs his sleep, and we'll need to rise early in order to get breakfast ready for Caleb before he leaves."

"Oh, no need to put yourselves out." The last thing Caleb wanted was to become a burden to them. "I'll take care of my own needs." He had supplies in the wagon and had cooked his breakfast almost every morning since that awful day.

"Nonsense," Mrs. Bell said. "That would be plumb foolish when we have an abundance to spare."

"Besides." Lilly spoke softly, as if she didn't want Teddy to hear her. "Don't you think you should make sure Teddy is okay before you leave?"

He squinted at her. She knew it was an argument he couldn't ignore, but why would she use it? Did she want him to stay for breakfast? Or was she only thinking of Teddy and how it felt to have a father leave you behind? He studied her gentle smile a moment, but she revealed nothing in her gaze.

For Teddy's sake, he would accept their invitation.

"It's most generous of you." He would pay these people for their kindness.

Rose and Lilly went to one room. Mrs. Bell pushed the kettle to the back of the stove and fussed about tucking Teddy in again.

"I'll leave you that lamp." Mr. Bell nodded toward the one in the middle of the table, lit another and then headed for the bedroom.

"Good night," Caleb said. Mr. and Mrs. Bell said good-night before they closed their door and two voices called good-night from the other bedroom. He stretched out on his bedroll, his hands clasped behind his head. The sound of those friendly good-nights lingered in his head like a sweet melody.

"Papa?"

"Yes, Teddy."

"This is the nicest we've had it since Mama died." He sighed contentedly.

"Yes, it is." He never thought he would again feel the pleasures of home. A warning signal jolted up his spine. He jerked his hands to his side and closed his eyes tight. He felt like he was walking on a very thin board high above a raging storm with the Bell family following him. One misstep would send them all plunging into the turbulent waters below. Why should he feel this way? He accepted their hospitality with no intention of prolonging his visit beyond what was necessary. It was the best way to take care of Teddy.

Sooner or later, Ebner would discover what he was up to.

The tension in his spine increased. Surely Ebner wouldn't punish the Bells for helping him. Still, he couldn't shake the feeling of disaster.

His thoughts darkened. He'd brought pain into too many lives already.

God in Heaven, protect these people from any harm.

It was all he could do at the moment. He needed their help until he finished the job at the Caldwells' and took Teddy down east.

Rose turned out the lamp and darkness folded in on Lilly.

She tried to calm her thoughts, but they went round and round, faster and faster. Why had she told Caleb about their birth father abandoning them? It wasn't like she usually gave it any stock or let it fill her thoughts. Not like Rose did. No, she liked things exactly the way they were.

Her heart kicked up a protest.

Okay, there were things she might wish for, but she'd realized how foolish it was to have dreams that depended on other people.

Caleb would never leave his son. He was a father his boy could count on.

That did not, she warned herself, mean he was a man another person could count on.

"Lilly, why did you get so upset when Teddy cried?" Rose asked.

Lilly sat up and stared at her sister, though in the darkness she saw little but the shape of her in bed. "Didn't you?"

The shape moved and sat upright. "Of course I felt badly. But you acted like Caleb was leaving. Lilly, you haven't fallen in love with him, have you?"

She snorted. "Me? I think I can live without the risk of falling in love."

"What risk do you mean? Why are you afraid of falling in love?"

Lilly wasn't sure how honest she wanted to be. "Well, first there is what happened with Karl—"

"He doesn't count. We both agree he wasn't the sort of man you want."

Lilly didn't remember agreeing to that, but she knew it to be true. Karl had been more interested in Karl than in a life with Lilly.

Rose pressed her. "What if you found a man like Wyatt?"

"I don't think Cora would be willing to share him." Lilly's laugh sounded false, even to herself.

"You know what I mean. What's to be afraid of?"

"What are you afraid of?"

Rose grunted. "I'm not afraid. I'm just waiting for someone to come along who sees my value. What are you waiting for?"

Lilly sighed. How could she explain it to her sister? What better way than with her motto? "You get close to people, it'll just be one more loss down the road."

"I don't think you are talking about Karl."

Surprisingly, she wasn't.

"Now I see it." Rose's voice rang with victory.

"It's dark. How can you see anything?"

"You saw yourself in Teddy. You felt his fear that his father would leave him. And all this time you say you don't think about our past, don't want to try and find out who our birth parents were. You say you like things just the way they are—"

"And so I do."

"But don't you see the past is controlling you? It isn't Karl's leaving you that has you afraid. It's our father riding off and leaving us. You're afraid another man might do the same thing. Maybe that's why you pretended you cared about Karl. You knew he would live up to your expectation of eventually deserting you."

"Girls." Pa's voice was coming from the other room. "Some people would like to sleep."

"Yes, Pa," the twins chorused and lay back down.

"I'm right," Rose whispered. "And I think you know it."

Lilly didn't answer. Whether or not Rose was right didn't change a thing. Either way, she had no intention of opening her heart to more loss.

Though it might be too late in Teddy's case. She cared far more deeply for him than she knew was wise. Her heart would bleed more than a little when they left.

And Teddy's father?

She wasn't that foolish. All she felt for him was sympathy.

Within minutes she fell asleep, but sometime later, a sound startled her awake and she jerked up in bed.

Rose sat up, too, barely visible in the dark of night. "What was that?"

"Teddy's crying," Lilly murmured. She was grateful the darkness hid the sheen of tears in her eyes. In her mind a memory flashed, so sharp and painful she almost moaned. She had only been three at the time, but she remembered the fear that had threatened to rip her heart from her as she stood holding Cora's hand, looking down a long, empty road.

Teddy's sobs grew muffled and the low rumble of Caleb's voice calming him eased the tension from Lilly's spine. She lay back, her own painful memory fading into the night.

She woke the next morning to the sound of Pa starting the fire in the stove and Ma splashing water into the kettle, and she bounded from her bed.

Would Caleb have left already?

She was in her clothes and out of the room before Rose had even brushed her hair.

"Good morning," Ma said.

Lilly answered without looking at her, her attention elsewhere. Caleb sat at the table with a cup of coffee between his palms, his eyebrows knotted together in concentration.

Pa held the coffeepot and filled his own cup.

Teddy sat on the floor next to Blossom.

Caleb hadn't left. And he hadn't had his first cup of coffee. A grin tugged at Lilly's lips. "Good morning, Caleb."

He grunted.

Teddy held a finger to his lips. "He hasn't had his coffee yet."

She nodded. "I kind of thought that." Unable to resist the urge to tease him, she sat down across from Caleb. "Is it too hot to drink?" she asked in her most innocent voice.

He glowered at her and gulped a mouthful, gasping and waving his hand at his mouth to cool his burnt tongue.

She pressed her lips together to keep from laughing, but she knew he could see the amusement that made her eyes smile.

"Lilly, leave the man in peace," Pa said. He turned to Caleb. "Forgive her. She's not a coffee drinker, so she doesn't understand."

Lilly chuckled. "I can't help but feel a little sorry for Teddy. How does he put up with this day after day?"

Caleb cautiously swallowed more coffee. His eyes

slowly softened, and he sighed. "With a great deal more kindness than you've shown."

She grinned. "Sorry."

"You are not."

"You're right. I'm not. Like Pa says, I don't need coffee to make me cheerful in the morning." Was the man unreasonable if he didn't get that first drink?

"Papa didn't have coffee right away for the past few days," Teddy said. "He got up early and hurried to do the chores before everyone else was up. And he didn't even get mad at me."

Lilly widened her eyes. "Wow, I'm impressed."

Caleb quirked his eyebrows. "I'm really quite noble, you know."

Rose joined them. "Don't see how a noble person could work for the likes of the Caldwells."

Caleb shrugged. "They pay well, and besides, I didn't know I'd stepped into a feud."

"I suppose not," Rose acknowledged. "And maybe having you there will mean we will get some warning when they plan to do something."

Caleb's expression grew dark. "You're asking me to spy?"

"She is not." Lilly jerked to her feet. "Rose, how could you?"

Rose leaned close and spoke so quietly Lilly doubted anyone else could hear. "Don't be so naive. Don't you wonder if he is spying for the Caldwells?"

Lilly could only gape. It wasn't possible.

Rose continued, more loudly. "Besides, are you going to say that if you knew ahead of time they planned to chase your sheep into the river you wouldn't have stayed home to protect them?"

"Well, of course I would have," Lilly said. She sank

back to her chair. "I would have done anything to save my lamb."

Caleb sat back. "They did that?"

She nodded.

"And worse," Rose added.

"I wish I'd known before I took the job, but now—" He shrugged.

"Girls," Ma said. "This isn't appropriate table conversation."

"Yes, Ma," they chorused.

Pa refilled Caleb's cup. "We don't hold you responsible for what the Caldwells have done, do we, girls?"

Lilly answered quickly. "Of course not."

Rose mumbled something. Lilly knew she wasn't willing to overlook the fact that Caleb worked for the Caldwells.

Lilly set the table and Rose helped Ma prepare the food. Soon a hearty meal was on the table. Caleb ate hurriedly, glancing frequently at the window. As soon as he was done, he pushed away from the table. "I must be on my way." He knelt at Teddy's chair. "You be a good boy. I'll be back tonight."

"We'll expect you for supper," Ma said.

He hesitated a moment and then nodded. "Thank you. For everything. I'll certainly pay you."

Pa waved away his offer. "We'll see."

Lilly grabbed her shawl. "I'll show him the cross-country trail. It's much shorter."

They left the house. Caleb's long legs ate up the distance, forcing Lilly to trot to keep up.

He lifted a saddle from his wagon and tossed it on the horse. She pointed out the trail.

He swung into the saddle and paused to look down at her.

She patted his leg. "I'll take good care of Teddy. We all will."

"He has a special fondness for you."

The words melted her heart. "And I for him."

Caleb touched her hand and rode away. He lifted his hat at the crest of the hill and waved to her. She waved back and stood watching until he was out of sight.

He would return tonight, just as he said.

Because of Teddy, she reminded herself. Not because of her. She turned and retraced her steps as the truth of her words settled into her heart.

She would not expect any man to return to her. That led only to disappointment and pain. As Rose had pointed out, she'd learned that lesson at a very young age and she'd had it reinforced throughout her life.

Unless she'd simply trusted the wrong people. Or like Rose suggested, chose the sort of person she knew would leave her simply to prove her point. The thought felt so wrong she couldn't accept it.

No. It was in looking for and longing for what she didn't have that she found disappointment. She was more than content living on the farm with her family, tending the garden and the animals. But she'd accept the company and care of Teddy and his father for a short time, even knowing it couldn't last.

The pain would be worth the joy of the moment.

Chapter Eleven

Caleb kept his horse at a steady pace as he rode toward the Caldwell ranch. He reached the yard just as the other cowboys headed out from the cookhouse. Good timing. Ebner would have no cause for complaint.

He tended his horses and set to work on the barn chores. He had almost completed them when Ebner stepped in.

"Good to see you back at work."

"Did you think I would leave?"

Ebner grunted. "Then who would muck out the barn?" His tone conveyed the message that only Caleb would be desperate enough to take the job.

Caleb shrugged. He couldn't deny it was the sort of job he might have once shunned. Now all that mattered was doing all he could to pick up the pay.

Ebner listed a number of chores that would keep a man hopping all day. Caleb didn't care. He'd do them and leave. He smiled as he thought of the welcome he would receive at the end of the day. Teddy's smile, a hot meal and—

Would Lilly be gladder to see him than the others would?

He jabbed the fork into the muck so hard the shock jolted up his arm. It wasn't a thought—or rather, a hope—he could allow himself.

He worked hard all day, finished the list of assigned chores and then washed up at the pump.

Ebner hurried over. "You figure on leaving?"

Ignoring the challenging tone, Caleb answered. "I finished my day's work. I don't think you'll find any reason to complain about how well the chores were done. Now I've got a boy to take care of."

Ebner jammed his fists to his hips and scowled. If he could find a reason to order Caleb to stay at the ranch, he would, but Caleb only worked there. Neither Ebner nor the Caldwells owned him.

His horse stood saddled and ready and he took up the reins. "I'll return in the morning." He swung into the saddle and rode away before Ebner could find any reason to make him stay.

Not that Caleb could have been persuaded on any grounds. He meant to get back to Teddy and the Bells. And even if he only pictured Lilly when he thought of the Bells, he wasn't about to admit that.

Teddy was in the yard when Caleb rode in and waved and yelled. Blossom was huddled at Teddy's side. Lilly stood nearby, a basket of carrots in her arms.

A sense of peace and contentment came over Caleb.

"Papa, guess what?"

Caleb dropped to the ground and swept Teddy into his arms.

"Guess what?" Teddy demanded again.

Caleb set his son on the ground. "Let me see if I can guess." He studied him slowly. "I don't think you've grown since this morning." He turned Teddy's head from side to side. "Still just two ears."

Teddy giggled.

Caleb lifted his hands into the air. "I give up. What?"

"I got to help Lilly in the garden."

"Is that a fact?" So far he had avoided looking directly at her hovering by Teddy's side, but now he raised his gaze to hers. "So what did you do?" he asked the boy. "Dig carrots?"

"No, I couldn't with one foot, 'member?"

As if he could forget.

"I helped pick them up and then Lilly took them to their root cellar." He pointed to a dugout door. "She won't let me go in there. Says there are too many spiders. I'm not afraid of spiders, am I, Papa?"

Caleb's gaze held Lilly's. She tried to hide a shudder, and he chuckled. "Maybe Miss Lilly is afraid of them."

She gave a firm shake of her head. "Not afraid. I just don't like them." She let herself shudder visibly this time. "Creepy, crawly things. Ugh."

"Are you headed there now?" He indicated the basket full of carrots.

"Yes, I'm about to take in these carrots."

"Let me take them to the cellar for you." He reached for the basket.

Lilly eagerly accepted his offer and led the way.

Rose crossed the yard with another basket, this one full of potatoes. She laughed. "She's just a tiny bit afraid of spiders."

Lilly frowned at her sister. "So are you."

"Not like you. I'd never let it deter me from doing anything."

"I took my fair share of loads into the cellar."

Caleb leaned close to Rose. "Hang on a minute. There's something in your hair."

"A spider?" She practically screeched the word.

He laughed and flicked something away. "Just a leaf."

She jammed her hands on to her hips. "You did that on purpose."

Lilly crowed with laughter. "He called your bluff. Serves you right." She patted Caleb's shoulder. "Good job."

They looked at each other. He felt as if he could almost lose himself in her smiling, approving eyes.

Grinning, satisfaction warming his insides, he entered the dark, dank cellar and poured the carrots into the bin built against one wall. It held a goodly supply of carrots. More than he figured a family of four could eat in five winters.

He left the cellar, dusting his clothes to make sure no spiders came with him. "You planning to feed an army?"

Lilly chuckled. "We need lots to sell and give away."

"Who do you give them to?"

"Anyone who needs them."

He puzzled that a moment. "If you give them away, who buys them?"

"People we don't like." There was no mistaking the anger in Rose's voice.

"Rose, that's not true," Lilly protested. "We sell them at the store in town."

Caleb knew who Rose had been talking about, but he decided to let that particular conversation slip by without comment. "Do you want me to dump your potatoes?" He held a hand out to Rose.

"Thanks." She handed him her basket. Likely she didn't care to risk encountering any spiders.

He stepped in again and dumped the potatoes. That bin was only about half full—there were likely lots left in the garden still. If he had the time to spare away from his job at the Caldwells', he would help dig them. He stood admiring the bounty and shared in the sense of satisfaction, even though he wouldn't be one of those who benefitted from the Bells' garden. Seeing a root cellar full in preparation for winter brought to mind so many things he had lost—home, hope and dreams. He sighed and went outside again.

The twins were waiting for him, Teddy at their side.

"That's all for today," Lilly said.

Rose's eyes widened and she pointed to Lilly. "There's something in your hair."

Lilly shook her head. "I'm not falling for that trick just because you did."

"No, really." Rose backed away and shuddered. "Caleb, look. There's something there."

Lilly scowled. "You're not funny, you know?"

"Caleb, please," Rose begged.

He moved closer and leaned over. She smelled outdoorsy, like freshly turned soil and spicy fall leaves. He shoved his thoughts into proper order and squinted at her. A fat spider clung to her hair, a black intruder against the strands of blond.

"Don't move." He kept his voice calm.

She stiffened. "Do you see a spider?"

He caught the insect between his thumb and forefinger and pulled it off her. Stilling his own revulsion against spiders, he squeezed it and wiped his finger on his pants. "It's gone now."

She shuddered enough to shake her whole body. "Agh. I hate spiders." She rubbed her hands over her hair, wiped her skirt down and stomped a few times just in case.

Teddy had watched the entire proceedings with interest, his expression serious, but now he started to giggle.

Lilly stopped her anxious flitting about, planted her

hands on her hips and stared at him. "So you think it's funny, do you?"

He nodded. "You're a grown-up," he managed around his giggling. "You aren't supposed to be afraid of things."

"Who says?"

He sobered and looked a little confused. "Everybody knows that."

She snorted. "Well, everybody is wrong. Everyone is scared of something, even grown-ups."

"Not my Papa," chirped Teddy.

Caleb almost crowed. Having his son's high regard was just fine by him.

Lilly turned slowly to face Caleb. "Is that so?"

Uncertain how to interpret the challenging look in her face, he instinctively backed up a step.

"See that? I think he's afraid of me. Why, I think if Rose were to join me, we could make him very afraid."

Rose seemed to know what Lilly had in mind and came to her side.

Caleb looked from one to the other. Both wore challenging looks, but he riveted his attention on Lilly. He had no idea what they had in mind. Retreat seemed the wisest plan, so he backed up. For every step he took away, they took a step toward him.

"Papa, you're not afraid, are you?"

His son has interpreted his caution as fear. "Teddy, I assure you I'm not afraid. But I don't like the looks on their faces." He took another step backward. "Son, it's like this. You can never be too careful about how you act around women."

"Is that a fact?" Lilly drew her brows together. "Rose, what do you think?"

In tandem they stepped closer, forcing him to back up still more. That's when he discovered a wheelbarrow behind him. He landed backward in the bucket, his feet pointed skyward.

Laughing, Rose and Lilly grabbed the handles and pushed him on a mad ride.

He clung to the sides, afraid they would dump him out.

Teddy hobbled after them. "Don't hurt my papa."

Lilly called over her shoulder. "We'll let him go as soon as he admits he's afraid."

"I admit it," Caleb said, willing to do almost anything to get his feet back on the ground and restore his dignity.

The girls let the contraption come to a rest.

Lilly held out her hand to help him up. He scrambled to his feet.

"You two are a menace."

"Only to prideful men," Rose said.

"I'm not prideful."

"Nope," Lilly agreed. "I think we cured you of that."

The two of them laughed at him.

Caleb shook his head in mock disbelief, but their enjoyment of life and each other, and Lilly's sparkling gaze catching and holding his, caused a flower to blossom in his heart. He choked back a snort. What kind of cowboy thought frilly things like that?

The answer rose within him. A cowboy surrounded by beautiful, cheerful women. He'd defy any man—cowboy or clerk—to resist the joy the pair provided with their good-natured teasing and mutual love.

What would it be like to be included in that love the way Wyatt was?

Wyatt seemed to like it well enough.

But then Wyatt had no reason not to eagerly join that happy family circle. Caleb could think of at least two reasons it wouldn't be possible for him. Teddy and the need to get his leg fixed. And Caleb's own fear of failing at love.

It was a good thing Lilly didn't know of his deepest fear, though what difference would it make?

He'd given her no reason to expect anything from him and he certainly wasn't about to give himself one.

But still the question lingered.

What would it be like to be part of a loving family circle? To enjoy the love of a strong woman?

Lilly sensed Caleb's withdrawal and instantly regretted the way she and Rose had mercilessly teased him. "I'm sorry. We sometimes get carried away."

"We do not," Rose defended them both. "It was all in good fun."

Caleb waved his hand dismissively. "No harm done." He turned to his son. "Teddy, how are you doing?"

Teddy swung to his father's side so fast, Lilly reached out to catch him. But he didn't need her help. Caleb caught him up in his arms.

"I knew you weren't afraid." Teddy patted Caleb's cheeks. "You only said it to make them happy."

Caleb chuckled, a deep and pleasing sound.

"Sure, that was it," Caleb said.

Lilly and Rose looked at each other. Rose rolled her eyes and Lilly delivered their decision. "For Teddy's sake, we'll let him believe he's right."

"You are too generous."

"I know." Shaking her head, Rose headed toward the house.

"Tell me about your day." Lilly assumed he meant the question for Teddy, even though he looked at her as he spoke.

Teddy rattled off the many things he'd done. Help Rose

get the eggs. Feed the milk cows. "Just like Mama let me do." Sort bolts for Mr. Bell. Help Mrs. Bell make cookies.

"You didn't help Lilly do anything?"

"No, but she took me to the river and showed me where there are fishes. She said you should take me fishing. Will you, Papa?"

Caleb's warm gaze held Lilly's. Did he mean to thank her for helping his little boy enjoy the day? His gaze went on and on, as if looking for things hidden deep in her heart—truths she only sensed in some vague way. As he searched her thoughts, the truth grew stronger, almost clear enough for her to understand.

"I'll take you if Lilly agrees to come."

Teddy grabbed her arm. "Say you will, please."

"Of course." She knew her heart would pay a price when this connection came to an end, but she hoped the pleasure would be worth the pain.

"Now I have to warn you both," Caleb said. "You'll have to wait until I can get away from my job."

"That's okay," Teddy said. "Isn't it?" He directed his question to Lilly.

"Of course." Though she would be counting the days until it happened. A blaze of doubt flashed through her mind. Unless he was giving the promise carelessly.

But surely he wouldn't promise Teddy something and not follow through on it.

Because the cows were already milked, Caleb helped put away the baskets and tools used to gather the garden produce. By then supper was ready and they went inside.

After the meal, Caleb grabbed a tea towel and dried the dishes without being asked. He handed Teddy a towel as well and insisted he help. Not that Teddy minded.

Later, she helped do the poultice and exercises for Teddy. She could see no change in Teddy's leg and understood that Caleb was disappointed. It would take time. Something they had very little of. If Teddy didn't start to use his leg, Caleb meant to go down east with him. *God, help Teddy's leg get better.* If that meant they must leave, so be it. She'd never expected anything else. But if the poultices and exercises worked, wouldn't they be able to stay?

Why was she letting her hopes be raised? They would only be dashed.

She thought of what Rose had said about Lilly only letting herself care about people she knew would leave.

She shook her head. It wasn't so. Rose was getting far too fanciful.

She helped get Teddy ready for bed, marveling over his little boy smell and his father's strong arms as he tenderly washed Teddy's face and hands.

Blossom whined to be in bed with Teddy and she lifted the dog to Teddy's side. She glanced at Ma to see if she might disapprove, but the gentle smile on Ma's face said it all. Whatever this little boy needed to make him happy, Ma would gladly do it.

Teddy said, "I'm not sleepy. Can Lilly read to me?"

"Why, of course," she replied. "I'd love to if it's okay with your papa."

Caleb nodded and pulled a chair close. "Mind if I listen?"

"Not a bit." She felt her cheeks grow warm and hoped they hadn't turned pink. But the thought of sitting together caring for this little boy triggered longings that she didn't want to admit.

"Do you have storybooks?" Teddy asked, bringing her back to reality.

"I do somewhere, but I have an idea. Instead of reading a book, why don't we make up a story?"

"You and me?" He sounded excited and cautious at the same time.

"Do you think it would be fun? Shall we write it down?"

He nodded. "Then I can always have it."

She found paper and pencil and sat beside Teddy. "Do you have any ideas?"

"No. Do you?"

"Let's do a story about a dog."

"Like Blossom?"

"That's a very good idea."

Teddy snuggled close as she drew a dog somewhat like Blossom.

"What's the dog's name?"

"How about...Tiny?"

"Tiny, it is." She wrote the name across the top. "Let's get to know Tiny. Where does she live?"

She continued on with questions and drawings to match his answers. Who was in Tiny's family? What was her favorite food? What games did she like to play? Then she asked, "What's Tiny afraid of?"

Teddy sat back and stared at the page. "Tiny," he whispered, "is scared of bad men."

Lilly glanced at Caleb, noting his sudden alertness. She had no doubt the boy was referring to the bad men who had hurt his mama. But she continued. "What do bad men do to Tiny?"

Teddy wrapped his arms around Blossom's neck. "They do bad things. They hurt Tiny's family."

Lilly stared at the page. "I'm not sure what to draw."

He asked for the paper and pencil and scribbled dark, harsh lines. Then he gave it back. "I can't draw it."

She turned to a new page, wanting to shift the story to something happier. "Let's play a game with Tiny." She drew a ball with stripes. The ball was almost as big as Tiny. "What's she going to do?"

Teddy giggled. "Try to catch it."

Lilly did her best to draw the puppy tumbling over the too-big ball while Teddy continued to giggle. "She's happy now."

She drew Tiny on a bed. "Who is going to sleep with Tiny?"

"A little boy."

She wasn't good at drawing people, but she did her best to make a little boy who looked like Teddy.

Teddy nodded. "He's not scared anymore."

"That's good. I think Teddy and Blossom should go to sleep now, safe and sound in the Bells' house." She tucked the covers about him and kissed his forehead. She patted Blossom's head.

Teddy's eyes closed, a smile on his lips.

Caleb rose to stand next to Lilly. "Thank you," he whispered.

They moved away from the cot. Lilly wanted to talk about the experience, but only with Caleb. "Ma, Pa, I'm going to check on the sheep." Would Caleb want to accompany her? She toyed with the idea of asking him, but hoped he would offer on his own.

"I'll keep her company," Caleb said to her parents.

She turned to pull a warm sweater from the row of coats and such, hiding her pleased smile from her family.

Caleb planted his hat on his head and took his own jacket. They stepped out into the cool evening air.

They walked toward the pasture, both of them silent. Lilly's heart was full of things she wanted to say, but the words didn't come.

Caleb sighed deeply. "That was a good idea to use a dog and child to help Teddy tell us how he feels."

"It seems clear that he's talking about his life, don't you think?" They reached the fence and stopped. She ran a quick glance at the sheep, who were resting peacefully in the shelter of the trees.

"Sure seems that way to me." He shuddered. "Except it's Teddy who is afraid, not the dog."

"It's easier to talk about it through the eyes of someone safe."

"Like a pretend pet?"

"Exactly." She turned to study his face in the dusky light, looking for clues as to how Teddy's confession of fear had affected him. His jaw muscles were clenched. His brow was furrowed, which didn't tell her if he was worried or determined, or fighting pain and fear of his own. She figured it was a combination of all those things.

He must have felt so helpless at his wife's murder and his child's injury. She understood helplessness at another's actions. Having no control yet bearing the consequence.

"I know how horrible tragedies can leave a person feeling like there is no safe bottom to the life they live, no security for the future. For if these things happened once, what's to stop them from happening again?"

He brought his gaze to her, his eyes slowly focusing on her face as if he was bringing his thoughts back from a far distance.

"My abandonment was a small thing compared to what you and Teddy experienced." She took his hand, wanting him to see the truth that had freed her from her fears and uncertainties. Mostly freed her, she amended, for there remained certain fears about change. "I used to be so afraid any time someone in the family was gone. When Cora started school, it was very hard for me to understand. I was afraid she was leaving us."

He nodded. "You feared abandonment. With just cause in your case."

"But that's it. I'd been abandoned once for whatever reason. That didn't mean I should expect it again. Ma taught me a verse in Psalm 23. 'Yea, though I walk through the valley of the shadow of death, I will fear no evil: for Thy rod and staff they comfort me.' God's comfort and His promise to always be with us—surely that means something." Her conscience condemned her. Here she was telling Caleb how to find peace and comfort, letting him think she'd been successful in finding it for herself. Up until a few days ago, she believed she had.

Yet meeting Caleb and Teddy had brought all her fears and concerns back to life.

But if she could help Caleb and Teddy, she would do so. Her own fears she would also put to rest. She would be wiser when it came to choosing who to care about in the future, and she would not pick people who were leaving.

She ignored the fact she was doing exactly that at this moment.

Caleb shifted his gaze to a point somewhere in the distance. "If you can help Teddy find this same assurance, I'd be grateful."

"I pray you find it, too."

His gaze came back to her and a smile slowly creased his face. "You are such an encourager. You almost make me believe I can go back to the simple faith of my youth." He shook his head. "But life is so much more complicated than I once believed."

She chuckled. "You make it sound like you are a weary old man." She sobered. "I don't think you can go back to a simple faith so much as a stronger faith. One that has been tested and tried and comes forth like pure gold."

His eyes widened as if he'd never before considered

the idea. "Huh? A golden cowboy. That'd be something to see."

She smiled gently, amused but aware of the depth of their words. "Fortunately for you, the gold would be in your heart, unseen to gold hunters who would otherwise hammer away bits and pieces of you."

He chuckled. He lifted his hand to her cheek and cupped his warm palm to her skin. "I think I might end up coal, not gold."

She pressed her hand to his, holding it against her face. Her heart beat like a drum. "Coal has its purposes, too."

His eyes darkened. He studied her intently, but she did not lower her eyes as his look went on and on. Slowly, his expression changed from one of discouragement to one of hope. His thumb brushed her lips. Would he kiss her?

She swallowed hard. She hoped so.

Then he withdrew his hand. She liked to think he did so reluctantly.

"You've given me much to think about." He stuck his hands in his back pockets. "But it's getting late. We need to get back before your pa comes looking for you."

She tucked this information into her heart. Caleb was only being noble and concerned about her. Both admirable qualities. But a kiss would have been nicer, even though it would only have made it more painful when he left.

She'd allowed herself to go this far in caring about him and his son. There was no retreating now. Whatever was to happen to her in the future would be dealt with then.

She'd take each day as it came and accept whatever it brought. Even as she told herself so, her heart clenched like a fist inside her chest.

Was her heart about to be torn asunder?

Chapter Twelve

The Bells went to their rooms and Caleb spread his bed-roll beside Teddy's cot. As he lay staring into the darkness, he relived the events of the evening, lingering on the words Lilly had spoken. Coal or gold? Which would he end up being? Did he have any choice or would it simply happen? He didn't care for the idea that he had no say in the matter, though his life so far had revealed just how little control he had over anything. But hadn't she been talking about God's work? God had control. Surely, He would use the events in Caleb's life for good. He liked the idea of turning into gold—a golden cowboy, as he'd said to Lilly. Had she thought him foolish or had she understood what he'd meant?

Something about Lilly touched the corners of his heart like rain on barren ground, slowly causing his life to bloom. It was temporary, but why should he not enjoy the springtime of his soul while it lasted?

He left early again the next morning, eager to get to the Caldwells' so he could get his work done and get back to Teddy. *And Lilly?* his inner voice asked.

Maybe. After all, she was working with Teddy.

If Teddy would only start to use his leg again, there would be no need to go east. No need to leave.

He cut these thoughts short. Hadn't he decided to keep people at arm's length to protect them? And to protect himself from pain and guilt, he acknowledged.

Throughout the day, he often found himself smiling for no other reason than recalling the pleasure of the time spent with Lilly and her family.

He finished his assigned chores so early Ebner stopped him as he saddled his horse.

"Where do you think you're going?"

"I've done the work you laid out and I'm going to see my son."

"Huh. Guess I'm getting slack at assigning chores."

Caleb faced him squarely. "I worked double time to get done early. No other man would have worked so quickly, and you know it. I don't expect to have my load increased as a reward." He gave Ebner a look that said there'd be no compromise on the matter. Caleb meant to spend time with Teddy. And if Lilly was there, too, so much the better.

When he arrived at the Bells' farm he found them all in the garden digging the last of the potatoes. Teddy sat in the dirt, sorting them according to some system that had been explained to him.

Lilly stood up and smiled as Caleb approached. The others called a greeting but didn't stop working.

"Pa says there's a change coming in the weather. Says we have to get the potatoes in before it gets here," Lilly explained.

"I'll help. Let me take the baskets to the root cellar."

"You sure? I know you've worked all day."

This wouldn't seem like work. "I don't mind."

"Very well. The smaller potatoes go in one bin, the larger ones in another."

"Got it." He grabbed the full basket at the end of the row and headed for the root cellar. Back and forth he went—they filled baskets as fast as he could empty them.

Once he caught up, he grabbed a fork and started digging.

Lilly smiled at him. "Thank you." She turned to the side so the others couldn't hear. "We've been trying to get Ma and Pa to let us finish, but they insist they will stay until the end."

"Then let's get this done as quickly as possible." He'd been putting out all afternoon, but he kept up a steady pace until the last potato was out of the ground. He emptied the final basket in the cellar and stepped out, a sense of satisfaction easing through him. He liked helping the Bells.

With a grateful smile in Caleb's direction, Lilly turned to her parents. "Teddy's tired and hungry, Ma. You take him to the house while we clean up the tools. Pa, why don't you make a pot of coffee for Caleb? I expect he's in dire need of such."

"Sounds good," Caleb said, and he smiled as the elderly couple headed to the house with Teddy at their side.

"I can't thank you enough," Lilly said.

"Nor I," Rose added. "You're not half-bad for a Caldwell cowboy."

Caleb laughed as he helped put away the baskets and tools.

He paused to wait for Lilly to come alongside him. "Not half-bad for a Caldwell cowboy? Coming from Rose, that's high praise." He wondered what Lilly thought. Not half-bad? Real good? A golden cowboy? He almost hooted aloud at his foolish thoughts.

She patted his arm, a gesture he was enjoying more and more each day. "You're all right, Caleb Craig."

His chest swelled and his smile widened. All right! He liked that.

A few minutes later they trooped into the house for supper. Everyone ate with gusto. Made him wonder how long they'd been out in the garden without a break.

The main part of the meal over, Mrs. Bell said, "Who's ready for cookies?"

"Me. Me." Teddy practically bounced from his chair and Caleb didn't have the heart to scold him. He much preferred concern about the boy's manners over the continual worry about his leg.

Mrs. Bell gave Teddy four cookies and filled his cup with milk. Teddy took a bite of cookie and closed his eyes. "Good." He ate two and drank half the milk before he came up for air. He rubbed his tummy.

"Mrs. Bell, you are the best grandma in the world."

The woman's smile flattened and her hand flew to her chest.

"Teddy," Caleb warned. But it was too late to pull the words back.

Mrs. Bell's smile returned. "I don't have any grandchildren yet." She spared the girls an accusing look. "But I'd be honored if you'd call me Grandma." She squeezed Teddy's hand.

Teddy grew very still and slowly faced Caleb. "Can I, Papa?"

What could he say? If he refused, it would appear rude, even churlish. But if he agreed, wouldn't Teddy be hurt when they had to say goodbye to his chosen grandma?

He made up his mind. "So long as you remember it's only until we leave."

Teddy continued to stare at him, as if silently accusing him of robbing him of a perfectly good grandma.

"That's just fine," Mrs. Bell said. "And maybe someday you'll visit again."

"Would you make me ginger cookies if we did?"

"I'd be honored."

"Thank you, Grandma." Teddy couldn't have been more pleased, but Caleb was uneasy. Somehow he knew this wasn't going to end well, no matter what he did.

He sought Lilly's gaze. What did she think of this arrangement? She wore a cautious look, as if she shared the same wariness. Then she smiled and gave a little shrug.

He shrugged, too. There didn't seem to be any way he could renege at this point.

Mr. Bell took up his Bible. "Our root cellar is full. We have plenty to spare. God has blessed us abundantly and we give Him praise. But let us never lose sight of the fact that adverse circumstances do not mean God loves us any less. I want to read two verses from Habakkuk, chapter three." The Bible easily fell open to the pages as if Mr. Bell often read the passage. "Here we are. 'Although the fig tree shall not blossom, neither shall fruit be in the vines; the labor of the olive shall fail, and the fields shall yield no meat; the flock shall be cut off from the fold, and there shall be no herd in the stalls: Yet I will rejoice in the Lord, I will joy in the God of my salvation.'" He reverently closed the Good Book. "No matter what happens, God cares for each of us, and whether there are good or bad things in our lives, we are loved."

As Mr. Bell prayed, the words went round and round in Caleb's head. He had never considered that God loved him in such a special way. Thinking about it made the sorrow of his life fade in significance.

The next morning he rode away with a light heart, but

he also did so reluctantly. He would have liked to spend Saturday with the Bells, but Ebner had not given him the full day off, though he couldn't deny him the half day off he'd given to all the other cowboys on the ranch.

The chores the foreman had laid out for him kept him busy until past noon. By the time he finished, he was impatient as a kid on Christmas.

The Bells went to town on Saturdays to do their shopping and sell their produce. Would they be back yet?

He strained to find some clue as he approached the farm. When he saw Teddy and Blossom alone in the yard, he sank back in his saddle. Then he saw Lilly nearby and smiled.

"Hello," he called, and they both waved.

"Grandma and Grandpa and Rose went to town," Teddy said as soon as Caleb was close enough to hear.

"You didn't go?" he addressed Lilly.

She shrugged. "Teddy and I decided to stay home." Because she lowered her eyes, he couldn't gain any insight into why.

"Lilly thought we should wait for you," Teddy said.

"Is that a fact?" The idea pleased him clear to the soles of his feet. "Do you want to go now? I could hitch up the wagon."

She lifted one shoulder in a small shrug. "I've been to town plenty of times. Unless you want to go?"

"I've got no need to go to town." A strong wind tore at his hat and he grabbed it before it could blow away. "Besides, it's getting a mite cold."

"It's the change in weather Pa said was coming." She glanced down the road. "They should be home soon." She watched for a few seconds and then shivered. "We better go inside."

"I'll be along as soon as I take care of my horse."

A few minutes later he joined them in the house. She'd made coffee and poured milk for herself and Teddy. As usual, there were cookies to enjoy with the coffee.

She smiled at Teddy's enjoyment of the snack.

The boy finished and asked to be excused. He and Blossom went to the far corner of the room. Teddy pulled a handful of objects from his pocket and showed them to the eager pup. Soon they were engrossed in their own little world.

Lilly watched, a gentle smile on her lips. "Tell me what Teddy was like as a baby."

Lilly shifted her attention to Caleb when she asked about Teddy. He smiled and got a distant look on his face, as if falling into his memories. Hopefully, to a place that was pleasant for him.

"He said 'papa' before he said 'mama.' Amanda teasingly complained about that." Caleb chuckled. "I said it was because he knew that when he saw me it meant we were going to play. My, he did like to be tickled." He sighed. "No doubt you've heard it before, but babies grow up far too quickly. Especially when there aren't more little ones to replace them."

Lilly concentrated on the swirl of milk at the bottom of her glass. Would she ever know the joy of a baby? Not unless she found someone willing to settle for her, willing to stay long enough to see what Rose called her 'finer qualities.' This topic of conversation brought hard edges to her innards. But before she could think of something else to talk about, lightning flashed, filling the room with blinding light.

She jolted to her feet, her heart climbing to the back of her throat. The hair on her neck stood up, as her skin prickled. "I hate storms," she murmured, her words almost drowned out by the thunder that seemed to go on forever, rolling down from the mountains and echoing over the plains. Wind rattled the shingles and banged at the door. "I have to shut in the chickens." If she hadn't been distracted by Caleb's arrival she would have already done it. Now she had to go out in the storm.

She grabbed a slicker Pa wore in wet weather and shrugged into it. Never mind that it was miles too big and almost dragged on the ground. It would protect her from the rain that would surely come. Not to mention that wearing it, she felt safer, as if Pa's arms were about her. A floppy wide-brimmed hat completed her outfit.

Caleb followed her to the door. "Let me go. You stay here."

It was awfully tempting to agree. "Thanks, but someone needs to stay with Teddy, and I know what to do outside."

He stood at the door. "You'll be safe?"

A large portion of tension seeped away at the concern in his voice. "I'll be fine. You make sure Teddy is safe, too."

"I will." Still he did not open the door or step away so she could get out. She met his dark eyes, full of concern and maybe even regret, though she couldn't guess what he might regret. His gaze held hers as her heart settled into her chest with a sigh and then swelled with longing.

Lightning flashed again and seconds later, thunder rattled the glass in the windows.

She broke from his intense stare. "I must go."

Finally he held the door open and stood watching as she slipped loose the latch on the chicken pen. Lightning and thunder continued, but they seemed less frightening knowing Caleb was watching. She shooed the chickens inside and closed the door.

The barn door stood open. She needed to close it to keep the cows warm.

A glance at the house revealed Caleb still standing in the doorway. Then rain slashed down and he closed the door.

She couldn't remember feeling so alone before. But she had to take care of the necessary chores. Ducking her head against the wind and rain, she trotted to the barn.

She caught Caleb's horse and led it inside. Then she heard the loft door banging. It would not stay shut unless she threw the bar in place.

She stared at the ladder, trying to summon the courage to climb closer to the turbulent sky. She chanted Rose's words. "Just as safe up there as standing in the middle of a field." It didn't matter how true the words were. Fear didn't listen to reason, and Lilly had a huge fear of thunderstorms. However, she had to keep the barn dry for the sake of the animals. She'd do it for them. She let the huge slicker flap behind her as she planted one hand and then the other on a ladder rung. Gritting her teeth, she forced her feet to follow.

She found the length of wood Pa used to hold the door closed. Swallowing back a lump the size of a prize potato, she waited for the door to bang against the frame and then she caught it. Quickly she dropped the bar into place.

Lightning flashed and thunder sounded at almost the same time. Her scalp tingled. The smell of gunpowder filled the air. It had struck very close. She wanted to huddle in some safe corner, or rush back to the house and find comfort in Caleb's presence, but she could do neither. Her sheep would naturally seek shelter under the trees in the corner of their pasture. It was the most dangerous place they could be in a thunderstorm.

She must herd them to safety.

She clambered down the ladder and looked around to see if she could tell where the lightning had struck. She saw nothing damaged and no sign of fire, so she hastened onward to the sheep pasture. In her frenzied haste, she slipped on the wet ground, going down on one knee. She straightened and hurried on until she reached the gate of the pasture. What if lightning struck the moment she touched the wire? She'd be killed. Or at least thrown to the ground, her hair burned from her head.

She swallowed back a lump as large as a soup bowl. No one else would take care of her sheep. Ignoring the trembling of her limbs, she grabbed the gate, unhooked it and threw it back.

"Mammy," she called. The old ewe would be the only one to heed Lilly's call. "Mammy." Lightning flashed, allowing Lilly to look around her. There they were, huddled in the trees just as she suspected. "You silly sheep. You haven't got the sense to stay away from danger." She ran the length of the field, skidding and slipping. "Come, girls. Come, Boss." Maybe the ram would show his courage and follow her.

They bleated, but they didn't move. She grabbed a couple and shoved them in the right direction. They simply turned back to the shelter. "Mammy?" She located the ewe at the back of the flock and went to her side. "You're my only hope. Come with me and the others might follow. Please follow."

More lightning. More thunder. The sound crashed inside her chest each time. But she needed to get these sheep to safety.

She wrapped her arms about Mammy's neck. "You'll come with me, won't you?"

The ewe baaed.

Lilly took it as a sign of agreement. "Come along." She

clung to Mammy's neck, hoping the ewe would cooperate. They took a step. Two. Three. Mammy baaed again and Boss came running to investigate. She kept Mammy going forward, one step at a time. "Come on, you sheep. Come, come. I'll put you where you'll be safe and dry." Would they follow?

One of the younger ewes rubbed against Lilly's legs.

She wanted to look back and see if the others were coming, but she had her hands full keeping Mammy headed for the gate. They were as nervous as she, jumping at every crack, every rumble.

They were almost at the gate when a blinding flash and a thundering boom shook the ground. Balls of fire ran along the wire of the fence and into the ground. She cried out as fear exploded inside her.

Caleb stared out the window. The lightning was so close he could feel the electricity in the air and could smell sulfur. Lilly had been gone far too long. Where was she? Had she been hurt? Struck by a bolt? He shuddered and strode to the door. He needed to make sure she was safe. But did he dare leave Teddy? He returned to the window, staring into the darkness. In the continuing flashes he could make out the barn, his wagon and the other outbuildings, but he couldn't see Lilly. Had she taken shelter in the barn, meaning to stay there until the storm passed?

Perhaps she had welcomed a reason to avoid his company.

But how could he be certain she was safe?

He studied Teddy. Blossom watched the boy's every move.

He stared at the door. He had to find Lilly. But if both

of them were out in the storm, if both of them encountered trouble... What would happen to Teddy?

He looked back and forth between the door and his son, running his fingers through his hair until it grew so tangled his fingers caught.

She should have been back by now.

He made up his mind. He could not sit here wondering if she needed help. "Teddy, I have to go find Lilly. You stay here and don't go outside for any reason. I'll be back in a few minutes."

"Okay, Papa."

Still Caleb hesitated, torn between making sure his son was safe and making sure Lilly was. His chest tightened until it hurt to breathe.

He made up his mind. At the moment Lilly's needs were more urgent. "Blossom, you stay with Teddy."

The dog looked at him as if she understood what Caleb wanted of her.

Caleb grabbed his hat and stepped outside, immediately pelted by the slashing rain. He clamped his hat more firmly to his head and strode toward the barn. Lightning flashed. A bit of white to his right caught his attention. He turned and squinted, waiting for the next flash to illuminate the area. It came and he saw sheep gathered in a tight knot. What were they doing here?

Then he saw a black center amid the white. Another flash and he could make out the figure of Lilly. She was trying to get those silly animals to shelter.

But at least she was safe. He was so relieved he grinned as he jogged to her side. "Where are you taking them?" he called close to her ear.

"The shed on the side of the barn."

"Let's do it." He went behind the little flock and pushed at them as she led the way. They reached the barn, lightning flares showing the way to the shed. One by one, they managed to get the sheep inside, and then they closed the door.

It was quieter in there, and drier. He shivered in his damp clothes.

She made her way to his side. "Thank you. I couldn't get them to cooperate. Silly things. Especially after a bolt of lightning came within inches of us. You should have seen the fireball."

"Are you okay?"

"I'm fine." A blaze of light allowed her to see him clearly. "You're soaking wet."

"Yup. Might have been raining out there."

She snorted. "It's coming down in buckets."

"Is everything battened down?"

"As best I could."

"Then let's get back to the house." He took her arm. There was no way he would let her slip away and disappear into the storm for any reason.

"Teddy's alone?"

"Blossom is with him."

He pushed open the door, pulled her to his side and then, after making sure the door was firmly latched behind them, they dashed across the yard. They splashed through puddles they couldn't see, not realizing they were there, until the water slopped about them. They reached the house and Caleb pulled Lilly inside.

Blossom woofed gently, a greeting rather than a warning.

Lilly took off her slicker and hung it by the door. Caleb shook his hat and put it on the nearby cupboard to dry, and then stood there dripping.

She eyed him up and down. "You're certainly wet.

What provoked you to go out in the storm without protection?"

"You."

"Me? But I wasn't even here."

"Exactly. Didn't you realize how close the storm was? A couple of times the thunder sounded at the same time as the lightning hit." He was cold and wet and more than a little annoyed at the way she was regarding him, as if he'd acted foolishly. "You were gone far too long. I thought I might have to rescue you."

Her eyes softened. "From what?"

"The storm, of course." He'd worried in vain, it appeared. But remnants of his concern filled his mind. He caught her by the arms. "You could have been struck by lightning."

She shuddered. Stark fear filled her eyes. "I had to take care of the animals."

He pulled her close and then remembered he was wet, and held her inches away. "They're all safe and sound, and so are you."

She nodded, beginning to relax, and stepped back. "You must be cold. Come to the stove." When she kicked off her wet footwear, he did the same. He tipped his boots over the slop bucket to drain, and then padded after her.

She tossed wood into the stove and filled the kettle. "I'll make some of Ma's special tea. It will prevent you from getting a chill. She says it helps ward off a cold. It tastes just fine with a spoonful of honey. It's good for you."

Why was she rattling on at such a rate? Did his concern make her nervous? He watched her for a sign of what she was thinking, but she banged about in the cupboards, pulling out a tin of tea leaves and a small brown teapot.

Finally she looked at him, but only long enough to

sigh at his wet state. "Here. Sit down." She pulled a chair close to the stove and then dashed into one of the rooms off the kitchen, returning with a thick gray woolen blanket. She draped it about his shoulders and patted it into place. "You really should take those wet things off." Her cheeks flamed bright red at her words.

"I'll be fine. I've been wetter than this and survived." Without anyone fussing over him. Not that he minded. Her touch on his shoulder, her concern about his well-being warmed him more thoroughly than did the fire.

She stared at the kettle and then shifted her attention to the window. "I believe the storm is moving away."

He listened. "I believe you are correct." Lightning still flashed, but the thunder sounded distant. And the rain settled down to a faint patter. It had been a brief storm. It had come and gone in minutes, though it had felt much longer.

She brought her attention back to him and he smiled. "You don't like storms much, do you?" he said.

She shuddered. "About as much as cats like water." The kettle boiled and she bustled about making tea that she let seep for several minutes. She poured them each a cupful and stirred in generous spoonfuls of honey. "Here, try it."

The blanket slipped from his shoulders as he took the cup and she rearranged it, tucking it about his neck so he could drink and not lose the warmth.

He sipped the hot drink. "It's good." He meant more than the tea, but he wasn't about to confess that aloud. "I've never tasted anything quite like it. Dare I ask what's in it, or will that ruin it for me?"

She chuckled. "Depends how fussy you are." She waited for him to answer.

"If you stop to consider that for months I've been mak-

ing my own meals, mostly over a campfire, you'll understand I'm not the least bit fussy."

"Okay, then, I'll tell you. The main ingredients are
rose hips. I'm afraid I can't tell you the other things Ma
puts in it or she'd have my hide for revealing her secrets."

It was his turn to chuckle. "Wouldn't want that."

She grinned at him, her eyes sparkling so much it
seemed as if the skies had cleared and the sun had come
out. "Let me assure you it wouldn't be pretty."

He sucked back another mouthful of tea and almost
choked in his haste to dismiss his fanciful notions. "Has
your Ma always been a healer?"

"A healer? Why that's a very nice way of describing
her. Much kinder than some descriptions I've heard."

"Really. Like what?"

She studied her cup, from which she had yet to take a
drink. "A lot of people consider her odd. Actually, they
consider both my parents odd." She looked past him. "I've
even heard it said that they stole us or somehow caused
us to suddenly appear out of nowhere so they could have
children. Some have said awful things about Ma and Pa
and about us." She grew fierce. "People can be so cruel."
Her gaze returned to him, full of sorrow and regret. "I'm
sorry. I guess you know that better than most."

His fingers tightened around the cup. He knew he must
have appeared angry. She'd take it to be about Amanda's
murder, and it was. But distress raged through him at the
way people had treated Lilly and her parents. "Do people
still act that way toward you?"

She shrugged. "Mostly they accept us. People have
come to value Ma's medicinals."

Blossom sat up and barked, looking toward the door.
Both Lilly and Caleb hurried to the window to see an

approaching wagon, Mr. Bell guiding the family home through the gloomy dusk.

Lilly hurried to the door. "You're back safe and sound." Pa helped Ma to the ground and Rose scurried from the back.

"It was a cold, wet journey home," Rose moaned.

"You appear to be dry."

"'Cause Pa saw fit to bring along some canvas. He's the only one who is wet. Pa, get inside and get warm."

Lilly stuck her feet into her boots and dashed outside. "Yes, Pa. Rose take Ma inside. I'll tend the horse."

Rose hustled their parents inside while Lilly led the horse away. A few minutes later, she hurried back to the house and went right to her father's side. He was sitting before the stove, now in dry clothes. Rose poured him a cup of the hot tea.

"I hope you don't get a chill," Lilly said.

Pa waved away her concern. "I'm right as rain."

She grunted. "Not sure how right the rain was." She told her family about the lightning on the fence as she had been trying to get the sheep to safety.

Rose hustled to her side. "Lilly, you might have been killed."

"Guess it wasn't my time."

"God protected you," Pa said. "I pray He will always protect my girls and now Wyatt."

"What about me?" Teddy sounded hurt.

Pa patted his head. "Well, that goes without saying, doesn't it? I will always pray for you and your papa."

Teddy nodded and settled back, his new pet resting her head on his knee. The boy had a look of such contentment on his face, Caleb was tempted to forget about the crutches at his son's side.

Could Teddy learn to be happy and productive with only one good leg?

Caleb ducked his head, hoping no one would notice the way his jaw had clenched and his lips had pulled down.

How could he think of staying here with Teddy in his present state? He stole a glance at Lilly, who hovered by her father's side.

It had been a purely selfish thought because he liked the idea of becoming a permanent part of this family.

He drove the admission away as quickly as it had come. Hadn't he failed enough people already? Hadn't he vowed to never let himself care for another person? It would only give him another chance to prove his inability to protect them.

Despite his vow, despite his fear and caution, Lilly had cracked open his tightly locked heart.

He would leave except he needed the job and he needed the Bells to help with Teddy. Surely there was no harm in enjoying Lilly's company and the comfort of her family for a few days.

What could possibly go wrong?

Chapter Thirteen

The rain stopped before they went to bed, and the next morning the sun was warm. By the time they left for church, all but a few puddles were dried up and the day promised to be glorious.

Lilly sat in the back of the wagon with Rose, Caleb and Teddy. The youngster bounced up and down, peering ahead. "Are we almost there?"

She'd never known a child so eager to attend church, though it was all she could do not to bounce up and down as well for an entirely different reason. Ever since the storm yesterday, her nerves had twitched with an awareness of Caleb. Glibly she put it down to coming so close to being struck by lightning. But she knew it was more than that.

It had begun when he'd come looking for her, concerned about her safety. The feeling had grown more intense when he'd pulled her close, stopping just short of holding her against his chest. She understood it had been because of his wet clothes, but she wouldn't have cared if she got a little wet. Well aware that she was treading perilously close to the dangerous precipice of caring more deeply for him than she should, she had covered him with a blanket, her fingers lingering one second longer than was necessary to secure the wrap.

Seeing him across the table, helping him with Teddy's care, observing the way he tenderly dealt with his son, had all added one hot coal after another to her feelings. Finally she wondered if she could contain—let alone control—them any longer.

They entered Bar Crossing at that point, so thankfully her thoughts were diverted. She watched the familiar buildings pass.

Church would give her something to think about besides Caleb. She'd concentrate on the sermon and that would make her forget everything else.

But she soon realized that was easier said than done. Again, Teddy made sure she walked in beside him and his father and he sat between them. He turned to whisper to her, "I like this church."

"Me, too," she whispered back. "Pastor Rawley is a very kind man. Mrs. Rawley is Ma's best friend."

His smile lit up his face. "I like them, too."

Lilly stifled a chuckle. In Teddy's mind, any friend of Ma's and Pa's was a friend of his. She glanced up at Caleb, seeing by the way he grinned at her that he'd heard the conversation and come to the same conclusion.

Their gazes locked long enough that Rose jabbed her in the ribs and whispered, "Stop making eyes at that man. Have you forgotten you're in church?"

Heat raced up Lilly's neck and she ducked her head as if needing to smooth her gloves. She could only hope Caleb hadn't heard Rose. But her sister was right, and she again vowed to concentrate on the service. Thankfully, at that moment Pastor Rawley went to the pulpit and announced the first hymn.

Lilly turned to share Rose's hymnal, but Rose had

already offered it to Lonnie on her other side. That left her no choice but to share the book Caleb was holding toward her.

Their fingertips brushed under the cover. Her throat tightened so much she squeaked out the first note, but she cleared her throat and continued. She had always enjoyed singing, especially with her sisters. Wyatt couldn't carry a note in a bucket, but Caleb's deep voice echoed in her ears in perfect harmony. She could go on singing with him all morning.

But after two more hymns, the song service ended and Pastor Rawley announced the text. She'd brought her Bible, as had her sisters and Ma and Pa, and she shared the Book with Caleb.

It was smaller than the hymnal and his fingers didn't just brush hers, they maintained contact throughout the reading. For the life of her, she couldn't concentrate on the words.

What was wrong with her? She had never felt this way before. Certainly not around Karl. Why, the few times he had sat beside her in church, he'd kept his hands on his thighs and shaken his head when she'd offered to share the Bible or hymnal. It had always made her feel isolated, as if he had built a wall around himself that he didn't want her to breach.

There had been moments when she'd minded, but on the whole she'd welcomed the distance between them.

Not so with Caleb. Unfamiliar feelings bubbled inside her. A longing to touch and to be touched, to be held, to have no barriers between them. Those longings were exciting but at the same time, frightening. She knew the pain of being left behind. The feeling of not being enough to make people stay or have any regard for her feelings. Blame always came from her heart—she must have done something to drive them away. And she always vowed to do better, be better.

Most of all she promised herself to never again care so much.

She'd broken that promise. She cared about Caleb and his son so much it hurt. And it would hurt a thousand times more when he left. She pressed her fingers to her lips. Let anyone who noticed think she was moved by the sermon, though she couldn't have repeated a single word of it.

All she really heard was the final "Amen."

She rose and followed the others out, answering Teddy's questions, responding to the comments offered to her. But inside, she concentrated on telling herself how things would be. She'd allowed herself to care for both Teddy and Caleb, but no one would ever know to what depth.

After dinner at home, with Cora, Wyatt and Lonnie also in attendance, her older sister edged forward on her chair. "I'd really like to go to Chester's Pond this afternoon. It's such a lovely day, and who knows how many more chances we'll get. What do you think?" She looked at Pa for permission.

Pa nodded. "It's a nice afternoon for an outing. Ma and I can have a long lovely nap while you young people enjoy the day."

Caleb looked uncertain, as if he didn't expect to be included in the invitation.

"You, too, of course," Cora said to him.

"How far is it?"

"Take the wagon," Pa said.

Lilly and her sisters made short work of the dishes and packed a little snack. "It's tradition," Lilly explained to Caleb and Teddy. "We always have a picnic of sorts."

Teddy grew so excited he was in danger of falling facedown as he swung back and forth on his crutches.

Cora and Wyatt went to get the wagon, while Rose and Lilly gathered everything they'd need for an outing. In a few minutes they were loaded in the wagon and on their way.

Wyatt drove with Cora beside him. They followed the river for a few miles.

"You two rode together the last time we went," Lilly pointed out.

"Last time we were there, I kissed Cora." Wyatt's voice was husky.

Cora shook her head. "I thought I kissed you."

They laughed together.

Lonnie shook his head with mock disapproval over the way his brother adored Cora. "Well, I found an arrowhead."

"Papa, maybe I'll find one, too. Will you help me look?" Teddy's eyes widened with excitement.

"We'll all help you look," Lilly promised. "We're almost there."

A trail led through a grove of trees to the body of water. The twins sat up and watched as they drove closer.

Lilly sighed. "This is one of my favorite spots."

"Me, too," Rose echoed.

"October is my favorite month, when every leaf is a flower," Lilly said. And now she'd have even more reason to like the month.

With a start, she realized there were only a few more days in the month. She shivered. Would Caleb leave in November, making that month her least favorite?

She quickly dismissed the notion. She would not let such thoughts ruin this day.

Caleb jumped from the wagon as soon as it stopped and held out a hand to help her to the ground.

She placed her fingers in his strong palm. Warmth raced up her arms and pooled in her cheeks. She kept her head lowered as she stepped down. Only after she'd swallowed hard and adjusted her skirt did she glance up and thank him.

He nodded, a smile clinging to his eyes, and then he turned to lift Teddy to the ground.

"Where did you find the arrowhead?" he asked Lonnie. The pair headed to the shoreline.

They all followed, splitting off in various directions.

Cora and Wyatt disappeared into the trees.

Lilly stared after them. Was that where they had kissed? When had they known they loved each other? How had Cora been sure her heart would be safe with him?

She didn't have the answers, nor would she ask the questions. Whatever happened between Cora and Wyatt was particular to them. Neither she nor Rose could hope to copy it.

Caleb walked by her side. "It would be nice to find an arrowhead for Teddy."

"There's bound to be something around here." They traipsed about the pond for half an hour and saw nothing of interest, so they turned back.

When Lilly caught her shoe on a rock and stumbled, Caleb caught her before she fell. "Are you okay?"

She clung to him as she found her balance. And if she held his hand longer than was necessary, he didn't seem to object. Rose watched them from a few yards away and Lilly slowly withdrew, but her gaze remained locked with his.

Their look went on and on as if time had no end. Her

heart unfolded like a flower before the morning sun. Thoughts that she'd kept hidden all her life took flight and flew upward. She longed to share each of them with Caleb, but now was not the time or the place.

She lowered her gaze. "I'm fine. Thank you for saving me from that fall." There would never be a time or place. Not with him leaving.

She pushed the secret thoughts back to the dark recesses of her mind. She'd never felt safe enough with anyone to open her heart fully. Although she found she had to remind herself of that fact on a frequent basis when in Caleb's presence.

The rock that had almost tripped her lay overturned at her feet. "Look." When she had kicked it, she had by chance uncovered an arrowhead. "Let's call Teddy and let him find it."

Caleb's warm smile thanked her more than words could.

She slid her eyes away from him. "Teddy," she called. "Come and see what we found."

"An arrowhead?" he called, hopping so fast over the rocks that her breath caught partway up her throat. If he fell...

"Teddy, slow down." Caleb's firm words did not completely disguise the fear in his voice.

Teddy slowed marginally. Lonnie stayed close to him, one arm outstretched, prepared to catch him if he stumbled.

Teddy's crutch caught on a rock.

Lilly gasped, expecting to see him hit the ground.

Caleb sprang forward, but Teddy righted himself and got the crutch safely back in place.

Lilly's breath whooshed out. Her heart continued to

beat double time. She'd envisioned him crashing to the ground, further injuring himself.

How had he prevented the fall? She replayed the scenario in her head. Had he used his injured leg to catch himself? She stared at him, his leg now hanging limply. Was she mistaken? But she didn't see how else he could have stopped the fall. Was his leg able to do more than he thought?

She'd add a few things to his exercises and see if his leg could bear any weight.

He and Lonnie reached them.

"I think I saw something special on the ground here." Caleb pointed at the ground.

"What? What?" Teddy got on his hands and knees. "I don't see it."

"Maybe it's on this side of the rock," Caleb said.

Teddy saw the perfectly formed black arrowhead. He scooped it up. "Look, Papa. Look, Lonnie. Lilly, see what I found."

She squatted beside him. "It's very nice."

Lonnie looked over Teddy's shoulder. "It's a better one than mine."

Teddy fairly glowed with pleasure.

Lilly turned to Caleb. At the tightness in his expression she straightened. He looked about ready to break in two. She touched his arm gently. "Caleb?"

He shook his head and moved toward the water's edge.

She followed. "What's wrong?"

"Everything." He scrubbed at his neck.

"I thought you'd be happy that Teddy found an arrowhead."

"I am." He turned to face her, his eyes full of dark torment. "But don't you see? This is everything I ever wanted for him—people who care about him, enjoyment in life, a home, a family—" He broke off and shook his head. "And he has none of it. No family. No home. And how can he enjoy life to the fullest when he can't walk without crutches?"

His grief twisted her insides into a cruel knot. She reached for him, wanting to offer comfort and encouragement, but he shook his head.

"You've made me want to have and be what I can't."

She dropped her hand to her side. "And what is that?"

Rather than answer, he turned to stare at the water. "Life here is so simple. So...so..." He shrugged. "For want of a better word, sweet."

"And you object to that? Seems to me it's something a person would want."

"Wanting and having are two different things."

"I don't understand."

Slowly he brought his gaze back to her. She guessed he was trying to hide his feelings, but she saw the dark sorrow that filled his eyes.

"I can't have those things. I tried once and failed. Now it's just me and Teddy."

She thought of how she suspected Teddy had caught himself using his injured leg—the one that had forgotten to work. "What if Teddy's leg gets better without the help of a doctor? Then would you allow yourself those things? A home, a family, a sense of belonging?" *Love?*

The darkness in his eyes deepened. "I don't know. What if I fail again?"

He wasn't making sense. "How did you fail?"

His jaw muscles clenched, and the skin about his eyes pinched into harsh wrinkles. "My wife is dead. My son is injured. And you can ask how I failed?"

She backed away a step. He must have loved Amanda a great deal to mourn her so deeply, feel her loss so keenly.

She could never hope for that depth of love. Especially from Caleb. But her heart went out to him, lost as he was in all that pain. "Caleb, you must not give up hope. I believe Teddy will walk normally again. Just as your heart will someday heal." She wanted so much more for him. "Someday you will find joy in your present life, hope in your future and forgiveness for your past. I pray the day will be soon."

He looked right at her, an unhurried, gentle melting coming through his eyes until they flashed what she could only interpret as the hope she had asked for. A slow, powerful smile caught his lips and her heart.

"Lilly Bell, if I could borrow just a fraction of your attitude I might see life as the joyful gift you believe it to be."

"You can have the same attitude I have. It's free to everyone. It's a matter of choice."

"Choice, huh? Sounds too easy."

"It is and it isn't."

His eyes crinkled with amusement. "How do you explain that?"

She tried to focus on what she meant to say, but she was distracted by the smile in his eyes. "Our doubts and failures get in the way of believing."

He nodded, his expression serious, as if he understood what she meant.

But did he only understand the difficulties? She pressed the point. "Do we believe the possibilities or the failures?" Perhaps she meant herself as well as him. Could she believe in a future that held the things she wanted while guarding her heart against them?

"Lilly, Caleb," Cora called. "Come have tea."

"Coming," she responded, but she wished she'd had a

few more minutes with Caleb to see him choose to start life over again.

On second thought, perhaps she should be grateful. Cora's call had pulled her back from the dangerous territory she had been venturing into—a place that beckoned with all the things she yearned for but feared to believe were possible.

Wait. She reminded herself she longed for nothing more than what she already had—her parents and sisters and animals. Only it got harder and harder to believe it.

Caleb stole glances at Lilly as they sat around on logs, ate cookies and drank warm, sweet tea brought in jars. Teddy talked incessantly about the arrowhead he'd found.

Caleb was content to listen to the hum of conversation around him as he mulled over his discussion with Lilly. She wanted him to believe in life—and love? She hadn't said so, but her words had seemed to indicate it.

Did he dare believe he could have family and love again? Or was he looking for things beyond his grasp? Was he asking for another dose of pain and failure?

He knew he should listen to the warning words inside his head, but he couldn't keep himself from wishing he could have the very things he'd wanted for as long as he could remember.

Was it possible, if only temporarily? Was temporary enough? And why not? Why not enjoy the present, with Lilly filling it as she was with joy? He could relish the moment and let the future take care of itself.

Satisfied with his decision, he settled back to listen to the others talk.

Rose spoke. "I still think we should try to find out who our birth parents were."

Cora sighed. "I really don't see what we could do. Our

mother is dead, and our father didn't want us when we were little. We don't need him now. We have our Ma and Pa, and each other. And now I have Wyatt."

Rose swirled the contents of her cup around. "I understand our mother died. But there must be some good reason for our father to have left us in the middle of nowhere for two days and a night."

Caleb jerked forward. "You were left alone? Overnight? You must have been terrified." He glanced at Teddy, who had gone back with Lonnie to search through the rocks along the edge of the water. He couldn't imagine leaving his son alone for any length of time.

"Exactly," Cora said. "I don't think we want to know what kind of man would do that to his children."

Caleb looked at Lilly, who had so far not joined this conversation about her birth parents. "That's dreadful. I can see why Rose would like to find out what had happened. There must be an explanation for such callous behavior. It's just not normal."

Lilly gave him a look fit to stall every thought he had. "I don't want to know. We have a perfectly good life here and now. Why complicate it with things we might not want to know?"

He opened his mouth to protest and then closed it again without speaking. How could he say anything about her running from her past when he had done the same thing? It was no wonder she clung to the security of her family, but somehow it seemed wrong when she did it.

Likely she would say the same about him. Just when he'd thought there was a bridge across the gulf between them, the gulf had widened.

But did he have to let that happen? Maybe it was time both of them stopped running. And what better place than here? And what better time than now?

Cora turned the conversation to other things—plans for the fall, things the girls wanted to make during the winter.

He sat back and watched them. Lilly came alive when she talked about her sheep and all the wool she would card that winter. She really did have the power to forget the past and enjoy the present.

What else had she said? Hope for the future.

For the first time in many months he allowed himself to think of doing the same, thanks to her.

The afternoon cooled and they headed back.

A soft breeze blew from the southwest as they returned. Grub and Blossom waited in front of the house. Blossom got stiffly to her feet and trotted over to greet Teddy, while Grub twirled about in excited circles, making them all chuckle.

In the garden, the dry cornstalks swayed and rustled. Cora looked in that direction and sighed. Rose and Lilly exchanged knowing looks.

He wondered what they were thinking.

Teddy hurried as fast as he could to the house, calling, "Grandma, Grandpa, look what I found." He stepped inside to show off his arrowhead.

Caleb went with Wyatt to put away the horse and wagon and the rest of them followed Teddy indoors.

"How's the boy doing?" Wyatt asked.

"He's the happiest he's been in ages, but he still doesn't use his leg."

Wyatt clapped him on the back. "Don't be in a hurry to give up on what Ma and Lilly can accomplish. This place sure helped Lonnie and me."

"How's that?"

"You haven't heard my story?"

"Just that you and Cora married and moved to a little ranch with Jack Henry." A simple life.

"We were running from our past. You see, I spent a year in jail before I came here."

"What? How can that be?" So much for assuming the man had led a simple life.

"Our pa was mean as a rattler. Sometimes a person can only take so much before they snap. I got charged with assaulting him."

The two men studied each other and something in Wyatt's face let Caleb know Wyatt wasn't telling him everything.

"When I got out, my pa was dead. My ma lived only long enough to see me set free and then we buried her, too."

"I'm sorry." This man had seen more than his share of trouble.

"We were on our way out of the country, trying to get away from all the people talking about my time in jail, when we landed here with a mare too heavy in foal to continue. I'd say God brought us here to help us. I'd say He brought you here for the same reason."

"Huh? What reason would that be?" He'd never been in jail or beat a man. Though he'd shot the two intruders in self-defense.

"Why, to find a reason to start over."

Lilly had said much the same thing. Was it possible to forget the past and start over? "I need to take Teddy to the special doctor."

"Like I said, don't be in a rush to leave. Now, shall we join the others?"

Caleb didn't move. "Did you really beat your father so badly you were sent to jail?"

Wyatt's eyes hardened. "He was fortunate he didn't

die. Like I said, you can only push a man so far before he strikes back."

He thought of all he knew of Wyatt and Lonnie and all he'd observed of their relationship. "I'm guessing the man you said was being pushed around wasn't you."

Wyatt shrugged. "It's water under the bridge. Now I have Cora and a beautiful future."

"That's nice." Caleb would not say anything about their past. They deserved the chance at happiness.

Maybe he did, too.

He accompanied Wyatt to the house, where Teddy was still talking a mile a minute to Mr. and Mrs. Bell, with Lonnie adding details to the story.

The three sisters were preparing supper, glancing often to the four at the table, exchanging smiles of approval at how Teddy and Lonnie were entertaining their parents.

Caleb allowed himself to enjoy the scene. Home. Family. Belonging. Was it possible to put his failures and disappointments behind him?

Or was he foolishly begging for more trouble?

Chapter Fourteen

Lilly watched the play of emotions on Caleb's face. Her heart leapt within her. Did his contented expression mean he was thinking about staying? She stilled her eager thoughts.

If she had a lick of sense, she'd not be pinning her hopes on such.

She turned to stir the pot of soup Ma had started.

Cora was staring out the window toward the garden. Wyatt went to her side and wrapped his arm around her. "What is it, dear?"

She smiled up at him. "It's nothing, really. I'm just remembering how we used to enjoy running through the dry cornstalks trying to scare each other." She shrugged. "But I suppose I'm too old for that now."

He chuckled. "Yes, you are such an old lady."

Cora gave him a playful shove.

Lilly watched them together, her heart almost bursting with a long-buried longing. Oh, how she ached to be loved like that. She stole a glance at Caleb and saw he was watching the pair, too.

Did they want the same thing? A family, a home, a

forever love? But he'd had already it and lost it. That's probably what he was thinking.

Wyatt turned to the others. "Who'd like to run through the cornstalks?"

Lonnie and Teddy answered in unison. "Me."

Lilly and Rose waited.

Cora sighed. "Thank you for offering, but it's only fun if we do it at dusk, and we need to be on our way home as soon as we have supper." She grinned at the twins. "Remember how I used to scare you."

Lilly laughed. "She was so sneaky. She'd hide and not make a rustle and then jump out to frighten us."

"Sounds like fun," Lonnie said. Both he and Teddy looked disappointed that they wouldn't be able to play the game.

Wyatt rubbed his chin. "Well, let's see now. I think I'd like to be part of this fun. There's no reason we can't travel home after dark."

"Really?" Cora smiled up at him. "You'd do that for me?"

Wyatt nodded, looking at her in such a way that Lilly wondered if he even remembered the rest of them were in the room.

"Hello," Lonnie said. "We're still here, you know. Hey, can Teddy play, too? You know, with his crutches and all?"

Teddy gave Caleb a pleading look. "I can, can't I, Papa? I'll be careful. Besides, even if I fall I won't hurt myself." He sat up straight and looked around importantly. "I've fallen lots of times and I'm okay."

Caleb raised his eyebrows and met Lilly's glance. Of course, he wasn't okay, but that wasn't because he'd fallen. "I guess you can join in on the fun."

"Then let's get supper done." Rose set the table while

Cora sliced a loaf of bread and Lilly dished soup into each bowl.

Teddy sat between her and Caleb and it felt exactly as it should. The family around the table. Even if Caleb and Teddy weren't truly a part of the family. But she'd enjoy the evening without worrying about what tomorrow might bring.

By the time the meal ended and the dishes were done, the sun filled the sky with streaks of red and pink and orange.

"Let's go," Cora said, and all but Ma and Pa hurried outside to the corn patch.

Cora and Wyatt disappeared into the rustling stalks.

"You'll have to stop giggling," Lilly called. "Or we'll know where you are."

Rose slipped away as silently as a shadow.

Lonnie went with Teddy, the clump of moving crutches letting everyone know which direction they were headed.

Lilly and Caleb glanced at each other and then Lilly slipped away. At first the rustle of leaves signaled her path, but then she drew back out of sight, stilling her breathing so she could listen. To her right she detected a movement and she jumped out. "Boo!"

It was Rose she frightened, and they giggled and tip-toed away in opposite directions.

A few minutes later she did the same to Lonnie and Teddy, who screamed. Next, she leapt out at Cora, and giggling, the two collapsed into each other's arm. Then Cora went off to stalk Wyatt through the corn plants.

Lilly stood still. Where was Caleb? She hadn't heard him since they'd entered the corn patch. She tipped her head to the left. Did she detect a noise? It had to be Caleb since she knew where the others were, so she eased in that direction. She was an expert at this game. She'd sneak up on him and give him a fright.

At the thought she pressed her hand to her mouth to silence her laughter.

Inch by inch she moved forward, guided by a faint rustle, her own noise so muffled she hoped he wouldn't hear her. To her right, the sound of the others laughing and screaming and crashing through the plants helped cover her approach.

Then the guiding sound stopped. She held perfectly still, holding her breath. Where was he? Something tickled her ear. A spider? She shuddered and brushed at the side of her head.

The tickle moved to her other ear. She shuddered. Had she walked into a nest of spiders? Were they crawling all over her? How she abhorred the creepy crawly creatures.

She couldn't stand it any longer. Not caring who heard her, she pushed away from the nearest plant and turned around to see what she'd run into.

"Boo."

Her heart crashed against her ribs. Her lungs refused to work. "Caleb. I thought you were a spider." Her voice trembled, revealing just how much he'd frightened her.

"Gotcha good."

Her heart and lungs and emotions released in a whoosh. "You scared me." She shoved him hard.

"Whoa." He stumbled backward, clinging to her arms to keep from falling, but to no avail. He went down like a ton of potatoes, taking her with him.

She lay sprawled across his chest, looking into his eyes, made twice as dark by the fading light. "You are one awfully big spider," she managed.

He brushed her hair back.

"Please tell me there isn't a spider in my hair."

"Only me." He trailed his finger along her cheek to her chin and let it linger there.

Her heart fought for the next beat and the one after that, as if it had gotten lost in the warmth and tenderness of his touch. She wanted to feel him stroke her face again. Wanted to turn her face into his palm and kiss it. Wanted to—

"I can't get up until you do." His words cut off her fantasies.

"Of course." She scrambled to her feet, her mind in total disarray. What had she been thinking?

Only that she wanted him to hold her. Only that she longed to open her heart and soul to him and let him see every fear, every hesitation, every ache of longing.

He pushed to his feet. "That's better." He caught her upper arms and pulled her to his chest. "When I kiss a girl, I prefer to do it standing on my two feet."

"Kiss a girl?"

"I mean you." He caught her chin and lifted her face toward him. "Unless you object."

"Object?" She could think of no reason she wouldn't want his kiss. In fact, she'd been wanting it for a long time. Maybe all her life. "No, I've no objection."

"Good." He lowered his head slowly, as if savoring the anticipation as much as she was.

She closed her eyes and breathed in his scent, his nearness. And then his lips caught hers, firm, full of today and tomorrow. And forever? Never mind silly questions right now. All that mattered was this moment, when time stopped to allow them to give and take of this kiss.

She wrapped her arms about his waist and pressed her palms to his back, reveling in the power and warmth she was feeling.

And then it ended. He broke off, but he didn't move

away. She stayed safe and secure in the shelter of his arms. Their foreheads touched and they breathed in unison, as if their entire beings had found union in the kiss.

"Lilly," he murmured.

"Yes, Caleb?" His name was sweet nectar on her tongue.

"I shouldn't have done that, but I can't say I'm sorry."

"Nor can I." She and Karl had kissed, but it had been a mere brushing of their lips. Cold and lifeless. In no way comparable to this.

"Papa." Teddy's call jerked them apart. "I can't find you." The corn plants rustled nearby.

Caleb brushed his knuckles along her jawline. "I have to say I really like playing in the cornfield. I'll never forget it." He lowered his hand slowly and then responded to Teddy.

"I'm over here. Come find me." He eased away from Lilly, leaving as silently as he'd come.

She stood rooted to the spot until Teddy and Lonnie came crashing through the plants. Then she slipped away, not wanting to see anyone until she had her senses about her again.

Would that ever happen?

She felt as if Caleb's kiss had forever changed her.

Caleb stepped into the dark cornstalks. He needed to consider what he'd done.

He'd kissed Lilly. Likely he shouldn't have, but he sure didn't regret it. She'd come readily enough into his arms and lifted her face for the kiss.

He closed his eyes and made himself take slow, easy breaths, though they did nothing to still the racing of his heart. He'd kissed a woman before. After all, he'd been married for more than six years. But he couldn't recall a kiss that had claimed him so completely that he could barely recall his name.

A rustling nearby signaled someone's approach. He held his breath, not ready to desert his thoughts. Rose tiptoed past, unaware of his presence, and he let a fraction of tension ease from his limbs.

His name? Right. He was Caleb Craig. A widower with a five-year-old son who had a leg that didn't work. He was in the employ of the Caldwells, feuding neighbors of the Bells. He had to keep the job to earn enough money to take Teddy to a special doctor.

He recited the long list of reasons he could not let one kiss influence his thoughts. But all the reasons failed to quench the longings the kiss had awakened. It had the power to erase every rational thought from his mind. He wanted a new beginning and a love to fill his life with passion and meaning.

He shook his head. What he wanted and what he could have were not the same.

His nerves tensed as the cornstalks behind him rustled and Lonnie and Teddy jumped out yelling, "Boo."

Teddy giggled madly. "We scared you, didn't we?"

"You sure did." He scooped Teddy into his arms and tickled him as the boy squirmed and laughed. This was all that mattered. Taking care of his son. He could not allow anything to make him forget that. Especially the yearnings of his foolish heart.

The play continued for a bit longer and then Wyatt yelled out. "It's time for us Williamses to head home."

Caleb called out, too. "It's time for little boys to go to bed."

"Aww," Teddy answered.

Caleb met the boy at the end of the corn patch and together they headed for the house.

As Caleb prepared the poultice for Teddy's leg, his thoughts continued to war inside his head. He could imagine himself and Teddy living here. If not for the fact Teddy needed to see a special doctor, Caleb might consider staying in the area.

But some things would remain the same. He would still have to deal with his failure to protect those he loved.

Rose and Lilly entered the house a short time later as Caleb prepared to remove the poultice from Teddy's leg.

Lilly hurried to his side. "How is it?"

He looked into her gaze as she bent close. The air between them grew still. A longing as fierce as a winter storm gripped his heart at the blue welcome he saw in her eyes. The kiss had changed him. Perhaps it had changed her, too. But there were barriers he couldn't ignore. He tried to remember what they were, but the details eluded him at the moment. He knew he would recall them later and wonder how they could have slipped his mind.

She looked at Teddy's leg. "I'd like to try some different exercises tonight if you have no objections."

"None at all," Caleb said. She could have asked him to dance a jig in the middle of the room and he'd have had no objections. Thankfully, she didn't, for he really had no wish to make a fool of himself. He'd come perilously close to doing so as he'd stood there in the cornstalks all moon-eyed.

He blinked and focused on what she was doing.

She had Teddy sit on the side of the bed and press his foot to the floor. "Does that hurt?"

Teddy shook his head and patted Blossom.

She pushed on his ankle. "Try and keep me from moving your leg."

He pushed back.

She did it in every direction. "Very good."

She had him lie back and then she did the original exercises. "All done. Good job."

Mrs. Bell watched from her chair. "I see progress."

Lilly nodded. "I do, as well."

Caleb wanted to ask what they saw, but he didn't care to discuss it in front of Teddy. "Son, it's time to get ready for bed." It was past bedtime, but he wouldn't have robbed his son of the pleasure of that particular evening.

A smile tugged at Caleb's lips. Had Teddy had as much fun as his papa had? He hardly thought it possible.

"Can Lilly do Tiny's story with me tonight?" Teddy asked.

"'Fraid not, son. It's much too late."

"Ahh."

"We'll do it again tomorrow," Lilly promised, smiling at them both.

"Okay." Teddy settled into bed.

As soon as Teddy had prayed and bid good-night to all the Bells, Caleb turned to Mr. Bell.

"Sir, may I walk outside with Lilly? I'd like to ask her about—" He tipped his head toward Teddy.

Mr. Bell nodded. "'Tis a fine evening for a stroll."

Lilly hurried over to get a shawl.

Rose cleared her throat. "Don't suppose you'd like company?"

Caleb hesitated. He could hardly say no.

Lilly pulled the shawl close and didn't answer immediately. Then she nodded. "You're more than welcome to join us."

Rose laughed. "No, thanks. I was only teasing."

Lilly gave her sister a tight smile. "One of these days your teasing will get you into a heap of trouble."

"Not a chance." Rose grinned as Lilly and Caleb stepped into the night.

A gibbous moon lit the yard, gilding every leaf and branch in silver.

"It's a beautiful evening," Lilly said.

"I like your game of playing in the cornstalks." His voice rumbled in his chest, deepened by his memory of the other game he and Lilly had played in the corn patch.

They walked along the path that led to the barn and beyond.

"Do you mean the game of chasing and scaring each other?" Her voice was deceptively innocent. "Or were you referring to another game?"

"Both." He caught her hand and turned her about to face him, placing his hands on her upper arms. He resisted the urge to pull her into his arms and kiss her again. There were things that needed to be said. In the moonlight he could not read her eyes, so he was unable to see if she was longing for the same things he was. "I can't promise you anything but the here and now."

She nodded. "It's all I've ever had."

The words troubled him. Her pessimistic attitude was in such contrast to her assurance that a person could choose to live life to the fullest. Or was it? Perhaps she was simply being realistic and forging ahead despite the challenges of life.

"I'm sorry I can't offer more, but Teddy—well, Teddy has needs that must come above everything else."

"Of course they must. But his leg is improving."

His grip on her arms tightened. "What do you mean?"

"Those new exercises required he use his muscles and he did." She flashed a smile. "The muscles are responding to the treatments we've been doing." She planted her hands on his arms and squeezed. "Isn't that great?"

Hope leapt within his heart. Could it be possible? The flame of hope died as suddenly as it had sparked. Doctors had suggested that they'd seen positive changes before, but Teddy still didn't walk on that leg. He wasn't about to see Lilly's observation as a cure just yet.

He patted Lilly's shoulders. "It's a real good start." He needed still to keep his sights set on his goal of taking Teddy to the special doctor.

It was time to end the evening, so he turned back to the house, tucking Lilly in at his side.

He paused at the door. "It's been a lovely evening. Thank you."

"And thank you, too." They stood inches away from each other.

He wanted to kiss her again, but he feared doing so would make him lose all sense of his priorities. Still he ached to hold her and claim her lips. Feel again the depth of emotion that had rocked his world.

No, he must remain guarded, keep his head on straight. Not be led from his path by his heart.

"Good night, then." She opened the door and stepped inside, and he followed.

He'd waited too long, argued with himself until she'd taken the choice from him. He should have been relieved. Not filled with stinging disappointment as he was.

Chapter Fifteen

Lilly hurried into the bedroom, where Rose had already prepared for the night.

"How was your moonlight walk?" Rose asked, smiling as she teased her sister.

"We discussed Teddy. Did you see how the strength is coming back to his leg?"

"Don't get your hopes up."

Lilly didn't know if Rose was referring to Teddy's leg or to the possibility Caleb would see the improvement in his son and decide to stay. She took her time hanging her dress and pulling her nightie over her head. She didn't want to discuss the evening with anyone. It seemed Caleb only meant to enjoy a quick kiss and move on. He had even dismissed the notion that Teddy's leg was getting better, as if he needed to cling to that excuse for leaving.

Well, she should be relieved. At least he was being honest about not offering her anything more. And he was honorable enough not to kiss her again.

To her dismay, she wished he had. Even knowing he meant to move on. Even knowing her heart would break in a thousand pieces when he rode away.

Rose sat up on one elbow and watched Lilly. "I just don't want to see you get hurt."

Lilly purposely misunderstood her. "How would I be hurt if Teddy's leg doesn't fix itself? I never offered any assurance to Caleb or myself."

"You know I'm not talking about that."

"How could I know that?"

Rose chuckled. "Because we know each other so well. I meant Caleb, and you know that."

Lilly wouldn't give Rose the satisfaction of admitting it.

Rose sighed. "I see the way things are between you two and I'm afraid. You've been hurt before."

"I thought we'd decided Karl didn't matter."

Rose gave her a hard look. "You always say you're happy with things the way they are. You don't want to change for fear life could get worse."

"Uh-huh. So?" She crawled between the covers and picked up her Bible, hoping Rose would take the hint and drop this subject.

"It's just your way of avoiding dealing with something painful. You hide from it."

She opened her Bible. "I got over Karl a long time ago."

"But why did you pick him in the first place? Anyone could see you were only a convenient person for him to spend time with. His ambitions far outweighed any consideration he had for you. That's the very reason you accepted his courting, though it could hardly be called that."

Lilly stared at her sister. "Why would I do that?" Sometimes Rose pretended to understand a great deal more than was possible.

"To reinforce your belief that no one will ever stay with you. I guess you think it proves you aren't worth it."

"Huh. That's stupid." But the words edged into her heart and scraped away a protective scab. Her birth father had left her—not only her, of course—but the others didn't seem to feel the pain of that abandonment as deeply as she did. Or if they did, they didn't let anyone know.

"It is, isn't it?" Rose sat up and picked up her own Bible. "Maybe you should stop expecting to be left."

Ma had given them each a Bible and had written a verse for each on the flyleaf. Lilly turned there and read the verse even though she knew it by heart. Hebrews 13:5. "I will never leave thee, nor forsake thee." Then Ma had written her own words. *Lilly, I can't promise that Pa or I will always be with you, but I can assure you that God will never fail to keep His promise to be with you. My prayer is for you to surround yourself with others who will stand by you when we are gone.*

The words had stung Lilly when she'd first read them a few years ago. It had felt as if Ma was saying goodbye, as if she couldn't wait for that final farewell. Now she saw it only as Ma dealing with the inevitable, though the idea still pained Lilly.

She answered her sister. "I have you and Cora."

"Yes, you do, and we will always be here for each other so long as God grants us life. But don't you long for love like that which Cora has found with Wyatt?"

Lilly cocked her head toward the door—all that separated her from Caleb. Only there was so much more than a door between them. There was his warning that he wasn't offering more than the here and now. There was her fear of being left. No doubt Rose's statements contained much truth.

Lilly mused aloud. "I don't remember our birth parents, but I do remember standing beside Cora in the middle of the prairie and seeing nothing but grass and sky."

"I remember, too. Cora tried her best to comfort us."

"Do you remember when Ma found us?"

"Vaguely. I remember getting fed and feeling safe."

"For years I was so scared of being left that it must have driven Ma and Pa half mad."

Rose laughed softly. "Remember the little rag doll you clung to for so long? I wonder what happened to it."

Lilly snorted. "As if you don't know it's in my drawer. All tattered and torn."

"It was well loved."

"I guess I thought as long as I was holding it I was also holding on to Ma, because she'd made it. It doesn't make much sense now, but it did then."

"Do you think Caleb would stay if Teddy's leg worked?"

Lilly had been avoiding that question ever since she'd mentioned to Caleb that Teddy's leg was getting better and he'd ended the evening in response. He obviously did not welcome a reason to stay.

"I don't think so."

"Well, I'm sorry even though he is a Caldwell cowboy. I don't like to see you hurt."

"Who says I will be? Don't you think I've learned to be cautious?" She clapped her hand over her mouth as she realized her words had confirmed Rose's theory.

Rose chuckled. "Oh, indeed. But I think Caleb has managed to break through your defenses."

Lilly turned the pages of her Bible to signal the conversation was over. She was loath to admit it, but Rose was right. Despite Lilly's good intentions not to let herself be hurt again, something about Caleb had disarmed her and left her vulnerable.

It might be too late to prevent any damage, but she

would take steps immediately to contain it to one memorable kiss, one day of wishing and dreaming.

If only she knew how to accomplish such a task.

The next morning she had her resolve firmly in place as she hurried out of her room. She called a quick "Good morning" to everyone in general. Using every ounce of self-control she could muster, she kept her gaze slightly to Caleb's right to avoid direct eye contact.

Normally she waited until after breakfast and after Caleb had ridden away to do the milking, but today, without a backward look, she hurried out to the barn, grateful for the chance to be alone.

Breakfast was ready when she returned with the milk. Caleb followed her to the storeroom to help strain the milk. It was a task she could have managed on her own, but she couldn't refuse his help without being rude.

"You left in a hurry this morning." He sounded both curious and cautious and his smile barely lifted his lips.

She turned to watch the milk run through the cloth. "I wanted to get an early start on the chores. There's a lot yet to do to get ready for winter."

"I see." He waited as if he was hoping she'd say more.

She didn't. How could she explain when caution warred with sweet thoughts of last evening's kiss?

"Have I offended you?" He kept his voice low so those in the other room wouldn't hear.

She jerked her eyes to his. "Offended me? How?"

His lips twisted into a crooked grin. "By kissing you. By saying I couldn't promise you anything." He jammed his hands in the front pockets of his jeans. "Or maybe in other ways I haven't considered."

She chuckled. "None of the above." She grew serious. "But it seems to me neither of us is ready to think beyond today." At least in their relationship with each other.

He quirked an eyebrow in acknowledgment. "I don't blame you for wanting more."

In the way he left the sentence hanging, she understood he was wondering if she would say that was enough. But was it? Could she take temporary and not be hurt by it?

She was fully aware of the inescapable fact that she would pay a pretty penny in sorrow when he and Teddy left.

But why not enjoy what the present offered? Might just as well mourn a lot as a little.

"I don't know what I want." She headed for the door, ending the conversation.

If only she could as easily walk away from her thoughts.

Caleb reasoned with himself throughout the day as he did repairs on the oat bin at the Caldwell ranch.

He wasn't sorry he'd been honest with Lilly, telling her he could offer her nothing but the time he would be there. He could give no promises for the future. He clung to that fact as if it were a metal shield.

No expectations meant no failures.

He jerked back from nailing a board in place and stared out at the rolling hills. Did he avoid thinking of the future to make sure he couldn't fail?

Nah. He returned to his task. It was a practical decision.

He worked hard throughout the day, barely pausing to down water several times and grab a handful of sandwiches for dinner. He finished early and headed for the Bell farm.

Work hard, enjoy the evening with Teddy and the Bell family. A man could get used to that routine.

He snorted, realizing his thought was seriously at odds with his decision to avoid thinking about a future.

He shifted his attention to his surroundings. Ebner and the Caldwell cowboys had moved some of the cows down from the higher pastures. A dozen head grazed in a hollow to his right, another twenty or so on a grassy knoll to his left. The grass would prove adequate for several weeks unless it snowed a great deal.

The sky was clear and bright. He breathed in air heavy with the scent of fragrant grasses and ripe fall leaves. It was pretty and productive country. A man could look a long time to find a place that equaled it.

All his life he had imagined himself with a ranch of his own, a cozy home of his own and a family with which to fill it.

He sighed. He'd already tried that route. It was time to move on to something else.

But the feeling refused to be quenched.

The face that completed those dreams was not Amanda's, but rather it was Lilly's. Her lovely face smiled at him from inside his make-believe house.

"Hello."

A call behind him jerked him around in his saddle. What was Ebner doing out here? He'd said he would ride to the higher pastures and check on the cows.

Caleb reined in and waited for the foreman to reach him, though he could think of no one in the world he'd less like to see.

Ebner reached Caleb's side. "Howdy. Where you off to?"

"I'm done my work for the day." He wouldn't let Ebner know his destination.

"So if you're done, where you going now?"

"I thought you headed up into the hills. Did you run into trouble?" Was it possible to divert the man?

"Nah. But the boss and his wife should be returning this week. I figure if I can persuade the Bells to move on before he gets back he might be grateful enough to give me a nice fat reward."

The Bells! What did this man have in mind? "What kind of reward do you fancy?" He edged his horse around. He'd go back to the ranch before he'd let Ebner know his destination.

"I got my eye on a nice piece of land north of here. High in the mountains where a man can do what he wants and no one will say otherwise. Now, if I had me a few head of cows I might just say goodbye to this job and go claim that bit of land."

"Sounds like a fine plan."

Ebner cut off Caleb's retreat. "Why don't you ride along with me for a spell?"

Caleb considered his options. He could refuse and return to the ranch, but that would leave Ebner to go on his way to the Bells, and who knows what he might decide to do there. Besides, if he refused his boss, it might well get him fired.

Or he could ride along with Ebner and talk that man out of any mischief.

"Sure. Got nothing else to do at the moment." He hung back, letting Ebner lead the way.

They reached the crest of a hill that gave them a good view of the Bell farm. Fortunately, it was not so close as to draw the attention of those living there.

He made out the twins in the garden digging something. He couldn't see what from that distance, only that they were loading something into the wheelbarrow. Mrs. Bell was taking laundry off the line. Where was Mr. Bell?

Caleb swung his gaze wider. There he was, fixing the fence on the chicken yard. He couldn't see Teddy and prayed he would stay out of sight until Ebner left.

"Those gals are sure pretty things. Too bad they're as pigheaded as the old man. You'd think they'd be willing to befriend the one person who decides what happens to them."

Caleb understood the man meant himself, not Mr. Caldwell. He stifled a shudder. To even think of Ebner with Lilly made him feel dirty all over.

Grub loped across the yard, tumbling over himself.

"That's the dumbest dog I ever seen." Ebner chuckled. "Not that I'm complainin'."

"Uh-huh." Caleb didn't mean to give the man a reason to think he agreed with him. Nor did he want to arouse suspicion because he said nothing.

"I keep asking myself what it would take to persuade this bunch to leave. It ain't like they've been made welcome."

Blossom limped after Grub.

Caleb groaned in the depths of his heart. Would Ebner recognize the pup? Worse, would Teddy be chasing after the two dogs?

Ebner leaned forward over his saddle. "Say, ain't that the half-dead mutt you rescued? So you brought the thing here for the Bells to fix up, did ya?"

Before Caleb could answer, Teddy swung past the house and into plain view. If not for the crutches, Ebner might have thought it was any little boy visiting the Bells.

Ebner sat back. "Well, I'll be." He shifted to face Caleb, his face gouged with harsh lines. "Didn't I tell you to stay away from this bunch?"

Caleb kept his thoughts to himself. What he did on his own time was nobody's business but his.

Ebner's lips curled into a mocking grin. "Guess I can't blame you. I'd like to spend an evening or two with one of those pretty young things, too." The evil in the man's eyes made Caleb's fists into knots. But he faced the man without revealing what he was feeling.

Ebner turned toward the farm again, chuckling softly…a sound that grated across Caleb's nerves.

"You've been leaving your son here during the day and coming here every evening. Now ain't that nice. I could fire you for consorting with the enemy."

Caleb said nothing.

Ebner studied the farm long enough for tension to squeeze the back of Caleb's neck. He hadn't known Ebner long, but long enough to be aware that when the foreman spent more than a few minutes in thought someone wasn't going to like the words that came out of his mouth. Caleb knew he wouldn't like what the man had to say.

"I could fire you," Ebner repeated. "Or I could use this to my advantage."

Caleb clenched his teeth. He did not like the sound of that.

"Yup. Having you here every day might be a good thing." He faced Caleb with narrowed eyes. "You can tell me what they're up to. Let me know when they're where I can do them the most damage." He stared down at the farm again. "I tried drowning those smelly little woolies, but those people came home in time to rescue them. But if they happen to go visiting and we know ahead of time…" He didn't finish his sentence. Instead he turned his horse and pressed right up to Caleb's side. "Do we understand each other?"

Caleb met him look for look, not blinking, not giving in to Ebner for even a heartbeat.

Ebner snorted. "I think you get my meaning. Just remember your job is at stake here." He spurred his horse and galloped away.

Caleb slowly brought his gaze back to the farm.

Rose was standing there, pointing in his direction. Lilly was turned toward him, her hand tented over her eyes.

How much had they seen? There was only one way to find out.

He rode to the farm, and Teddy hurried toward him. Caleb lifted him up to sit behind him on the horse. He hooked the crutches on the saddle horn and continued toward the garden, where he lowered Teddy to the ground.

"Son, go wait in the house." He dropped to his feet.

Teddy looked at him and then at the twins. Their calm expressions stilled any protest and Teddy hobbled away.

"Howdy," Caleb said. From the scowl on Rose's face and the uncertainty on Lilly's, he knew they'd seen him with Ebner, but he'd let one of them reveal how much they had seen and what they now thought.

"Never had any use for a Caldwell cowboy," Rose said.

"'Spect you've got good reason," he replied. Ebner had made it clear he'd done everything he could to drive them out.

Lilly looked past him to where he and Ebner had been. "What does Ebner want?"

Rose snorted. "As if we don't know. He wants us out of here and will stop at nothing to accomplish that." She drilled Caleb with her look. "But you! After we've offered you hospitality and Lilly has helped your son."

Lilly's eyes met his, confused, silently asking for an explanation. Her uncertainty tore at his soul. If only he could promise to always protect her from men like Ebner... He'd give the only promise he could. "I work for the Caldwells, but that doesn't mean they have the right to tell me what I do in my own time. Ebner is the foreman. He doesn't own me." He drew himself tall. "I am not part of this feud, nor do I want to be."

"Words. Let's see if actions follow." Rose stomped away.

Lilly ducked her head.

"Lilly," he said, "I would never do anything to hurt you or your family."

He wanted to see her face, gauge what she was thinking. He caught her chin and lifted it. "Lilly, you believe me, don't you?"

For a moment more she kept her eyes lowered. The breeze caught her hair and blew strands across her face from her loose braid. She caught the wayward lengths and tucked them behind her ear. His fingers curled. What would it be like to see her hair unbraided and tumbling down her back?

He scrubbed his lips together and sighed. When he realized she was watching him, he brought his thoughts and attention back to her.

"I don't trust Ebner."

He waited, his hands at his side, as she searched for what she meant to say.

"I'm sure he wants you to be part of the Caldwell campaign against us. But I don't believe you will do anything to harm us while Teddy is here."

He rubbed his hands against his legs. "You think it's only for Teddy's sake?" He studied her a moment, relieved to see her shift her gaze away from him, revealing she wasn't being entirely honest with him or herself. "Do you really think I'd want harm to come to you or your family?"

Her eyes jerked back to his, full of what he could only

think was longing. It hit him square in the chest and knocked his breath out.

What did she want from him?

He wanted to promise her the sun, the moon and her very own star. He forced his lungs to work and his thoughts to remain in the realm of reality. He couldn't promise her anything except for what he already had—the present.

She seemed aware of what he was thinking and gave a tight smile. "You couldn't stop Ebner even if you wanted to. Even if you were here to do it." She stepped aside and turned to the full wheelbarrow.

Turnips. They'd been digging turnips.

"But seeing as you'll soon be gone…" Her voice contained a shrug.

He opened his mouth to protest but closed it without saying a word. He wished he could promise he'd stay and help her, take care of her, protect her from men like Ebner. He wished not only that he could promise it, but that he could have faith he would follow through on it.

But his past had shown nothing but failure on his part. He didn't believe he could live up to his expectations, let alone the expectations of others.

Something Lilly had said sprang to his mind. Was it that he didn't have enough faith or that he was looking for faith in the wrong places? In his own strength and abilities?

But what else did he have?

If he couldn't protect and provide for those in his care, he would continue to suffer both loss and failure.

Still, he wanted to offer Lilly some kind of assurance.

"While I'm here, I won't let Ebner do anything harmful to your family."

She stopped picking up turnips and faced him. "Is that a promise?"

He nodded. "It's a promise." She didn't say whether or not she believed him, instead simply turning back to her task.

The sight of Amanda bleeding and dying filled his mind. He recalled Teddy, white with shock and fear.

He tried to ignore the heavy lump in the pit of his stomach.

He'd promised to protect them, too. And look how that had turned out.

Chapter Sixteen

Lilly followed Caleb as he pushed the barrow full of turnips to the root cellar. She waited outside while he dumped them into the bin.

His promise to see no harm came to them while he was there had made her smile. For a few days they could forget about the Caldwells.

She sighed. And then what? Things would be back to the way they had been. Nothing would have changed.

Wasn't she always saying she didn't want things to change? Except when it came to the Caldwells. If only they would just leave her family alone.

Rose came over. "You made him take the turnips inside, didn't you?"

Lilly chuckled. "I see no reason to do it if someone else will."

Rose stared at the doorway. "I don't trust the Caldwells."

"I don't either. But Caleb assured me he would see nothing happened while he's there."

"And you believe him?" Rose stared at her like she'd suddenly sprung an extra head.

"I do. He doesn't seem the kind of man to break a promise."

Rose stomped away.

Caleb stood in the doorway to the root cellar, a look of surprise and delight on his face. Then his expression gave way to guardedness. "I wouldn't intentionally break a promise." His words were low and husky. "But I failed to protect my wife and son."

A great need to comfort him welled up inside her and she followed her instincts. "Caleb, you can't blame yourself for what evil men do." As she spoke she rubbed his arm, relieved when she felt the stiffness in his muscles ease.

"But I do. I failed them."

"You must have loved her very much." Each word clawed its way out of her throat.

He swallowed hard. "We loved Teddy."

Her heart lurched at the wording of his reply. Did he mean he hadn't loved his wife? But how awful that would have been for both of them. It was certainly nothing for her to be pleased about.

She sought a way to comfort him and assure him he wasn't a failure. "Does not God promise to keep our feet from slipping and to put us on a solid rock?"

"Does it say that in the Bible?"

She nodded, trying to recall the exact verse. "I think it's in Psalm 40, but it's a theme repeated throughout the scriptures. He is able to keep us from falling, and that's in Jude."

"I'll have to find it and read it for myself." He rubbed at his neck. "But it doesn't explain what happened to Amanda."

"How do you explain evil in the world? And yet it exists." She could have told him some of the cruel things the Caldwells had done, but what would have been the point? He had firsthand experience with how cruel people could be.

They tidied up the garden tools and he went with her to bring in the cows.

Grub followed, getting in the way as he chased a butterfly and tripped in front of Maude, who mooed at him as she sidestepped to avoid him.

Teddy and Blossom followed as she led the cows to the barn and into their stalls.

Caleb took one of the buckets she had brought out. "I'll help. Which cow should I milk?"

Her mind went blank for the space of two full seconds.

"Do you object to my help?" He sounded hurt.

"Just surprised. Thanks for offering. You can milk Maude."

He took his place at the cow's side, and in moments the white streams plunked against the bottom of the empty pail.

At the sound, the cats ran into the barn. They saw Caleb doing the milking and skidded to a halt.

Her hungry cats were expecting fresh milk, so she hurried to Bossy's side and began to milk as well, squirting streams to each waiting cat.

Teddy giggled when one cat missed and got a faceful of milk.

Caleb attempted to squirt milk to the cats closest to him. He missed by a mile, sending Teddy into a fit of laughter that had him rolling on the floor. "Papa, you don't know how to milk a cow."

"Anyone can do it." Caleb tried a couple of more times and missed, while Teddy continued to giggle. Then Caleb shifted the direction and shot a stream of milk at Teddy, managing to hit his open mouth.

Teddy's laughter ended on a gulp. He sat up, swallowed the milk and stared at his father.

Caleb laughed, a full-throated, deep-chested laugh that rang through the barn and echoed in the loft.

Teddy's eyes widened and he giggled so hard he got the hiccups.

Lilly grinned, leaning her forehead into Bossy's flank. It felt so good to see the pair relax and enjoy themselves. They both deserved a home and a family.

But Caleb had been clear as springwater that he would be moving on.

Unless something happened to change his mind. She guessed it would have to be something more than Teddy using his leg. He thought he'd failed his wife. And now Teddy. Would Caleb ever be willing to try again?

Oh, if only it would be so. For Caleb's sake. And Teddy's, too, of course.

And for her sake as well. She wanted to deny it, but she couldn't. Something in her heart cried out to know him more deeply and thoroughly. To hear him laugh more often. To talk about their faith.

They finished milking and turned the cows out.

She took the buckets of milk to the house, a smile clinging to her lips.

Rose noticed before Lilly had the presence of mind to change her expression. "Lilly, you are going to get your heart broken and you know it."

Lilly sobered. "I won't let that happen."

Only it was already too late, and there was absolutely nothing she could do about it. She could not deny herself one moment of time with Caleb and Teddy.

She did her best to keep her distance the rest of the evening and to avoid looking at Caleb throughout the meal.

Then it was bedtime. She couldn't avoid being close to

Caleb as they helped Teddy prepare for bed. She'd promised to continue writing the story they had begun. Almost every evening they'd added more to Tiny's adventures, things that the dog was scared of and what made him feel safe. Sometimes Teddy asked Lilly to correct a picture, so she knew he was truly involved in the spirit of the story.

Every evening she silently prayed that the story would help Teddy find the healing he needed as well, for she understood his little heart must be full of hurt and confusion after witnessing his mother's murder.

Tonight Teddy wanted to talk about what would happen if Tiny got hurt.

The request stunned her so much she didn't answer immediately. She glanced at Caleb and saw her surprise reflected in his face.

She brought her attention back to Teddy's request. "What sort of hurt?"

"A broken leg."

It appeared Tiny was going to mirror Teddy's injury. Where would this lead? She could only follow his direction and pray for wisdom as she did so. "Poor puppy." She drew the dog with a splint on one front leg. "What happened?"

"Take it off." He indicated the splint and she obediently erased it.

"Maybe it isn't broken." Teddy sounded confused.

Caleb met Lilly's gaze over Teddy's head as the boy rubbed his fingers along the picture of the dog. She felt Caleb's hope and fear, a reflection of her own. Silently she prayed. *God, help this little boy find healing.*

Teddy sat up. "I don't think it's broke. Just hurt."

"Can he walk on it?"

Teddy shook his head.

"Is he in pain?"

Again Teddy shook his head. "But he'd like to run and play with his boy."

The boy had never been given a name. Just "boy."

Teddy studied Lilly. "What can we do to help him?"

The question caught her off guard. She'd hoped Teddy would be the one to say how he or the puppy could be helped. She glanced to Caleb for guidance. When he shrugged, she understood what he couldn't say with Teddy listening…he'd already tried everything to no avail.

She glanced at the others in the room. Pa had nodded off in his chair. Rose had her nose buried in a book. Only Ma was paying attention, and she smiled her encouragement. *Follow your heart,* she'd say. Or would it be to follow her instincts? Either way Lilly needed to answer Teddy's question to the best of her meager abilities.

"Do you think Tiny would like to play a game? Or would that hurt his leg?"

Teddy considered the question. "He's afraid it will hurt."

"I see. Then we'll have to do our best to see what will work. Has Tiny tried taking little steps?"

Teddy shook his head. "That might not work, and if it didn't he'd fall down."

"Maybe the boy could help him."

"Maybe." Teddy sounded doubtful. "I think he has to keep resting until it's all better."

Teddy was clearly afraid. She feared pushing him too hard. "Then we'll let him rest. It's time for Tiny to go to bed. Maybe the boy should pray for Tiny's legs to get better." She drew a picture of the boy kneeling at his bedside with the dog curled up beside him.

"What will the boy say?"

"What would you say to your papa?"

Teddy turned to Caleb. "Papa, can you make Tiny better? Can you make him forget his leg doesn't remember how to work?" He had used the same words he used to describe his own leg.

Lilly's heart twisted at the agony in Caleb's face. She hadn't expected Teddy to be so direct.

Caleb swallowed hard. "Son, I'm afraid I can't make Tiny better."

"Well, who can?"

"Only God," Lilly said.

Teddy shifted his questioning eyes to Lilly. "Then I'm going to ask Him." He hesitated, stroking Blossom's head. He gave Lilly a shy look. "Will you help me pray?"

"I'd love to." The words caught in her throat. She often helped him say his good-night prayers, but this time felt different. She reached for his hands.

He squeezed his eyes shut.

"Dear Jesus," she said, and he repeated her words. Silently she added a few more of her own. *Help me guide this child.* "I know You love me always and forever," she prayed aloud.

"Always and forever? Even when I'm bad?" Teddy asked.

"Yes, even then, though He's sad when we do bad things because He knows bad things aren't good for us."

"Okay." Teddy bowed his head again and continued his prayer. "I know You love me. Even when I'm bad and I'll try not to be bad too often." Teddy's sweet trust tightened Lilly's throat, but she continued.

"Our friend, Tiny—" She'd almost said Teddy but had caught herself. "He has a hurt leg. Can You please help him?"

Teddy repeated the words.

"Thank You for always hearing me."

Teddy again repeated the words. Then he added, "Good night, God." He tilted his face up for a good-night kiss from Lilly.

She kissed his soft cheek and gave him a hug. Her heart swelled against her ribs with love for this child. She wanted to hold him tight and never let him go. But he wasn't hers. She forced herself to release him and leave his side, and then she went to the table and sat down.

Caleb tucked him in and kissed him good-night.

He joined her at the table.

She ached to squeeze his hand or pat his back to show she understood how difficult the past few minutes had been, but she was acutely conscious of the others, so she kept her hands clutched together in her lap.

"Teddy is telling you about himself through Tiny," Ma said. "It's a very clever way to help him."

Lilly pulled her emotions under control. "I just follow his lead." She meant both Teddy's and God's.

Ma folded up the mending she'd been doing and put it in the basket. "It's been a long day. I expect you're all ready for bed."

Lilly and Rose immediately headed for their room as Ma wakened Pa. Just before she closed the door behind them, she glanced over her shoulder. Caleb was watching her, his eyes dark with—

She ducked inside and leaned against the door.

Rose looked at her. "What's wrong with you?"

"Apart from having a few sore muscles after digging in the garden all day?"

"You know that's not what I mean."

Lilly pushed away from the door and slipped out of her dress. "Right now it's enough." She didn't want to think of the rush and tangle of emotions that knotted her insides.

Rose grunted. But thankfully she did not press the matter.

A few minutes later Lilly lay in the darkness. What had she thought she'd seen in Caleb's eyes? Longing? But what could he long for that he couldn't have?

Her heart answered that question.

He had a boy who didn't walk and a heap of guilt over his perceived failures. No doubt he wished he could erase parts of his past.

If he could, would he wish for more than just that? A family, a home, love?

She turned on her side, facing the wall, and pressed her fist to her mouth. Those were her heart's wishes, not his. Wishes she must keep silent. Unless, as Rose continually reminded her, she wanted to be hurt.

This time she knew her pain would reach new depths, and she hugged her arms around her, wanting to prevent it.

Knowing she couldn't.

Throughout the next day, Caleb's thoughts bounced back and forth as he tackled the list of chores Ebner had given him. The list grew longer every day, as if Ebner hoped to force Caleb to quit in order to spend his evenings at the Bells.

By midmorning he was chopping wood and stacking it. His mind wandered to the time he'd spent with Lilly.

He'd heard Lilly say she trusted him. He liked that.

But guilt darkened his pleasure. Would he prove himself worthy of her trust?

She'd assured him God would keep him from failing. He scrubbed at the back of his neck. God surely didn't take responsibility from a man, leaving him free to live a lackadaisical life.

Chunks of wood flew before his ax as his thoughts continued to wander.

He'd made a promise to make sure the Caldwell cowboys didn't bother the Bells. The first promise he'd made since he vowed to himself that he would not give up looking for help for Teddy until his son could walk.

Would he fail to keep either of those promises?

Sweat trickled down his back and dripped from his forehead. He was chopping wood as fast as he could.

Teddy and Lilly had made up a story about a pretend dog, Tiny. Caleb had seen the similarities to Teddy's own situation and, as they'd bent over the paper, he'd held his breath and prayed for something wonderful to happen.

But Teddy had grown weary of the story without giving any suggestion that he knew how to fix Tiny.

Caleb jerked upright, the ax hanging from his hand. Something wonderful *had* happened. Last night, for the first time since Amanda's death, Teddy had not cried out in the night with a nightmare.

Caleb grinned. He hadn't even noticed. He could hardly wait to tell Lilly. She'd be as pleased as he was.

"Grinning like a fool don't get the work done." Ebner crossed toward the wood stack.

"Just taking a breather." Caleb swung the ax and split a log neatly.

Ebner moved close enough to force Caleb to stop working.

"You need something, boss?"

"Yeah. What can you tell me about the Bells? They got anything planned I should know about?"

Caleb planted one boot on the chopping block and considered the foreman. He wasn't about to tell the man what he thought. That he had no intention of spying for him. Instead, he took his time wiping his brow and answered, "Well, now. Seems to me they did mention they meant to finish digging the turnips. You should see the crop they grew. Some of those turnips were as big as a bucket. I imagine they'll taste real good about the middle of winter." He managed to answer the man's question without giving him any useful information.

Ebner made a rude noise. "Who cares about turnips?"

Caleb pretended surprise. "Why, I expect the Bells do, and likely people in town who buy vegetables from them do, too. Hear tell they give them away. Say, you ever buy stuff from them?"

"Anything I want from them, I'll take."

Caleb put another log in place and edged back, waiting for Ebner to move aside so he could swing the ax.

Instead, Ebner planted a boot where the ax would have landed. "I'm counting on you to keep an eye on them Bells and let us know when an opportune time arises for us to persuade them it's in their best interest to leave."

Caleb touched the brim of his hat in a little salute. Let the man think what he would of it. He could take it as agreement if he so chose. For Caleb it meant that though Ebner might be the boss, Caleb wouldn't be following an order like that.

Ebner gave Caleb a steely look and then walked away.

Caleb returned to chopping wood. It would be a frosty day in July before he'd do anything to help Ebner chase the Bells from their land.

His arms ached by the time he called it a day. There was more wood to chop, but even Ebner couldn't expect a man to keep at it any longer. He glanced about. No sign of the foreman. Good. He might be able to slip away without running into him.

He dashed to the well and pumped water. He downed several dippers full, then washed up as much as he could.

By rights he should grab some clothes from the wagon when he got back to the Bells and take a trip down to the river for a good scrubbing.

He realized he was standing there grinning at the thought of seeing Lilly and her family, and he quickly sobered, lest anyone see him and draw their own conclusion.

A few minutes later he swung into his saddle and trotted from the yard. His nerves twitched until he was out of sight of the buildings, but even in the open he glanced over his shoulder repeatedly and checked the horizon for any sign of Ebner.

Not until he reached the Bell farm did he take a full, satisfying breath. He had not seen Ebner. Had not been reminded of what the man wanted.

"Papa, Papa." Teddy hurried toward him, swinging his crutches so fast Caleb feared he would fall.

"Slow down, son. There's no fire."

Teddy reached him. "But there will be."

"Will be what?"

"A fire. There's gonna be a fire tonight."

Lilly crossed the yard to join them. She smiled.

He forced himself to continue unsaddling his horse, though his hands felt a mile from his brain at the sight of the welcome light in her eyes. "What's this about a fire?" Caleb asked.

"And a party." Teddy practically danced a jig on his one foot. "A real party. Miss Lilly says they do it every year. Isn't that right, Lilly?"

He didn't correct Teddy about using Lilly's name as she ruffled Teddy's hair. "We've done it for a long time." She turned to Caleb. "We burn the cornstalks. It's such fun we started asking our friends to come. They seem to enjoy it."

"I see." He tried to imagine where he would fit in this picture. He was an old man compared to Lilly and her friends. Even compared to Wyatt. An old man with a child and heavy responsibilities.

Teddy pressed close to Caleb. "Lilly said everyone can come. Us, too. Right, Lilly?"

"Everyone is welcome." She met Caleb's eyes and no doubt read the eagerness in them. "You are most sincerely welcome." She lowered her eyes as pink stole up her throat and stained her cheeks in such a beguiling way he grinned and dipped his head to see full into her face.

"That sounds like an invitation I can't refuse."

She looked at him through the curtain of her lashes. "I'm glad."

"Me, too."

"I can stay up for the party, can't I?" Teddy asked. "Lilly said I could if you agreed."

"You may stay up for a reasonable amount of time." He finished caring for his mount.

Teddy hung his head. "I 'pose you decide what's reasonable."

Lilly laughed. "That's your papa's job. To take care of you."

Caleb held her assuring gaze. His heart beat hard against his ribs. His job. He needed to remember that his responsibilities must come before anything else.

Lilly patted Teddy's head and then rubbed Caleb's arm. "You remember that you have a very good papa who cares deeply for you."

Caleb stood motionless. Had she purposely praised him in response to what he'd said yesterday about his failures? Or had she spoken spontaneously?

She squeezed his arm. "Now, don't get all serious and

cautious. This is an evening meant for fun and celebration."

"What're we celebrating?" Teddy asked.

"The harvest." Lilly swung her arms in an all-encompassing gesture. "The crops are in. The garden has filled our root cellar to bursting and there is still more to bring in. The sheep and pigs are ready to sell. And—" She caught Teddy's chin and tipped his face to grin at him. "We have friends and family to share our joy with."

Caleb held his breath, hoping she would touch his face as she had Teddy's, but she only smiled at him.

"Would you like to help us prepare for the party?"

He nodded. "What do you need done?"

The three of them left the barn. Blossom and Grub waited at the door and joined them. Blossom still limped when she walked, but she was improving every day.

"We need to get a place ready for the fire." Lilly led them to a spot in the middle of the garden. "Right here, where we don't need to worry about the fire getting away."

"Do you want me to pull out the cornstalks?"

"Oh, no. That's part of the fun. But we need something to sit on." She pointed to the planks and lengths of logs and together they made a wide circle of benches.

Caleb's stomach rumbled. It had been hours since he'd grabbed a quick dinner, and it had already worn off.

Lilly heard and pressed her hand to her mouth to cover a giggle.

He rolled his eyes.

"We are going to eat," she assured him. "Everyone brings their own sandwiches and Ma makes us hot cocoa."

A wagon rumbled toward them.

"Here are the first ones." Lilly hurried toward the

wagon. When she saw that Caleb was hesitating, she waved him forward.

Mr. and Mrs. Bell and Rose came from the house and joined them as they went to greet the visitors.

Lilly introduced the preacher's daughter, and several other young ladies. Caleb forgot most of their names almost as soon as they were given.

Behind them came a second wagon. With relief Caleb recognized Wyatt, Cora and Lonnie. At least he wouldn't be completely surrounded by strangers.

Lonnie and a Miss Ellen smiled shyly at each other and headed to the circle of benches.

Some young men arrived on horseback. Was one of these Lilly's beau? Or a man who wanted to be? She greeted them all exactly the same way and drew him forward to introduce him.

The crowd seemed made up of school chums and church friends. Caleb again felt old in comparison.

But Lilly didn't allow him time to worry about it. "Come on. We're going to start the fire."

Everyone gathered round with Mr. Bell in the center next to a small stack of kindling. He lifted a hand to signal for quiet and then spoke.

"Welcome to everyone. It's always a joy to celebrate our bounty with friends and neighbors."

Caleb noted that one bunch of neighbors was conspicuously absent—the Caldwells. Too bad they wouldn't forget their feud and join in on the fun.

Mr. Bell continued. "Let us pray." He removed his hat and the men in the crowd did the same.

"God of all the earth, You have blessed us abundantly in this land. You bring the rains. You give us the sunshine and You cause the seeds to break forth into new plants.

Everywhere we see evidence of Your great love for us and we thank You. Amen."

Several echoed his amen.

"Let the fun begin." He lit the fire. "Now remember not to put too many stalks on at once. You want to enjoy a nice fire, not a scorching blaze that could get out of control."

"Come on." Lilly drew Caleb and Teddy with her toward the corn patch and they wrestled the stalks from the ground. "Knock off the dirt." They did so and then took their stalks to the fire.

One by one the young people did the same while Mr. and Mrs. Bell sat and watched. Dusk descended and the fire blazed brighter. Sparks flew upward.

Teddy sat by Mrs. Bell, her arm around him, and watched with amazement.

Caleb paused a moment, too, watching the light of the fire reflect in Lilly's face. She smiled at him. Flames burned through his veins.

But he dared not hope that she meant to encourage his interest. He could not allow himself to think this tender feeling, this sweet regard, this full-bodied enjoyment would someday grow into more.

He had followed his dreams once before and his dreams had proven to be made of dust.

Someone tossed another stalk into the fire and the flames shot into the sky. Lilly shrank back from the heat.

Caleb turned away.

He needed to quench this yearning of his soul before he failed, before she shrank from him as she had from the fire.

Chapter Seventeen

Lilly hurried after Caleb. She had sensed from the start of the evening that he was fighting a war with himself. But she was uncertain as to the cause. Did he fear enjoying himself? Perhaps he saw that as a way of inviting disaster. She reached him and caught his arm to bring his attention to her.

"Caleb, don't take things so seriously. This night is meant for fun."

Others dashed past them bearing stalks to toss on the fire, but she paid them no mind.

Caleb studied her for a long moment. "I can't lose sight of my responsibilities."

She pressed her hand more firmly to his arm. "I wouldn't for one moment think you should. I know there are things you must do for Teddy." If his leg didn't start to work then Caleb needed to take him east and seek help. "A father should always put his children first."

His expression softened and he covered her hand with his own. "On that we agree." His fingers curled about hers, offering much more than his words did, as if he understood her concern about a father's devotion.

She allowed herself a moment of sweet comfort before

she returned to her original intent. "You wouldn't be neglecting Teddy by enjoying this evening."

He drew in a long breath while she held hers, waiting for him to come to his own conclusion. Then she filled her lungs, knowing even before he spoke that he would agree.

"Enjoy the evening, you say?"

"Your responsibilities will be waiting for you come morning, but there's nothing you can do at the moment."

He nodded and headed for the corn patch, her hand firmly clasped in his. "Then, by all means, let's enjoy the evening." He laughed, filling her heart with shimmering warmth.

They gathered cornstalks, throwing them on the fire and laughing at the way the flames rushed into the air. Teddy sat with Ma and Pa, watching and laughing.

Lilly found herself glancing at Caleb more frequently than not, each time catching his dark gaze and something more. She couldn't name it—hope, anticipation? But whatever it was made her aware of her own needs and wants and dreams in a way that made the flames pale in significance.

The night deepened. Cool air crept closer, drawing people toward the fire.

Pa moved to the center again. "Who's hungry?"

A general call indicated that everyone was.

"I'll ask the blessing and then we'll eat."

She bowed her head and added her own silent words of thanks to the prayer. Thanks for the way Caleb was enjoying himself. Thanks for her own enjoyment of the evening. A warning sounded in her brain, but tonight she would follow her own advice and enjoy herself without thinking of the consequences.

Rose and Ma had made sandwiches for the Bell family as well as Caleb and Teddy, and Rose brought them out as the guests retrieved their food from wagons and saddlebags.

Lilly sat between Caleb and Rose. Teddy sat on Caleb's other side.

She wondered how the boy managed to eat three sandwiches despite his constant chatter. For her part, she was content to be in this place at this time without considering what tomorrow might bring.

Harry Simmons sauntered over. "Mind if I join you?" he asked as he looked at Rose.

Lilly stared. Harry! She couldn't believe he had an interest in Rose. Unless Rose hid it well, she certainly didn't have any interest in him. But stranger things had happened.

She shifted so Rose could make room for Harry at her other side. The movement pressed Lilly close to Caleb. He angled his body so he could look directly at her.

"*The* Harry Simmons?" he whispered for her ears only.

"Pardon?" She didn't know what he meant.

He leaned closer. "Who sings like a bullfrog?"

Then she recalled what she had said about the poor man. But pleased he had remembered, she chuckled. "One and the same."

Rose had been listening to something Harry was saying, but she turned at the sound of Lilly's chuckle. "What's so funny?"

"I'll tell you later."

"Uh-huh."

She turned her attention back to the food, but her arm brushed Caleb's each time she lifted her hand to her mouth. She grew so aware of every movement she could hardly swallow. Her nerve endings tingled.

"Girls, let's get the hot cocoa," Ma said.

Lilly bounced to her feet and rushed after her. The distance gave her a chance to gain a tenuous control over her emotions.

They carried a big pot of the hot drink back with them and filled each one's cup. If Lilly's hand seemed a little shaky, no one seemed to notice.

Then she stood before Caleb and her tremors increased. She held her breath so as not to spill the hot liquid on him, and managed to fill his cup.

Only then did she meet his gaze. The firelight reflected in his eyes, burning away secrets and barriers. She felt as if she could see straight into his heart. Her breath stalled at the depth of longing and love she saw there.

Did he want her to be part of what she saw? Did he think she could satisfy at least part of his longing?

Rose nudged her and they moved on, filling Harry's cup and continuing on to the others.

But something had shifted inside Lilly. It no longer mattered if caring about Caleb brought her pain in the end. This moment, this evening, these past few days would be the source of so much joy that they would outweigh anything else.

Caleb ate the sandwiches offered him and drank the hot cocoa that Lilly had poured. *Enjoy the moment,* she'd told him. It was good advice. His responsibilities wouldn't suffer because of an evening of ignoring them.

He watched Lilly circle the crowd with Rose and her ma, ladling out hot cocoa for each.

He grinned as she made someone laugh and bent close to others as if sharing some heartfelt confession. He grew thoughtful. She'd done the same for him—made him laugh, made him share things from his heart. Made him care. It was her sweet way.

He should be worried about how she'd pulled so many feelings and confessions from him. Perhaps he should have been pulling them back.

But that night was made for enjoyment.

She finished with the cocoa, and Rose took the pot to the house. Lilly returned to his side and his heart filled with warmth.

Teddy leaned against Caleb.

"It's time for you to go to bed," he said to his son.

"Aww." But the protest was halfhearted.

Mrs. Bell pushed to her feet. "We're going in. The night is for young people like yourself. Let me take care of him tonight."

He turned to Teddy, but he didn't need to ask his son if he approved of the idea. Teddy had already taken Mrs. Bell's hand.

"I'll go with Grandma and Grandpa," he said. "You stay and have fun with Lilly." He patted Caleb's hand.

Lilly chuckled.

Caleb shrugged. He didn't mind that Teddy approved of his friendship with Lilly. In fact, it eased his mind greatly.

Someone pulled out a guitar and started strumming it. A young man took a mouth organ from his pocket and sat beside the guitar player, and they played a lively tune.

A young lady across the fire called out a song and the musicians played it. Voices rang out in chorus. Caleb had already heard Lilly and her sisters sing, knew them to have fine voices, but sitting beside Lilly, he felt like the two of them sang a duet.

The fire threw off welcome heat and filled the area with dancing shadows. Stars rivaled the sparks for attention. It was a night made for love.

Whoa. Caleb was not letting his thoughts head down that trail. Love carried responsibility and risks.

And, his hopeful side suggested, joy and satisfaction.

Caleb argued back. It was a package deal. You couldn't have one without the other.

Then Harry Simmons joined the singing and Caleb's attention came back to his surroundings. He choked back a chuckle. The man indeed croaked like a frog. He nudged Lilly in the ribs and they grinned at each other.

No sooner had one song ended than someone called out a request and another began. Caleb knew many of the songs and sang along. He enjoyed listening to Lilly sing those he was unfamiliar with.

Someone requested "The Girl I Left Behind Me." He had forgotten the words. But as the crowd sang, each word wailed through his head. A girl with golden hair and eyes like diamonds. And a wish to get safely back to her. He closed his eyes as the ache inside him swelled with every note.

He would miss Lilly when he left. As the song said, like a bee that could no longer taste the honey, or a dove that had become a wanderer.

The song ended and for a moment people were quiet, allowing Caleb to consider what he was to do.

Not that he really had any choice. One promise he would never forget and for which he would never accept failure was getting help for Teddy. He would not stop until his son could again walk on two legs.

He needed to ignore the sweet call of Lilly's beauty and spirit in favor of his son's needs.

A reveler requested another song and the evening continued for some time.

However, the songs seemed to grow fuller and fuller

of love and angst and sorrow, until Caleb thought his heart could not contain it.

Lilly edged closer. "Are you okay?"

He nodded, his heart too swollen to answer.

"Does this music make you miss Amanda?"

He jerked about to face her. The fire filled her eyes. "Amanda!" It shocked him that she'd thought that. "Amanda and I didn't—" He could hardly say they didn't love each other. Not only did it make him sound mean-spirited, but it besmirched her somehow. He shook his head. "We weren't like that."

From a few feet away Rose was watching them, but he was certain she couldn't hear their words over the music, so he continued. "All my life I've wanted what you have here—a home, a family, love. Now it is out of my reach."

She ducked her head before his intensity then slowly brought her gaze back to his, her face full of fierceness. "It sounds like you're giving up."

"I have given up on my dreams. All that matters now is getting help for Teddy." He scrubbed his lips together. It was no longer true. His dreams had never died. They'd only lain dormant. "You have made me wish things could be different."

She smiled so gently his throat tightened. "Caleb, maybe they can be different. Maybe you just have to be willing to look for ways to make it so."

He drank in her look of hope and encouragement. "Teddy didn't have a nightmare last night."

"Well, there you go. Things are changing for the better."

"If only he could walk."

Her eyes bored into his until he saw nothing else but her, heard no sound but the twinning of their breath. "If Teddy walked, what would you do?"

He stared as hope flourished like a drought-stricken plant soaked in life-giving water. Then he pushed reality into his thoughts.

"I've never considered it." He turned and faced the fire. He didn't dare let his thoughts drift in that direction. He might be tempted to take a wait-and-see attitude toward Teddy's healing.

She correctly read his withdrawal and turned her attention back to the sing-along. He couldn't help but notice that she shifted to her right, putting a few inches between them so their arms no longer were no longer brushing.

He should be glad. He didn't want to encourage her to think he was offering more than he was. All he could offer was friendship and gratitude.

But there was no gladness in his heart. Only a gut-wrenching regret.

The guitar player stood. "Best be going."

His announcement echoed around the circle and the company slowly drifted away except for Cora, Wyatt and Lonnie, who had planned to stay overnight.

Wyatt grabbed a shovel and tossed dirt on the fire. Caleb helped him. Each shovelful quenched the flames until nothing remained but the smell of smoke.

Caleb took the tools and carried them to the shed, his footsteps slow and heavy.

The flames in his own heart also needed to be put out. He had to set aside the dreams he had allowed to flare to life and again focus on the tasks before him, working to get enough money to take Teddy down east.

But the sweet fragrance of memory would remain.

Cora and Rose lay in their beds on either side of Lilly. Wyatt and Lonnie slept in the other room with Caleb, Teddy and Blossom. Lilly smiled with contentment. "It's almost like it used to be."

"It's nice," Cora said. "I miss you two."

Rose made a jeering sound. "From what Lonnie says, all you talk about is Wyatt. Wyatt this and Wyatt that."

Lilly chuckled. "He says Wyatt is just as bad. It's always Cora this and Cora that."

Cora laughed. "That doesn't mean I don't miss home at times. Lots of times."

Lilly sat up on one elbow. "Is it as you hoped?" What she meant was: Did the change make life better? Or did it make life scary? Did she ever wonder if Wyatt would leave her?

"I love Wyatt and can't imagine life without him. Every day is full of sweet surprises as we get to know each other better. More and more I am impressed with what a good, noble man he is. And my, what good times we have. He—"

Rose groaned. "We get the picture."

Cora laughed. "Sorry. Lonnie's right. I do talk about Wyatt a lot." Her voice grew serious. "There's one thing I want to say to you both. Don't ever be afraid to love."

Neither of the twins said anything. If Cora had pressed her, Lilly would have had to confess she was afraid of falling in love. What if it led to more disappointment?

Cora continued. "Don't let our past control your future."

"Funny, but I said the very same words to Caleb." The words were barely out of her mouth before she wished she'd held them back. Her sisters would demand details.

But maybe she'd said it because she wanted to talk about Caleb.

"I expect he has good reasons for his past to influence his future," Cora said, her voice thoughtful. "He's had to deal with a lot. How are your treatments working on Teddy's leg?"

"I see improvement in his muscle strength, but he won't use the leg. It seems to me he's afraid to, and I don't know how to help him deal with that." She told her sister about the story she and Teddy were making up and how she hoped talking about Tiny would give her clues that would help Teddy. "All he says is his leg has forgotten to work."

"So what are you going to do?" Cora asked.

Lilly smiled. Her big sister was back, even if only for the night. She'd always felt she could go to Cora for anything from a little scratch to a big fear. "I think I'll play some games with him. Something that will give him an opportunity to express whatever is holding him back." She had talked to him plenty over the past few days, saying much the same things as she had said to Caleb, only in simpler, more direct ways. Like bad things in the past don't mean bad things in the future, and how evil things make a person fearful, afraid to change or try new things.

With a start that almost brought a cry from her mouth—a cry that would surely have made her sisters demand an explanation—she realized she had been speaking from her heart and to her heart as she talked to Teddy.

She was afraid of things changing. She didn't want to try new things. Rose was right. Being abandoned on the prairie had left an indelible mark on her. Not that it surprised her that it had. It only surprised her that the event had the power to flavor every thought she had.

Was it something she could change, or was her past so much a part of her that it would always make her fearful of change and of trusting others?

Chapter Eighteen

"I hear there was a fire at the Bell place last night."
Ebner gave Caleb a look that made Caleb's skin tighten.
He wished the man would go away and leave him alone
to relive the joys of the previous evening. He didn't even
have to close his eyes to recall every detail—the way
the firelight had pooled in Lilly's eyes, the way she had
smiled when she'd talked to him, the way her eyes had
lowered with shyness and then blinked wide open with
assurance. The way his heart had willingly gone down
pleasant trails with her.

"Don't suppose you set it."

Caleb's muscles tensed with horror. "Nope." He managed to keep his tone neutral.

"Too bad. It's fine idea."

"Have you forgotten my son is staying there?" His taut
and commanding voice should have alerted Ebner that
he wouldn't tolerate putting Teddy at risk.

"He won't be there forever."

Caleb didn't like that answer. He would divert Ebner
as best he could while he was there, but then what? Ebner
meant to get the Bells to move by fair means or foul. And
he guessed Ebner preferred the latter.

"What have you got against the Bells? It isn't like they own enough land to affect the Caldwell ranch. Just a few measly acres."

"It irks me that anyone could be so stubborn. The boss has tried to reason with them. He offered them ten times what the land is worth, but that old man refuses to budge. You know what he says?" Ebner snorted.

Caleb held his counsel, though he guessed the man didn't expect an answer.

"He says God meant the land to be put to good use and that's what he's done." Ebner snorted again. "Like he and God have a special arrangement." Ebner looked ready to gnaw the arm off someone.

Caleb backed away. "I best get to work. It won't get done on its own."

"Yeah. You do that." The man stomped away, muttering to himself.

Caleb shook his head. He didn't want Ebner to become a problem for either himself or for the Bells, though the Bells had already experienced trouble from him.

He tended the list of chores Ebner had assigned then headed for the woodpile.

Ebner rode into the yard and jumped from his horse. He jogged toward Caleb. "I got something for you to do."

Caleb groaned inwardly, but outwardly he kept the appearance of patience. Ebner had gone out of his way all week to keep Caleb from getting finished in time to have supper at the Bells'. Likely he meant to try again. "What do you need, boss?" he asked as Ebner drew closer.

"Need you to go to town. Get some oats from the feed store. Those horses coming in from working the range all summer deserve a good feed." Ebner headed away and then turned back. "Best see if the cook needs anything for the kitchen, too."

"Yes, boss." As Caleb trotted to the barn to hitch up the wagon, he did a little figuring. If all went well, he should be able to get to town, pick up whatever was needed, get home and unload the wagon and still get to the Bells' in decent time. Though he might not make it for supper.

Would Lilly be disappointed? Would she set aside a plate of food for him?

A few minutes later he was on his way. At the fork in the road, he took the right-hand one that led to town, but he glanced longingly to the left and wished he could follow it to the Bells' farm.

In Bar Crossing, he jumped down from his wagon and clambered up the steps, his boots ringing on the boards. He hurried for the door of the store, stepping aside to allow several young ladies out.

They studied him with interest. "Hello, Caleb," they chirruped.

He touched the brim of his hat. "Afternoon, ladies." They had been at the bonfire the night before.

One pretty little thing with eyes as dark as the night sky glanced past him. "You're alone?"

"I am." Why should she care?

The girl sidled up to him, her friends surrounding him. "Maybe you'd like some company while you're in town."

He scrambled for a way to inform them he had neither the time nor the interest without being rude. "Ma'am, I wish I had the time to enjoy your company." He let his glance skim over the four of them without meeting a single pair of eyes. "But the boss is mighty particular about me getting back in good time."

The girls stepped back, the dark-eyed one pouting openly.

As he reached the door, one of the others spoke loudly

enough for him to hear. "I think there's something not quite right about a Caldwell cowboy courting Lilly Bell."

Courting? The word blared through his mind.

He gave the storekeeper the list the cook had given him.

"I hope you don't mind waiting," the man said. "I have three other orders to fill and I don't have anyone to help me today."

"I have to get some feed and a few others things, so I'll be busy for a while." Caleb left the store and jumped into the wagon. Surely the order would be filled by the time he had picked up the other things.

He smiled as he thought of returning to the Bells in a few hours. His mind scurried back to the conversation with the young ladies in front of the store.

Did he mean to court Lilly? Maybe he had been doing so without realizing it. He shook his head. As soon as he got his paycheck he would be going east with Teddy. There would be no time for courting.

He pulled up to the feed store and loaded the sacks of oats and then drove to the hardware to get nails and two new ax handles.

When he returned to the mercantile, the order was ready. He carried the boxes to the wagon, ready to be on his way.

He hadn't left town when someone flagged him down. "Mister, you got a loose wheel."

Sighing back his frustration, Caleb thanked the man and got off to inspect it. Indeed, the wheel was crooked.

He scrubbed at the back of his neck. This would mean a delay, but at least it hadn't happened out on the trail. He turned the wagon toward the blacksmith shop.

An hour later the wheel was repaired and he was again

on his way. He glanced at the sun already halfway down to the horizon. Would he make it to the Bells' before dark?

"Let's play catch," Lilly said to Teddy as she tossed a ball back and forth from hand to hand.

"Okay." He grabbed his crutches and followed her out to the yard. He leaned on the crutches in order to free his hands.

Lilly tossed the ball gently to him. She had no wish to see him tumble to the ground, but she hoped to again see him use his right leg when he wasn't conscious of it.

If Teddy's leg would work again, Caleb wouldn't need to leave.

Would he then stay in the area? He'd hinted he might. She allowed herself to dream of the possibility.

He giggled as she missed his wide toss and had to chase after the ball. After that, it turned into a game of how far he could make Lilly run, until, panting for breath, she finally called a halt.

"Let's see if Blossom would like to play." She found a stick and handed it to Teddy. "Call her over and show her the stick, then toss it just a few feet away from you. Let's see if she will bring it back."

Teddy looked troubled. "Won't it hurt her to fetch it?"

"Don't throw it very far." This could be a chance to talk to Teddy about injuries. "She needs to use her muscles to keep them strong."

"Won't she be afraid?"

"You mean of the pain?"

"I guess."

She squatted before him and held his shoulders. "Did your leg hurt a lot when it happened?"

He nodded.

"Are you afraid it will hurt if you walk on it now?"

He looked into her eyes as if seeking something.

She wanted to hug him, but she needed for him to think about her question. She'd seen enough evidence to be convinced he could use his leg if he tried. He had to get over his fear.

Teddy looked at the stick he was holding. "My mama's dead." The agony in Teddy's voice brought the sting of tears to Lilly's eyes and she hugged the child.

"I'm so sorry." She felt powerless in the face of his pain. The child had endured so much physically and emotionally. No wonder he feared to trigger any more pain by using his leg.

Rose wandered by. "Pa's out digging turnips." There were several rows still in the ground.

Lilly understood Rose's unspoken message. Pa shouldn't have been doing it on his own. In fact, since his fall from the ladder a few months ago, they'd done their best to persuade him to leave most of the physical work to them. Not that he had listened.

Lilly straightened. "Teddy, you stay here and play with Blossom while I help Rose and Pa." She grabbed a digging fork and hurried after Rose.

They knew better than to ask him to leave, so they set to work alongside him. The more they dug, the less Pa would have to do.

An hour later, when they were down to their last ten feet, Lilly felt the ground rumble.

"Did you feel that?"

Rose nodded and they looked about for the source. Over the hill raced a herd of stampeding cows.

"The Caldwells." Rose spat out the words.

They raced for the house.

Lilly stopped. Where was Teddy? She spotted him up

the hill, right in the path of the thundering cows. "Teddy!" she shrieked.

The boy stared at the approaching herd.

"Run, Teddy, run."

He took one step. Two. Then froze.

Lilly's heart stalled. He'd be trampled unless she could reach him. She picked up her skirts and tore across the yard, with Rose behind her hollering, "Hurry!" Then Lilly heard nothing but the pounding hooves, the snorting and bellowing of the cows.

She measured her progress against that of the cows and forced another burst of speed to her feet. She reached Teddy, snatched him into her arms and continued her headlong flight to the barn.

The ground shook. The air rang with a noise that she knew would fill her nightmares for days to come.

They reached the barn, falling through the slit in the door. She sat on the floor, rocking Teddy as the cows rushed past. The door shuddered as an animal banged into it. Something creaked from the pressure of the surging animals.

The pigs squealed. Chickens squawked. She wondered if any of them would survive.

Finally the noise lessened. A set of hooves cracked against the wall and then the thunder passed. Dust and the smell of cattle droppings filled the air.

She held Teddy, her arms locked in position. Weakness filled her until she thought she might throw up.

"Lilly, come quick." Rose's urgent voice gave strength to her limbs and she stood up and pushed the barn door open enough to exit easily.

Teddy's crutches lay nearby, one broken in two, the other soiled so badly it would require a good hard scrubbing.

Debris and disaster lay everywhere. The fence around

the chicken pen was torn down. She saw at least three dead chickens. The garden was flattened, the turnips they'd dug but not picked up trampled to pieces. Ma's herb garden was a mess, the flower gardens by the house torn. One step of the porch was broken.

"Lilly." Rose waved from the garden, where she was bending over something.

The bottom fell out of Lilly's stomach. Pa lay on the ground before Rose.

Her feet leaden, her heart full of dread, she carried Teddy to the house. Ma's hand was clamped to her mouth, her eyes wide with shock.

Lilly put Teddy on a chair and led Ma to another. "Ma, you and Teddy stay here."

Ma's eyes focused on Teddy and she nodded. "Go see to things."

Lilly hurried from the house and did her best to avoid the cow droppings as she crossed to the garden. She knelt by Rose and looked at her pa. "How is he?"

Rose shook her head. "I don't know."

Pa groaned and tried to sit.

Lilly and Rose gently pushed him down.

"Pa, lie still until we see if you're injured." Lilly turned to Rose. "What happened?"

"He was right behind me, but when I got to the house he wasn't there." Her voice quavered and she reached for Lilly's hand. They held on tight, comforting each other.

"I tripped," Pa said. "Silly old man that I am."

"Did the cows—" Lilly couldn't finish the question. She couldn't bear the thought of Pa being trampled by the herd.

"Where are you hurt?" Rose asked.

"It hurts to breathe."

Rose and Lilly exchanged fearful looks. That could

mean a number of things, from bruised ribs to severe internal injuries.

"Take me to your ma."

"You wait here while we get something to carry you on."

The fact that he didn't protest indicated how poorly he felt.

The girls hurried to the barn to get a piece of canvas and wrap it around two poles, and then they raced back. Neither of them spoke. Lilly knew Rose was as reluctant as she to express the truth—that Pa might be seriously injured. *Please God. Please God.* She uttered the silent prayer over and over, knowing God heard the cry of her heart.

They gently eased Pa to the makeshift stretcher and carried him to the house, where they laid him on the cot. Ma covered her mouth to muffle a cry as she rushed to his side.

"Bertie, Bertie, oh my dear." She bent over him, her hands hovering above him as if afraid to touch his skin.

Pa opened his eyes, full of stark pain. "Now, don't you worry. I'm okay." But the heavy tone of his words said otherwise.

Ma nodded and pulled herself together. "Girls, take Teddy and go outside while I see where your pa is injured."

Lilly took Teddy in her arms and the three of them left the house.

The devastation before them brought a groan to Lilly's lips. She would have sunk to the ground, but there was no place fit to sit. "It's awful," she whispered.

"Why'd those cows do that?" Teddy asked, his voice small and full of fear.

Rose grunted. "The Caldwell cowboys had a hand in this. That herd was purposely led here."

Lilly shushed her, tipping her head toward Teddy to indicate they should be cautious how they spoke around him.

Rose hushed, but her scowl informed Lilly what she was thinking.

"Where's Blossom?" Teddy's words rose with panic.

"I expect both she and Grub were smart enough to get out of the way." *Oh please, God. Let the pup be okay.*

"Blossom," Teddy called. "Come here, girl."

Lilly held her breath and waited. But there was no sign of either dog.

"Grub," Rose called. "How about some food?"

"Look." Lilly pointed toward Pa's workshed, which was relatively unharmed except for patches of green manure dotting it. Blossom stepped out, Grub at her tail. As soon as they saw it was safe to venture forward, they trotted across the yard.

She put Teddy on the ground and he wrapped his arms around his dog, laughing as she licked his face.

Ma opened the door and joined them on the step. "Your pa is badly bruised. I can't tell if he's injured inside. We'll just have to wait and see. I pray God will spare him."

Lilly took her hand on one side and Rose on the other. "Amen to that."

Ma looked about the yard. "Oh, my!"

There wasn't much else to say. Lilly added, "Rose, let's get started cleaning up. I'm going to get Teddy's crutch cleaned first. Teddy, you'll have to make do with one until your other can be repaired."

"Okay." He happily played with Blossom.

Halfway across the yard it hit her. Teddy had walked

at least a step or two. His leg did work. For a second she rejoiced. Then she stepped in a fresh cow pie. "Ugh. It's going to take hours to clean this place."

"The sooner we get started, the sooner we finish," Rose said, her expression grim.

A tremor of fear skittered up Lilly's spine. "Rose, what are you thinking?"

"You have to ask?" She faced Lilly squarely. "What part did Caleb have in this?"

"Rose, how could you think that? Why, he'd never do anything to hurt...his son." She almost said he'd never hurt her. But could she be so certain? Hadn't he promised they'd be safe from a Caldwell attack while he was working there? Why hadn't he stopped this, or at least warned them it was coming? Perhaps tried to turn the cows away from the farm?

But he'd been conspicuously absent.

"I expect he was counting on one of us to make sure Teddy was okay." Rose looked about.

"I'm sure there's another explanation."

"I'm not planning to accept just any old reason." She kicked at a board torn from the chicken house. "Not after this."

Lilly scrubbed Teddy's crutch and took it to him. Then with shovel and wheelbarrow she tackled the cow manure. Green droppings smeared the outside of the barn that had been built just that summer. It would take a good rain to wash them away.

Meanwhile they would remain as a reminder of this dreadful day.

She and Rose repaired the chicken house and buried the dead chickens. They were about to start work on the fence when Ma called out.

"Pa says to salvage what you can of the turnips."

The girls crossed to the garden and picked through the damaged vegetables. Some could be used immediately. A few were whole, but most of them were trampled to a juicy waste.

All the while she secretly waited for Caleb to appear, and hoped he could provide an explanation of why this had happened.

She couldn't believe he'd had a part in it. But she'd been wrong before in trusting people.

Was she to be proven wrong again?

Chapter Nineteen

Caleb glanced at the sky, again assessing the amount of daylight he had left. He drove up to the Caldwell barn and unloaded the sacks of oats. He'd take care of the horse and wagon and then he would be on his way. He had a good chance of making it to the Bells before dusk descended.

A few minutes later he rode from the yard. He saw no sign of Ebner or any of the other cowboys who normally hung about the place.

As he neared the Bells' farm he saw evidence of many cows having trampled the grass. Odd they had bunched up together like that. Just that morning they had been scattered in small groups across a large area.

The closer he got, the more intense the signs grew. His jaws clenched. If he wasn't mistaken the herd had headed directly for the Bells'. What would have spooked them in such a fashion?

Or who? A shudder snaked across his shoulders. Why hadn't he seen Ebner back at the ranch?

At the top of the hill overlooking the farm, he could see the cows had run right through the yard, trampling it into a dirty mess. Had Ebner done this?

Stampeding cows were dangerous. They could as easily trample a child as a flower. He scanned the yard in a quick second. No sign of Teddy. He spurred the horse forward, leaning over the saddle horn. *Teddy, Teddy,* he silently cried.

The boy was all he had left. If something happened to him—

He couldn't even finish the thought. He should have never left him there. Should have kept him at his side, no matter what.

When had the distance down the hill grown so far?

The horse's hooves pounded, the sound reverberating in his chest.

Then Teddy appeared, limping along, Blossom at his side, and Caleb sat back to catch his breath.

Anger pounded against the back of his eyes. His son could have been hurt. If this had been a deliberate action—

He rode more slowly toward the farm.

Rose and Lilly were kneeling in the garden. He couldn't be sure what they were doing, but they appeared to be picking up turnips. Strange. Why would they do that when there was so much cleaning up to do?

He dismounted when he reached his son, swung Teddy into his arms, and went to join Lilly and Rose.

Rose jolted to her feet, gave him a look of pure displeasure and stalked away.

He saw they weren't picking up turnips so much as looking for undamaged ones to salvage from the mashed mess. The cows had done this.

Lilly stared at him, her sorrowful expression tinted with both hope and despair.

"How did this happen?"

"You need to ask? Where were you that you didn't stop it? You promised."

Rose had not gone far, and was listening to every word. "Yes, let's hear your explanation."

He didn't want Teddy to hear this conversation. He put him down. "Go to the house." He waited until Teddy went inside, walking with one crutch, and shut the door.

"Ebner sent me to town." His suspicions grew. The blacksmith had wondered why the wheel had been loose, suggesting someone had deliberately tampered with it.

Ebner had planned it all along.

"I see now he meant to keep me out of the way because he knew I'd oppose him."

Rose snorted. "Well, I hope he's happy. The place is a mess. Pa is injured."

"He's injured? How badly?"

Lilly's eyes misted. "We don't know. He might have internal injuries."

"Lilly, you must believe I had nothing to do with this."

She averted her eyes.

He knew she was having trouble believing him.

He wheeled around and headed for the house.

Rose trotted after him. "Where do you think you're going?"

"To check on your pa."

"Ma can do that."

Lilly followed hard on Caleb's heels. "Rose, for pity's sake. You can't blame Caleb for every evil the Caldwells have inflicted on us."

"Right now I can't see why not."

Caleb ducked into the house. Mr. Bell lay on the cot, pale as the sheets.

Mrs. Bell glanced up. Caleb had never seen her look so drawn and old.

"How is he?"

She responded the same way Lilly had. "We'll have to wait and see. I've given him something to ease the pain."

"I pray he'll recover."

"Thank you."

Caleb saw no accusation in Mrs. Bell's eyes and was grateful. He didn't dare look at Lilly again for fear of what he'd see.

"Can I leave Teddy here for a bit? I have something I need to take care of." He didn't wait for their answer, knowing Teddy would be well cared for in his absence. If they'd let him, he'd return and help clean the place up. But they might never want to see him around again. At least that was the impression Rose had given.

Did Lilly see things differently?

He'd soon find out.

He swung back into the saddle and retraced his route through the cow droppings, over the hill and onward to the Caldwells' ranch.

He rode directly to the cookhouse, where he guessed the men would be gathered. He swung down and stomped in.

Ebner looked up and glowered. "Thought you'd gone to join your friends."

"What you did was lower than a snake's belly. You chased a herd of cows over the land of an old man, an old woman and two innocent girls." He took a step forward, his fists clenched at his sides. "Even knowing my son is there, a crippled little boy who can't run from the stampede. That's about the most cowardly thing I've ever heard of." He would not mention Mr. Bell's condition, lest Ebner feel he should take advantage of the Bells while they were down and hurting. "I'll not work for an outfit like this."

A dozen men observed them. It helped ease Caleb's

tension to see half of them hang their heads in shame. The other half, however, sneered. A cowardly, dangerous bunch.

"I'll take my wages now if you care to give me them."

Ebner rolled his shoulders. "'Fraid that's up to the boss."

"Right. When do you expect him back?"

"Say, didn't he and the missus ride in this afternoon?" The man who spoke had a face as cruel as a tornado, but he was one of those who hadn't looked pleased about Ebner's actions.

"Shut up, Stu," Ebner growled.

Caleb didn't nod his thanks to Stu. No point in making things worse for the man. "I'll be collecting my wages, then." He strode from the cookhouse, mounted the steps to the main house and banged on the door, ignoring Ebner as he hollered at him to stay away from there.

A man opened the door. "Mr. Caldwell?" The man had a fine head of silver hair and wore a suit that had obviously been tailored to fit him to perfection. He lacked the menacing air Caleb expected.

"Yes, what can I do for you?"

"Name's Caleb Craig. I've been working here a month, but I quit and I've come to collect my wages."

"You quit?"

"Yes, sir. I can't work for an outfit that deliberately attacks innocent, helpless people. It goes against my grain."

"I see. Well, come in and we'll settle up."

Caleb followed the man across the hall to an office with a big mahogany desk, mahogany wainscoting and shelves lined with leather-bound books.

"Have a seat." Mr. Caldwell pointed toward a black leather armchair.

"I'll stand." He held his hat in hand.

"Suit yourself." He wrote on a piece of paper. "Perhaps you'd care to tell me what you're in such a high dungeon over."

Caleb considered whether or not to tell him, then decided it might help him judge the character of this man to see his reaction. "Your crew stampeded a herd of cows over the Bell farm, even knowing my son who has a crippled leg was there."

"Was your son injured further?"

"No, but it was no thanks to your cowboys." Again he decided against telling Mr. Caldwell about Mr. Bell's injuries. "I'll not be part of a crew that acts in such a cowardly way."

"You have proof my men did this?"

"Who else would?"

Mr. Caldwell gave him a piercing look. "Cows have been known to stampede for lots of reasons, many of them not man-made. It seems you're jumping to conclusions."

Caleb nodded. So that's the way it was to be. "I'll take my pay."

Mr. Caldwell handed him the paper. "Present that at the bank in town and they'll give you what's owed you."

"Thanks." He strode from the room without another word and crossed the yard to his horse. He didn't say anything to Ebner, who followed him demanding to know what he had said to the boss.

He swung into the saddle and rode back toward the Bells'.

Could be they'd ask him to move on.

Welcome or not, he'd help them clean up before he left.

Was it just that morning he'd been smiling at what he'd interpreted as Lilly's acceptance of him?

Would she welcome him now or side with Rose in wishing him gone?

He'd soon enough know.

For the first time he looked at the script Mr. Caldwell had given him and sat back. Twice what he'd expected for a month's work.

His first instinct was to turn around and ride back, demand to know why he had given Caleb that generous amount. Was Mr. Caldwell trying to silence his criticism with a bribe? He stared at the paper for a minute. It was enough for him to go east with Teddy and see that special doctor.

Was this how it was meant to be?

He'd promised Lilly he'd make sure she and her family were safe while he was there. He'd failed. Again. He folded the script, tucked it deep into his pocket and rode on.

Dusk had fattened the shadows by the time he reached the Bells'. He put his horse in the barn, grabbed a shovel and set to work. He scooped and smoothed the dirt, then when he finished that, he lit a lantern and untangled the wire for the chicken yard.

Lilly came from the house. "Caleb, it's dark. Come inside for supper."

He stopped hammering. "You sure I'm welcome?"

She nodded. "Where did you go?"

"I went to the Caldwells' to quit."

Her eyes were wide, the lantern light revealing surprise and—dare he hope—gladness.

"What about taking Teddy east?"

"Mr. Caldwell paid me generously. I can afford to take him to that special doctor."

"The Caldwells are back?"

"Arrived today." He pulled at the wire, trying to un-
tangle it so he could nail it to the post.

She grabbed the end and pulled it tight.

He drove in the nails and moved on to the next post.
In a few minutes they had the chickens securely shut in.

There was something he needed to know. "You don't
believe I had any part of this, do you?"

"No. After all, Teddy is here."

He leaned closer. "I wouldn't hurt you, either. Didn't
I promise you that?"

She ducked her head. "I hope Pa will be okay."

He understood what she meant. She would be hurt if
her pa was hurt.

"Come in for supper," she said again.

"I'll be there as soon as I put the tools away."

She didn't move. "A person can't always keep their
promises." With that, she hurried to the house.

What good were promises if a man couldn't keep
them? What sort of man failed repeatedly to protect those
he cared for? If he'd been paying attention, he would have
known Ebner meant to do something, but he'd walked
around with his head in the clouds, thinking he could
forget his past.

It was impossible to forget his failures.

A little later he went to the house and joined the family for supper, but the meal was somber with Mr. Bell
lying on the nearby cot.

Lilly had a troubled sleep, awaking in a sweat with the
sound of angry cows in her ears. Twice she woke when
Rose called out, and she knew her sister's dreams were
also troubled.

Finally she gave up on sleep and stared into the dark.
Her insides twisted and turned in turmoil.

Caleb had enough money to leave. He'd given no indication he wished it could be otherwise.

A blackness to rival that of the moonless night crept into her heart. He'd never given her any reason to think he would stay. Not even if Teddy used his leg again.

She gasped and sat up in bed then lay down again, waiting to see if she'd disturbed Rose. Thankfully Rose continued to breathe quietly, because she didn't want to discuss her latest thought with her sister.

Teddy had taken at least two steps on his leg. Would Caleb stay if he knew?

Or did he want a reason to leave?

Would he stay if she asked? Why would she? She hugged her arms about herself as the answer grew clear.

Because she cared for him and Teddy far more than she should have allowed herself to.

Cared? This feeling she had went far beyond that weak word. She loved them. The admission sang through her heart.

But love was so disruptive. It had taken Cora away.

Love often proved fickle. Karl had taught her that, though she'd never felt for him anything remotely like this feeling she had for Caleb.

But could love be trusted? Her birth father had given her that doubt.

The next morning, she rushed from the room to see how Pa was doing. He was sitting at the table.

"I'm fine," he said. "Just sore. Thank God for His mercies."

She raced around to hug him, then paused, afraid to hurt him, and settled for squeezing his shoulder. "I'm so grateful."

"Me, too," Rose echoed, patting Pa's arm.

"Grandpa is going to be okay, right?" Teddy said.

Ma ruffled his hair. "I believe he is."

Where was Caleb? Certainly not in the house. Lilly glanced out the window. With a broom and water, Caleb was scrubbing the soil off the side of the barn.

He came for breakfast when she called him, but he had little to say over the meal and returned to scrubbing the barn as soon as the meal ended.

He finished at noon. After he'd eaten, he made an announcement. "I'll be leaving this afternoon. I'll get whatever supplies we need, sell the horse and wagon at the livery stable then get the train headed east."

Teddy's face sagged. "We're leaving?"

Caleb planted his hand on his son's head to silence him.

"I'm most grateful for everything you've done." He pushed from the table, signaled Teddy to follow and left the house.

Lilly stared after him, every thought in her head frozen.

Rose sighed. "Well, that's the end of that."

"I'm sorry to see him go," Pa said. "He's a good man."

"I guess now that he's not a Caldwell cowboy he's okay," Rose allowed.

Lilly bolted to her feet and fled through the door. He couldn't leave without saying goodbye. That was the very worst way to end things.

As she approached the wagon she could hear Teddy asking, "But why do we have to go?"

"I'm taking you to see the doctor your grandparents found. He'll help your leg work again."

"No, Papa. We don't need to go."

Lilly reached them. She wanted to rush to Caleb's side and beg him to stay. But would her asking change his decision?

Teddy saw her. "Tell him, Lilly. Tell him I can walk."

Caleb turned to her then, allowing her to meet his eyes. In them she saw despair and determination. "He used his leg when the cows were coming. Seemed to work just fine."

"I'll show you." Teddy climbed from the wagon and took five faltering steps right into Lilly's arms. "See? It doesn't hurt anymore. I was scared it would, but it doesn't."

She hugged him tight, laughing and crying at the same time.

Teddy wiped her tears away. "Don't be sad."

"These are happy tears."

Teddy looked toward Caleb for an explanation.

Caleb leaned back, a wide grin on his face. "Son, it's something women do."

Teddy looked confused for a moment. "See, Papa? We don't need a doctor. We can stay here. Can't we? Please say we can."

Teddy left Lilly's arms and walked to Caleb, who swept him into a bear hug. Tears glistened in Caleb's eyes.

"Papa, are those happy tears?"

"The happiest in the world."

"Can I go show Grandma and Grandpa?"

"Yes. But take your crutch just in case."

Teddy hopped away with a combination of leg and crutch movements.

Caleb wet his lips. "It isn't just about his leg."

Lilly waited for him to explain.

"I can't promise I can prevent disasters."

"Isn't that why we trust God to take care of us?"

"But a husband's job, a man's responsibility, is to protect and guard his loved ones. I have failed so many times."

"You can't hold yourself responsible for what happened to Amanda."

"Or what happened to you and your family?"

"I don't blame you."

He scrubbed at the back of his neck. "Life is full of so many risks."

"That's why we must leave the future to God."

He moved closer. "Do you really believe that?"

She nodded, somewhat confused by the question and by his nearness. They stood so close she could touch him with a mere flick of her hand and yet they were separated by so many doubts.

"Do you believe strongly enough to trust love?"

"I—" Had she not asked herself almost the same question? And now she saw the answer as plainly as if God had written it in visible letters across the sky. She gave a joyful little laugh. "Of course. Our future includes our responsibility and our relationships. How foolish I've been to think I had to guard my heart so tightly, when all along it was safe in God's keeping. Like it says in the Psalms, 'What time I am afraid, I will trust in Thee.'"

"Are you afraid of me?"

She shook her head.

"Even if I can't prevent the Caldwells from further mischief?"

She smiled up at him, her heart so ready to love that she could hardly contain the urge to hug him. "It wouldn't be fair to blame you for what others do." She touched his cheek. "It's not fair for you to blame yourself for what others do, either."

"I'm beginning to understand that." The air between them shimmered with unspoken promise and possibility.

"Lilly, I know you've been hurt before, but do you think you can learn to trust love?"

"I believe I already do."

"You do?" He swallowed audibly. "Dare I hope?"

Her smile came from a heart and soul overflowing with joy. "I believe you dare."

It took him about two seconds to understand her meaning, and then he laughed, a sound of joy she knew she would cherish forever.

He wrapped his arms about her. "Lilly Bell, sweetest thing I've ever found, I love you. I love you to the heights and depths of this world. I love you with every breath. I will love you as long as my life shall last and I pray God will give us both a long time to enjoy love." His smile faltered. "Am I getting ahead of myself?"

She chuckled softly. "No. I'd say you're right on target, because—" She cupped her hands to the back of his head. "Caleb Craig, I love you with everything I have and am. I trust your love." It was wholly true. Once she stopped holding on to her doubts, they had dissipated like early morning dew. "Nothing I have ever known compares to the love I feel for you."

"Are you going to marry him?" Teddy called from the corner of the wagon.

"Would that be okay with you?" she asked, amused that he had come back to spy on them.

"It would be just right."

"Son, go back to the house and let me ask her on my own."

Teddy studied his father for a moment and then nodded. "I guess you can do it without any help."

Lilly and Caleb held their laughter until Teddy reached the house.

Then Caleb sobered. "Lilly, will you marry me?"

"I thought you'd never ask."

"So did Teddy," he murmured before he claimed her lips.

Lilly sighed beneath his kiss. This was the love she had ached for since she was three years old. A love of her own. A love given by a man who would cherish her and care for her so long as their lives should last.

Epilogue

A month later, Lilly stood in the anteroom of the church.

Cora wiped a tear from her eye. "You look lovely in our dress." When Cora had married, the girls had agreed they would all wear the same wedding gown.

Rose adjusted the veil Lilly was wearing. "You are a beautiful bride."

Lilly hugged each of her sisters in turn. "You both look lovely, too." She sighed. "My only regret is how things are changing."

"It's time to grow up and move on," Cora said. "That's how life was meant to be." She turned to Rose. "I wonder who you'll find to marry."

Rose snorted. "Who says I plan to?"

Cora and Lilly both laughed.

Rose shrugged. "Look at me. Red hair like my head is on fire." She shrugged again.

Lilly could not stand to think of her twin sister being sad on her wedding day. "Rose, someday a man will come along who thinks your hair is the most beautiful thing he's ever seen. And he'll fall so madly in love with you he won't be able to think straight."

Rose laughed at Lilly's impassioned description of love.

Pa stepped into the room. He'd recovered his strength and showed no ill effects from the cattle stampede. "Are you girls ready?"

Together they said, "Yes, Pa."

He pulled them close and touched his forehead to each of theirs. "I've always known this day would come when one by one my girls would leave me. I've prayed you'd find good men and I've prayed I'd be strong and brave when I walked you down the aisle." He paused as his voice grew shaky. "I'm doing my best to live up to my plan."

They hugged their pa and then the organ music changed.

"It's time," he said.

Cora left the room to walk down the aisle and then Rose followed.

Pa held his arm out for Lilly to take. "You've found a good man."

"He found me," Lilly said.

"You found each other with God's help."

They stepped into the sanctuary. Lilly smiled at Teddy and Wyatt at Caleb's side and then she met Caleb's gaze and nothing else mattered.

She walked down the aisle and joined hands with him. Their hearts were already joined in joyful love. And now their lives would be joined as they began married life together.

They had decided to take a house in Bar Crossing for the winter so Teddy could start school without having to walk far. In the spring they'd find a bit of land and start a ranch, God willing.

One thing she'd learned was life was easier and happier if she entrusted her future to God.

She repeated her vows, as did Caleb.

"You may kiss the bride," the pastor said.

Caleb kissed her gently. She understood what he didn't need to say. He, too, had learned to forget the past, leave the future in God's hands and enjoy what the present had to offer.

"God has brought us to this day," he whispered.

"Blessed be His name." She would be forever grateful.

* * * * *

Dear Reader,

It's hard to trust God when things are going badly. At least I find it so. I tell myself I trust Him. But then I ask myself, Where is He? Why is all this happening? I recently went through a spell like that. My client was very ill. He needed extra care. At the same time I had a trip planned to visit my daughter, but I had to cancel it. I had a book deadline. Others in my family needed to be taken to appointments. Oh, and a crowd was coming for Thanksgiving. I'd wake in the middle of the night reviewing my to-do list. I felt like I was drowning in details. I'd like to say I calmly rolled over in bed, knowing God was in control and I could trust Him to take care of my needs. But I didn't. Like those in this book, I struggled to figure out how to trust.

I hope Lilly and Caleb's story encourages you, the reader, to trust God even when things aren't going smoothly.

I love to hear from my readers. You can contact me at www.lindaford.org, where you'll find my email address and where you can find out more about me and my books.

Blessings,

Linda Ford

Questions for Discussion

1. What about the Bell family attracts Caleb? Do his feelings toward them change over the story?

2. Caleb has been the victim of a terrible crime. Do you think it is a strong enough basis for his vow to never again care for someone? What other factors cause him to be so cautious?

3. Lilly was abandoned at three years of age. Do you think that is too young for it to have a bearing on the way she acts nowadays? Should she have simply gotten over it? Is it that easy? Why or why not?

4. Rose believes she understands why Lilly chooses people like Karl. What does Rose think? Do you think there is truth in her belief? Were there times in your own life when you acted in a similar fashion?

5. Teddy doesn't use his leg even though there is no sign of a continuing injury. Why is that? How does he explain it? What do you believe is, or could be, the real reason?

6. The Caldwells are determined to drive the Bells out. What is their reason? Is it justified? Do you think Mr. Caldwell knows what his foreman does? Why do you think this?

7. Lilly challenges Caleb's faith. What does she suggest he is trusting in? Do you find yourself doing this at times? How and why?

8. How is Lilly's faith challenged? By whom? Do her own words condemn her? Can you recall instances?

9. Teddy reminds Caleb of what they used to have. Does Caleb have good memories?

10. What leap of faith do both Lilly and Caleb have to take in order to accept the love they have? Is this lesson final, or will they struggle with it in the future? What things do you think might challenge their faith? Do you face similar issues? Can you learn something from Caleb and Lilly's story?

SPECIAL EXCERPT FROM

Love Inspired HISTORICAL

*As a widower, Sheriff Colt Garrett has his hands full
with a rambunctious son and daughter. Could feisty
schoolteacher Allison Grainger be the missing piece in
their little family?*

Enjoy this sneak peek at Penny Richards's
WOLF CREEK FATHER!

"I think she likes you," Brady offered.

Really? Colt thought with a start. Brady thought Allie
liked him? "I like her, too." And he did, despite their on-
again, off-again sparring the past year.

"Are you taking her some ice for her ice cream?" Cilla
asked.

"I don't know. It depends." On the one hand, after not
seeing her all week, he was anxious to see her; on the other,
he wasn't certain what he would say or do when he did.

"On what?"

"A lot of things."

"But we will see her at the ice cream social, won't we?"

Fed up with the game of Twenty Questions, Colt, fork in
one hand, knife in the other, rested his forearms on the edge
of the table and looked from one of his children to the other.
The innocence on their faces didn't fool him for a minute.
What was this all about, anyway?

The answer came out of nowhere, slamming into him
with the force of Ed Rawlings's angry bull when he'd
pinned Colt against a fence. He knew exactly what was up.

"The two of you wouldn't be trying to push me and

Allison into spending more time together, would you?"

Brady looked at Cilla, the expression in his eyes begging her to spit it out. "Well, actually," she said, "Brady and I have talked about it, and we think it would be swell if you started courting her."

Glowering at his sister, and swinging that frowning gaze to Colt, Brady said, "What she really means is that since we have to have a stepmother, we'd like her."

"What did you say?" Colt asked, uncertain that he'd heard correctly.

"Cilla and I want Miss Grainger to be our ma."

Don't miss WOLF CREEK FATHER
by Penny Richards,
available January 2015 wherever
Love Inspired® Historical books and ebooks are sold.

SPECIAL EXCERPT FROM

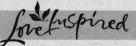

*When a rodeo rider comes face-to-face with an old love,
can romance be far behind?*

*Read on for a preview of
HER COWBOY HERO by Carolyne Aarsen,
the first book in her brand-new
REFUGE RANCH series.*

Keira wished she could keep her hands from trembling as she handled Tanner's saddle. What was wrong with her?

Seeing him again, his brown eyes edged with sooty lashes and framed by the slash of dark brows, the hard planes of his face emphasized by the stubble shadowing his jaw and cheeks, brought back painful memories Keira thought she had put aside.

He looked the same and yet different. Harder. Leaner. He wore his sandy brown hair longer; it brushed the collar of his shirt, giving him reckless look at odds with the Tanner she had once known.

And loved.

She sucked in a rapid breath as she turned over the saddle on the table. Tanner seemed to fill the cramped shop.

Keep your focus on your work, she reminded herself.

"So? What's the verdict?" Tanner asked.

"I don't know if it's worth fixing this," she said, quietly. "It'll be a lot of work."

Tanner sighed. "But can you fix it?"

"I'd need to take it apart to see. If that's the case, two weeks?".

"That's cutting it close," Tanner said. "Is it possible to get it done quicker?"

Keira would have preferred not to work on it at all. It would mean that Tanner would be around more often.

It had taken her years to relegate Tanner to the shadowy recesses of her mind. She didn't know if she could see him more often and maintain any semblance of the hard-won peace she now experienced. Tanner was too connected to memories she had spent hours in prayer trying to bury.

"I'm gonna need it for the National Finals in Vegas in a couple of weeks." Tanner continued.

"I heard you're still doing mechanic work, as well?" She was pleasantly surprised she could chitchat with Tanner, the man who had once held her heart.

"Yup, except last year I bought out the owner. Now I'm the boss, which means I can take off when I want. I took over the shop in Sheridan after a good rodeo run. The same one I started working on before—" He didn't need to finish. Keira knew exactly what "before" was.

Before that summer when she left Tanner and Saddlebank without allowing him the second chance he so desperately wanted. Before that summer when everything changed.

A heavy silence dropped between them as solid as a wall. Keira turned away, burying the memories deep, where they couldn't taunt her.

But Tanner's very presence teased them to the surface.

She looked up at him to tell him she couldn't work on the saddle, but as she did she felt a jolt of awareness as their eyes met. She tried to tear her gaze away, but it was as if the old bond that had once connected them still bound them to each other.

Will Keira agree to fix Tanner's saddle?
Pick up HER COWBOY HERO to find out.
Available January 2015, wherever
Love Inspired® books and ebooks are sold.

JUST CAN'T GET ENOUGH OF INSPIRATIONAL ROMANCE?

Join our social communities
and talk to us online!
You will have access to the latest
news on upcoming titles and special
promotions, but most important,
you can talk to other fans about your
favorite Love Inspired® reads.

 www.Facebook.com/LoveInspiredBooks

www.Twitter.com/LoveInspiredBks

Harlequin.com/Community

LISOCIAL

Love Inspired

Love the Love Inspired book you just read?

Your opinion matters.

Review this book on your favorite book site, review site, blog or your own social media properties and share your opinion with other readers!

Be sure to connect with us at:
Harlequin.com/Newsletters
Twitter.com/LoveInspiredBks
Facebook.com/LoveInspiredBooks